JUNCTURE

KEN MCALPINE

ISBN: 0991033442
ISBN-13: 978-0991033447

DEDICATION

To my best friend and wife Kathy, who has been with me every step of the way. And to all the heroes who are doing what they can to save this world.

Penetrating so many secrets, we cease to believe in the unknowable. But there it sits nevertheless, calmly licking its chops.

H.L. Mencken

ACKNOWLEDGMENTS

No writer has a better team of family and friends. Thanks to my amazing family - Kathy, Cullen and Graham - for always believing in my words and filling my life with so much happiness and love. Thanks to my father and mother, Harry and Betsy McAlpine, and my in-laws, Al and Dot McCart, for their amazing support on so many fronts. Thanks to my incredible cadre of intelligent readers - Kathy McAlpine, Donna Thonis, Pat McCart-Malloy, Jimmy Harvey and Lyn Tovar - who provided the extra eyes that caught my many mistakes (and a special thanks to Lyn, who painstakingly took on my poor punctuation). And finally, thanks to my special friend and creative genius, Hank Tovar, who continually reminds me what selflessness means.

Wreckage and Myth

I am the fomenter of fable. Over the centuries the tales have morphed to myth, though I still believe in myself. I continue to prey on man, but only when I must. Hunger, unlike loneliness, is an urge that cannot be pushed aside.

When I feed on your kind I try to be merciful and quick, but it is also true that hunger consumes me and I sometimes lose myself. You could say I see red, though really I don't see well at all. Smell serves me, the scent of the dead and dying carrying on ocean current breezes like apple pie resting on a windowsill. But mostly I feel and hunger for me is hollowness without bottom. See yourself saying goodbye to the ones you love most, knowing you will never see them again, though they blithely believe, as you all do, they will witness tomorrow's dawn. No telling them. No touching them. Just stepping away.

As you might imagine, such emptiness is a chore to ignore.

Hunger adds keenness to the scent, turning me madder still. The luscious renderings - fat, salty-sweet fluid, juicy-burst organs - of the human form crawl into my every pore. At this pressure cooker point, sadly mercy takes a back seat. I thoughtlessly part bone and flesh. I lose myself in the act, as you do when you murder or mate. Hate and love are twin sisters, both ugly and beautiful.

I exhibit mayhem and clinical efficiency: what little I don't ingest, the ocean's smaller creatures gobble, leaving only wreckage and myth behind. But here and there a sailor or a fisherman has survived, mumbling of reaching fingers, unable to turn their back to dark corners. One man chewed off his lips rather than give himself away. This suffering I regret. It is not always boon to be the survivor.

Opening your minds is difficult, a nudge by nudge process. Start with this. Do not be so quick to discount a lunatic's mumblings.

Sometimes a direct line runs from madness to truth.

Mother and Son

They stood together on the stainless steel swim step of the Wendell Holmes, the tips of their dive fins washed by water that matched their eyes. The bay's surface spread plastic wrap tight, the early morning waters not yet ruffled by the trade breezes. The water sluicing across the swim step was bright green in its thinness.

These days Cedar questioned herself constantly. But in this moment she knew her son was precisely where he belonged.

They watched the spinner dolphins rouse for the hunt. She glanced at Justin, his heartbeat visible beneath his skinny-smooth chest. *Now-now-now-now-now.*

She touched his forearm.

"Watch just a minute longer," she said.

"Too long," her son said, but he stayed where he was.

See this moment. Absorb every drop of lovely detail. She kept this to herself. Teenagers have a tipping point for life lessons.

Out on the water gray apostrophes appeared, bowed forms that skittered across the surface before disappearing in an equivalent wink, leaving a fingernail of foamy scrim behind.

"Just once, I'd like to swim like that," Cedar said.

"I'd just like to swim," said Justin. He coughed. "Carpe diem."

It was her expression.

"Sometimes watching is seizing," she said.

"Watching is pretty much waiting," her son said, but from the corner of her eye she saw the edge of a sly smile.

Justin wore the yellow mask his father had given him, the equally jaunty yellow snorkel poking up. Discounting proud five-year-olds, few divers sported yellow masks. Yellow stood out from the human stampede. Wyatt's every action bore a message. Her ex-husband couldn't be blamed. He descended from an unbroken and unyielding line of mid-Western alpha achievers. His father, a Chicago banker, had named him after the gun-slinging lawman. From the zygote Wyatt had been groomed to be quicker than the rest, metaphorical bullets bringing the Windy City's financial world to its knees. Soon it would be Justin's turn. They had agreed.

Sixteen-year-old boys aren't inclined to sunflower colors, but Justin loved his father and she did not want to discourage this.

Most of the dolphin pod still slept in their loose protective circle. The joy, as always, was in watching the first risers wake their brethren. Frenetic torpedoes, they leapt free of the water, their glistening forms suspended in the air until, with a last fanciful twirl, they struck the water with a wallop intended to put the spirit of the hunt into their slothful companions.

Joy is contagious.

"Watching is just waiting," Cedar said, shoving her son.

Even off balance, he pierced the water cleanly. She watched him descend through the water, a pale scalpel, fins together, performing an undulating beat. When he reached the sand bottom thirty feet below he remained clearly visible, his lanky form nearly as white as the sand. Justin dwelled in South Pacific sunshine, but Irish lineage resided firmly entrenched in his every pore.

Cedar always gave him a few minutes alone with the dolphins. Her gift to him. They dove with the dolphins several mornings a week, but the few minutes always made her anxious. Glancing down she saw her fingers coiling the drawstring of her gym shorts. She smiled. Being a parent was being unable to control your instincts.

She scanned the bay, for what she didn't know, and then she turned her attention back to the dolphins. They were readying to hunt, but this never overrode their curiosity. Beneath the clear waters three dolphins streaked for her son, their dark forms moving low over the sand in that bumping, playful, terrifyingly efficient manner that always trumpeted the fact that man was a clunky interloper in the sea.

As she watched, Justin rolled on to his back and blew three silver rings. In a wink, the dolphins redirected. Rocketing upward, each dolphin pierced its own wobbling molten ring.

Cedar laughed, took a last deep breath, and dove, morning cool waters scraping away the night's sweat.

The entire pod was awake now. Everywhere dolphins crashed past, making antic clicks. The dolphins veered closer to Justin, nearly brushing him. Standing on the bottom he turned slow circles, the dolphins whipping in and out. He did not reach out. Over the years she had had her share of New Age customers on the boat, folks certain of a karmic human-dolphin bond; more than once she had seen that certainty shatter in the face of aggressive dolphins.

Watching Justin, she wondered if maybe the New Agers were right after all.

For the first ten minutes she surfaced for air when Justin did, but after that she came up alone. At the last, exhausted, she floated on the surface watching the dolphins leap. An old Palauan fisherman had told her dolphins leap free of the water to enjoy the silence. She doubted this was true, but you could love a fable as much as a fact.

Soon enough the early risers made their point. On some collective signal, the entire pod rocketed off for the deeps.

Cedar looked down into the water. Justin stood on the bottom. Looking up at her he crossed his arms and scuffed the sand with a fin.

She was prying off her fins on the starboard bench when he pulled himself up the ladder.

"You could teach your mother how to hold her breath like that."

He smiled.

"You taught me."

"I've forgotten the part about not having to breathe."

If he heard her, she couldn't tell. He was humming, slipping off his fins. It took her a moment to recognize the song. She had tried to introduce him to music that mattered.

As a teenager she had fronted a band. She had possessed absolutely no aptitude for instruments, but she did have a surprisingly good voice. The band had covered David Bowie songs until the songs sang in her head. They'd experienced some small success. This was during Bowie's androgynous phase. She hoped all the pictures had been destroyed.

Well I, well I wish I could swim. Like dolphins, like a dolphin can swim.

Justin hummed.

We can be them, forever and ever. We can be heroes. Just for one day.

After the required debate and angst, they had named their band after Bowie's song.

"You probably don't want me to sing," she said.

"Now would be the perfect time."

She tried to look hurt.

"Before I was an embarrassment, I was your mother."

"You'll always be my mother." He reached for the fresh water hose. Before she could speak he said, "Sparingly."

"Perchance I repeat myself?"

"There's a chance."

She watched the water slough off his hairless body. He was thin, no doubt. In their e-mail exchanges, Wyatt was constantly telling her Justin was too skinny. *You can't make a man out of fish and papaya.* Perhaps this was true, but it was also true you could make three men out of steak and potatoes.

She saw that their debate was pointless. Justin's chest and back were beginning to thicken, long muscles spreading into each other like puddles.

He rinsed his fins, carefully placing them, one atop the other, under the bench. He had done this thousands of times, yet he performed every rinsing and placing with focused deliberation. On dry land her son moved slowly, always the observer. The afternoon of their arrival in Palau ten years ago she had staggered to bed, strung out and jet-lagged. When she woke she found her six-year-old son crouched in the drumming rain, watching water sluice off a palm frond twice his size. She had ushered him inside, toweling him off so that his hair stood out as if electrified, but the instant the rain stopped - as if someone had turned off a spigot -- he was out in the steamy afternoon, crouching now to watch dragon flies appear above the oily smooth mangrove waters.

These days she was an observer too. She watched her son, freezing each moment, storing them away for the departure that was coming. Wings. Every mother's wish and heart break.

Leaning out, Justin shook the water from his hair. In Chicago his hair would have been brown, but here it was bleached by the sun, filled with highlights women broke the bank for. It had grown long. It slapped about his head like a streaked towel.

For a long moment he looked quietly into the water.

She loved that he always did that. He never forgot the magic.

Turning, he waved the hose like a baton.

"Barely used a dribble," he said.

"Sixteen-year-olds are trainable?"

"Possibly."

"Lying is a synonym for being nice to your mother."

"Possibly."

He was humming again. Stepping forward, he kissed her forehead.

"You are my hero," he said.

Placing his hands on the railing, he swung down into the galley without touching the steps.

Walking to the bench, she bent, her hands shaking slightly.

"And we are all a work in progress," she said to the crumpled towel beside the arranged fins.

.

Tonight I am lucky. I encounter a saltwater crocodile, a fair size one too, which is a happy coincidence because I am famished. I watch her make her ropy-sway way across the starlit surface, intent on her own hunt. Self-absorption is her last mistake. I pull her down and squeeze her tight, feeling her heart race and rupture. Blood spins in her slack mouth. As the last spark leaves her, I regret my choice. Large saltwater crocodiles are rare here, females rarer still.

I do not need to eat often. I expend little energy swimming, for most often I swim slowly or simply drift. Actually, I sway more than swim. When it comes to swimming, I am no marlin or tuna. I am closer to a drunk at closing time. I feed on both the living and the dead; best to have a range of palatable options. The dead, of course, don't protest. The living creatures of the sea fight me, but they do not scream and lament and regret. In the last instant, as the water about them fills with their own wavy liquids, they accept their mistake. You, on the other hand, rarely accept your end. You deny your responsibility and your end right up to the last tick of consciousness. To the final moment, and probably on into wherever it is you may or may not go, you curse others. You curse me; you curse your gods; you curse fate. Once, a fisherman screamed his wife's name. I wish it had been a dying oath of love, but it wasn't. Through not insubstantial suffering, he screamed at her for making him fish at night.

You blame everyone but yourself. This explains so many of your troubles. It may be your most glaring weakness, and that's saying something.

Animals are harder to read, but, through muscle and sinew, they speak to me in their fashion. Holding the limp crocodile, I now know she had a vested interest in this world, for she fought me with surprising strength to the very last. You see the crocodile as a mindless predator, but in our world the female crocodile is known for the vigilant care of her young. On some loamy riverbank, her restless brood of hatchlings will now be answered by something unfamiliar coming out of the dark.

I wish I could give her back her life, but mawkishness is pointless now. I eat. After I finish, I don't descend immediately. It is a lovely night on an empty rolling sea. I drift above the reef, listening to the gravel-click of creatures feeding; gnawing, grasping, clawing, ingesting. It's what we do. What we have always done. It doesn't make us monsters. Overhead the stars wink. Such a lovely place we share.

I feel the tickle of outgoing tide. By the time you wake, what remains of the crocodile will be far out to sea, discovered only by descending birds.

At midnight Cedar still carried the electricity of their dolphin encounter. Justin was asleep in his cabin. She wondered if he was dreaming about the dolphins. More likely, his dreams comprised things a mother didn't care to entertain.

Water wrapped the dock pilings gently, passing with equal delicacy along the hull of the Wendell Holmes. Even by Palau's dreamy tropical standards it was a glorious night, a bright half moon poised like a tilted teacup in the silky black sky. She remembered sleeping on black silk. It had come with a price, but it would be nice again for a night.

The stars popped. It was a perfect night for playing the bagpipes, but she never played in the harbor. To quietly spite the members of the band formerly known as Heroes she had taken up the bagpipes when she and Justin came to Palau. Ten years later she still played terribly and she knew it. She only played out on the open ocean, where Justin could wear ear plugs and she winced alone. Still she loved the instrument for its elbows and knees look, and for the rare lovely note she wrestled from it.

She sat, sipping gin and enjoying the night, but slowly the sight of the tipped moon made her sad. Now it looked less like a teacup and more like a questioning smile. There was no turning back. She had made a promise. It was the right decision, which made things no easier.

She saluted the night with a last swirl of gin and tonic. Once a mother, forever a mother. It was the best of curses.

That afternoon, after Justin finished his schoolwork, they had made the run out to Long Drop-Off Reef, three raw Patti Jean frying chickens strung out - pink and glistening - in three identical three-foot-by-three-foot stainless steel cages on the bow. She didn't know why, but she still strung each fryer's stubby limbs so that they hung, spread-eagle in the center of the cage, like a goose pimply Fay Wray. In the beginning she had done it because *King Kong* was Justin's favorite movie. He had been obsessed with it. They had watched *King Kong* on the VCR in the galley every Friday night. It was their date; Justin eating Doritos and spouting the lines a second before the actors, pushing close to her and going quiet every time at the end. *It was beauty killed the beast.* Even at ten, she suspected he had a thing for Naomi Watts. She had certainly engaged in a fantasy or two regarding Adrien Brody. She had a weakness for the soft-spoken, cerebral type, still tough beneath the intellect. She didn't need a therapist to explain the attraction. Adrien Brody was the yin to the yang she had married. On more than several occasions she had entertained Adrien in her bed after the movie; her hands performing his magic, stifling her quick breaths.

In those days, when she strung up the chicken on the dock, Justin would prance about the cage banging out a drumbeat on the empty paint can he kept expressly for that purpose. He had painted the can black, with a white skull, more like a thumb print, at each compass point. The paint can was long gone, but Cedar still danced about. She did it partly to embarrass him and partly to hold on. She also did it because everyone should embrace a little prehistoric mystery.

Summon Kong.

It was beauty killed the beast, but it was life's mundane exigencies that strangled the thrilling possibility of the impossible. One day Adrien Brody might walk down the dock. One day she might play the bagpipes beautifully. One day Justin might pick up his towel.

Nudging the lemon slice with her tongue, Cedar scanned the night sky for an incoming patch of black. Jonathan almost always returned to the Wendell Holmes for the night. Justin was seven when they found Jonathan, perched one morning on the bowsprit railing, a tiny quivering thumb of furry fruit bat. With a wingspan of three feet, Jonathan was no longer tiny. He was wickedly smart and equally smelly. Perhaps this explained why he himself was drawn to particularly malodorous people. Having located a scent he found enticing, he proceeded directly for the armpits, turning things lively. She had posted signs on the pilings near their slip, warning divers of Jonathan's potential lack of decorum. She had put them up primarily for the benefit of Jonathan, who neither relished nor understood being swatted for his affections.

These days Jonathan slept hanging from a towel rack outside Justin's cabin. At first Jonathan had hung from a bookshelf above Justin's bed, but he had a habit of beating his wings in his sleep and Justin was a fidgety enough sleeper. Justin had protested bitterly when Cedar installed the towel rack outside his door, but watching her son fall asleep over school lessons, she had been firm. Jonathan hadn't been happy with the new arrangements either. For two weeks she had smeared the towel rack with overripe banana, but Jonathan had snubbed the roost, sleeping in the jungle. When he finally returned, she knew it was not for love of bananas, but for love of Justin. Animals were like children. They knew good things.

She should turn in, but the night whispered differently, the warm wind light as a kiss. Tomorrow they had a full day; eight sorely needed customers boarding the Wendell Holmes at 7am for the trip to Long Drop-Off and, if they were lucky, an encounter with the ancient past. She had named The Wendell Holmes in honor of Oliver Wendell Holmes senior. On the rare occasion when someone asked, she explained that she admired poets and philosophers more than barristers. More often, no one cared.

Divers just wanted to get underwater as fast as possible. On learning the origin of the vessel's name, the few who were interested often opined that naming a boat after a long dead poet was different. To which Cedar politely replied that living in the past was sometimes easier. This usually proved a conversation stopper.

She inhaled the night for twenty minutes before standing, stretching, and stowing the director's chair. The chair was a gag gift from the employees at the dive shop she had owned and run with militaristic efficiency. The shop was still there. She could see it now from the boat; dark save for the flickering fluorescent light under the porch awning. She had owned the dive shop for the first four years, long enough to decide she didn't like being a round-the-clock slave to business. Dive charters offered more freedom, but now she needed more business. You picked your shortcomings.

Hopping to the dock, she checked the lines a last time, although she knew Justin had tied them with just the right amount of slack. On some fronts he was meticulous, more like a tad obsessive, a curse from her side of the family. The glasses in the galley cabinet were arranged in ascending height; the books on the shelf in his cabin were arranged in the same fashion.

The tension in the lines was perfect.

A man's pleasant laughter issued from two slips away. The laughter rang in Cedar's ears longer than necessary.

Before retiring to her cabin, she went to the stern and looked up at the stars. Her son woke clear-eyed each morning.

"Thank you," she said.

A black smear wiped away a patch of stars. She braced herself, grabbing the railing with both hands.

Three feet of wingspan landed with an appreciable jolt.

"So," she said, as Jonathan fussed about on her shoulder, settling himself. "I suppose you'll require a meal along with a berth."

Jonathan rode regally on her shoulder into the galley, where she gave him a banana. Superstitious boaters believed bananas were bad luck, but Cedar believed it was worse luck to have a hungry fruit bat on your hands.

Jonathan accepted the banana as his due. He was much like a teenager. His eyes were clear, too.

He ate lustily, depositing drooly banana bits down Cedar's front. Already the galley was starting to smell like a high school locker room.

"You'd fill yourself up faster if you splattered less," she said, reaching into a cabinet to pluck two cereal bowls for breakfast. She grabbed a small plate too. "You can share a papaya with Justin in the morning, but only because you're impossibly charming."

Justin's name saw Jonathan's pointy ears prick up, but then he returned to eating.

Outside Justin's cabin, she lifted Jonathan from her shoulder and placed him on the towel rack.

He swung upside down and hung there, looking at her accusingly.

Bending to the bat she whispered, "I thought it was elephants who never forget."

Slipping into her berth, her gaze went to the tiny triangular shelf beside the porthole. The shelf was only big enough for her phone, her book of the moment, and the photograph in the handmade frame. Salt air and the passing years had seen the frame curl up at the edges. The glue beneath the shells was acceding now too; now and again a tiny shell dropped like an acorn. In the photo

Justin, maybe seven, held a conch shell to his ear, a happy light in his eyes. *Mommy, the sea is talking to me.*

For some reason she saw Jonathan's accusatory eyes.

"I refuse to apologize to man or bat," she said, closing her eyes. "It's a mother's prerogative to live in the past."

In the darkness my brethren take to the chicken as I once took to the sailors, before I became more cautious. The oceans remain a big place, but people cannot go missing willy nilly these days. In the days of sailing ships, leaving shore was dropping off the map. I had a field day. When a rare vessel happened by after the fact, splintered timbers and floating debris could be accounted for by so many things. For the sea farers of yore, disaster arrived regularly and in myriad forms.

Today your vessels are far sturdier and tracked incessantly by technology. A ship that disappears on a calm day draws attention. I must control my impulses, wait for auspicious conditions. Rogue waves? The perfect storm? The Bermuda Triangle?

Maybe. Maybe not.

The greasy spoor lacing through the darkness stirs me, begets a tinge of salivation. I watch my fellows push thoughtlessly into the cage through the one way funnel. Again and again they are trapped by their gluttony, worming through the funnel's wide end to get at the feast, only to discover the funnel's narrow end offers no retreat. Five of them already float in the three cages, gorging on the last of their respective chicken without a care in the world. In this case, their obliviousness is amusing, like watching a toddler closely pursued by a mindful adult, tottering toward a fall. Without fail, these particular cages have returned my companions safely. But even with these cages I feel a touch of hesitancy and trepidation. If I have learned anything in my long years it's that there are so many exceptions to every rule. But with these cages the risk of exception is worth the opportunity for a full stomach. In the ocean pickings are slim and growing slimmer, and my fellows do not possess my hunting abilities. Drifting, I cheer them as they tear and gobble.

In the beginning, only this boat visited the reef. Now there are several boats; and soon there will be more. This is how you work. I observe every boat closely, the individual lines, the singular tone of engine, the construction of the cages that sink into the deeps at night. Most of the cages are chicken wire and badly rusted, the chickens floating loose inside, spinning slow cartwheels. I have crushed more than a few of these slipshod cages, the wire dissolving under the first slight pressure. Perhaps because of my own longevity, anything that smacks of rush offends me. In these instances I help myself to some chicken, but not too much. I allow my companions the lion's share.

The original boat, her cages are stainless steel; the chickens are always tidily and humorously affixed. I could crush these cages too, but I let them be. The stainless steel cages -- three of them, never more -- sink down every third day. I also appreciate restraint.

Almost everything about her boat is different. She idles the engine back a hundred yards before she reaches the reef, and then kills the engine entirely as she nears, drifting up expertly on a mooring buoy. Most of the time her boat disgorges divers, but sometimes she arrives without passengers, just her and the boy with the similar airiness and scent. Occasionally she comes in rough weather, when the other boats opt for safe harbor. Often they go home before nightfall, but sometimes they stay, rocking out the night. These are my favorite times. I confess on a few of these occasions I have risen into the shallows, reaching out to gently touch the hull, tracing its shell-like smoothness with a pleasant shudder. It is fantasy; but why not? Rarer still, I have ignored my own rule and broken the surface. Several times, floating at a distance on still nights, I have heard the keening tumbling across the water. Despite hundreds of years of memories, the first time I heard the notes it took me some time to identify the melancholy sound.

A sound like memory. And heartbreak.

The woman plays the bagpipes terribly, without melody and only the barest trace of tune, but the music swells from her heart. If I knew how, I would smile. But it would be a bittersweet smile, for a woman who cannot carry a tune can be as sad as a woman who plays like a prodigy.

I know the captain of this vessel is a woman because I see her when she dives, but I would know this without the hazy visual acuity I possess. I cannot explain this to you. I do not understand it entirely myself. But when she is near I feel it as clearly as if you whispered "woman" in my ear, if I had an ear; a settling comfort, a balm of serenity, a soothing stroking, and something unconquerable and fierce too. I like how it feels. A steady, quiet strength; an intentness with limitless resolve. Resolve that will be needed.

The weaker sex? Now there is a joke without equal.

The woman and the boy, both with the sea green eyes, they soothe me. I do not feel what you call emotion, but I feel.

It is our connection and your hope.

Cheeseheads

The eight divers were from Green Bay, Wisconsin, men in their fifties, who, back when they had hair and incaution, were fraternity brothers. Given a choice Cedar preferred women divers, but diving, generally for the worse, remained a man's sport. Women paid attention to what they were doing and listened to instructions. In ten years Cedar had never had a woman jump in without a weight belt or a mask. Over the same ten years she'd seen men do both, and far worse, on a daily basis. Men competed on every stage, and a dive boat captained by a woman elevated the chest bumping to near hysteria. Too, there were few more testosterone-addled arenas than diving, with all the gear and the manly song of the sea. Every man was a Navy Seal until he realized his wetsuit was on inside-out. The other dive boat operators made fun of their customers behind their backs. She did not. Let the one without ego cast the first stone. Still, men generally made her job harder, and this included stifling smiles.

There were degrees to this testosterone tempest and the fraternity brothers fell on the tepid side. They clambered on board, toting the normal amount of gleaming, never-been-wet, state-of-the-art gear, and one of the men was so hung over the bags under his eyes resembled coagulated tomato soup. But they shouted Cheesehead at each other and made jokes at their own expense, and they stowed their gear neatly under the benches.

Justin moved about the deck, passing a clipboard from man to man. Each man scrawled something before passing the clipboard back to her son.

Her divers always signed their waivers at the dive shop before they boarded the Wendell Holmes. Perusing the waivers ahead of time allowed her to see the divers' experience, although most men lied about that too.

When her son passed close she said, "What's going on, Justin?"

Justin handed the clipboard to the next man.

"They're placing bets."

This man immediately made a quick notation.

"Don't need to be Stephen Hawking this time around," he said, handing the clipboard back.

"Bets on what?" Cedar asked.

The next man resembled a chubby-cheeked cherub.

"First to chum," the cherub said. "We *are* from Wisconsin, not known for its seafaring types. Everyone tosses ten dollars into the pot; winner take all. My money's on Alex," he scanned the paper, "and, surprise, I'm not alone." He consulted his watch. "In cases of an obvious front runner, we also bet on time."

Turning, he smiled at the tomato-eyed man seated beside him.

"Don't let me down now, Alex. I've got you at seven-thirty, and I have two boys in college." The cherub held out his watch for Alex to see. "That's three minutes, in case you aren't quite here in the present."

"I'd sooner swallow it down than see you win," said Alex.

"If you aspirate yourself can I have your dive knife?"

"Fudge you," said Alex and Cedar liked him instantly. They were just words and her son knew them all, but still.

Justin stood, embarrassed, before Alex.

"It's okay," Alex said. Taking the clipboard with a shaky hand, he wrote his name in big block letters. "Always believe in yourself, young man." He gave the cherub a waxy smile. "Seven thirty-one, loser."

They were tied to the dock, the engines slowly throttling. On a breezeless tropical morning the diesel fumes had nowhere to go.

A passing skiff set the Wendell Holmes rocking.

Cedar saw Alex go grayer.

"Give me the clipboard, quick," said the man on his other side.

"Up yours, legal beagle," said Alex.

Thrusting the clipboard into Justin's hands, he turned and puked over the side. The water made his voice echo slightly.

"Wendell Holmes," he said. "I hope it's the poet. Lawyers make me sick."

Today the South Pacific was smooth as glass. The Wendell Holmes skimmed across the surface like a skipping stone. Cedar was happy for the Wendell Holmes and Alex.

In calm seas it took forty minutes to get from Koror harbor to Long Drop-Off Reef. They could make the trip faster, but she had Ernan hold the throttle back. The price of gas kept going up as fast as Santy, the fuel dock owner, could add.

Usually Cedar joined Ernan up on the bridge for the first half of the trip. When Long Drop-Off was about fifteen minutes away, she would come down the ladder to hobnob with the divers. Conversation helped calm the nervous ones. If Justin didn't have schoolwork, she had him visit with the divers while she was up on the bridge. He was already better with people than she was. He was genuinely curious about everything and he had his father's charm. Sometimes her son's ease with strangers amazed her.

She backed down the ladder carrying a Tupperware container and a photo album. The brownies provided a jolt of energy; the album provided a test.

Alex ignored the brownies, but not the album.

He looked much better after thirty minutes of fresh air.

"What's that there?" he asked.

His inquisitiveness made her smile. It would be a black day when curiosity died.

"No peeking at the photos," she said.

"She might let you see them if you weren't breathin' three week old garbage," cherub cheeks said.

"Even those breathing fresh-baked brownies don't get to see the photos until after the dive," said Cedar, placing the album on the camera table.

"She didn't even let Heidi Klum see it," said Justin.

This called the fraternity to order.

"Heidi Klum was on this boat?"

A man in too short shorts moaned.

"Gaaaawd almighty. She's probably the only person in the world who looks good in a wetsuit. Got shots of Miss Klum in there?"

"I run a dive boat, not a modeling agency."

"Cruel fate to miss her," said the man in the shorts.

"She could have signed your belly, Arve," said Alex. "After she wrote out the Declaration of Independence."

"I'd bet she'd rather sign my belly than watch you puke."

"You already lost one bet today," said Alex.

Cedar said, "All you need to know about Heidi Klum is she had excellent buoyancy control and she paid close attention to the dive master. Help yourself to the brownies."

"We can't see the photos?" asked Alex. "Just so we know what's down there?"

Most dive boats showed their divers photos of what they might see. Cedar eschewed standard procedure. She wanted her divers to feel the first shock of loveliness in the world where it belonged. Almost always, though, there was someone who tried to steal a look at the photos. This little game let her know who might require closer shepherding below the surface.

Ernan cut the engine. Suddenly everyone's voice sounded louder.

Arve rubbed his belly as if it might bring him luck.

"We need to know what we're gonna see," he pleaded.

"If I knew what we were going to see, I'd show it to you," said Cedar.

She nodded to the unopened water bottle in Alex's hand. *I should have stayed below and watched him, made sure he was drinking on the way out.*

"Drink that bottle. Dehydration increases the risk of decompression illness, and you've lost some fluids."

"Alex Steiner performs the stomach serenade," said Arve.

Ernan maneuvered the Wendell Holmes up on the mooring buoy. Ernan was the best captain she had ever had. He was only twenty-two by his own best guess, but as a street orphan in Manila, he had grown up fast. What he lacked in a birth certificate he made up for with street sense and mechanical ability. It was as if he had been born inside an engine. Personable when he had to be, he preferred to keep to himself. He only left the bridge to do work down below.

Sprawled flat across the bow, Justin reached out with the gaffe and hooked the mooring line.

Cedar turned to Alex.

"You know what to do if you feel like you're going to be sick underwater?"

"Puke in Arve's alternate air source?"

It was a shallow dive. Cedar was willing to put up with a little joking. But she put on her serious face because bad things happened in shallow water too.

"If you're going to be sick, keep the regulator in your mouth. Everything goes straight out through the exhalation valve. You might want to make sure the first breath after you get sick is a light one, just in case there's some small semblance of leftovers." She lowered her voice. "And you don't have to dive at all if you don't feel up to it."

"I prefer to puke where it's cool," Alex said.

His tone was deferential. His eyes still bled, but his hands ably checked his gear.

"Fair enough," she said. "It won't get wasted down there."

She looked at the other men. Their faces were sufficiently sober.

She knew the spiel by heart, like a David Bowie song, but she made sure she never sounded rote.

"Listen closely, please. It's an easy dive. We don't go any deeper than forty feet because that's the top of the reef. We'll stay pretty much right under the boat since that's where the cages are. But you still need to keep a close eye on your gauges. When you get to 700 psi, signal me and head up. There's almost no current right now, but that can change, so everyone goes up the mooring line. No exceptions. And I still want a safety stop, three minutes at twenty feet. As for the magic while we're down there, wait for my okay sign before you handle them. Once I give you the okay, please be very gentle. They've made an ascent that would kill us and they've existed longer than we can imagine, but they're still fragile. Handle with loving care."

"Honeymoon night," someone said.

"This will be better," Cedar said.

She smiled, but she meant it. The sight of Earth's prehistoric past always filled her with joy and hope. A timeline unbroken.

But there was something else too and she felt it again as she stood, geared up, on the swim step. It was a feeling less in the heart and more down the spine, a buzz so faint she could almost discount it, a whisper from the end of a dark hallway.

The hiss of primal warning.

She didn't go in afraid. But she always went in aware.

Pressing her mask to her face, she jumped.

I know what happens on the boat. If I may be immodest for a moment, the interminable years have allowed me to develop skill sets beyond the pall. What was once impossible first become possible with tremendous effort, then a bit of concentration, and finally it is something I can do in my sleep, although I don't sleep. The best explanation I can think of is this. Imagine yourself standing in a dark room without distraction. Through the wall, you hear conversation. Some words reach your ears as a mumble, but you decipher the words that matter. And words, they are character. Sometimes they are actions. Standing in that dark room, with practice you can paint a crystal clear picture of what is transpiring on the other side. I still get things wrong, but not very often. These days, more often than not, you might as well be shouting inside my head. It is not a one way street either.

My skills are not confined to your species, but your species is far and away the most challenging and fascinating to decipher. Roaches, as you might suspect, have elemental motives. I can predict their actions as you can predict the sunrise. But man... well, what a trunk of tricks and sleights of hand you are. I place my ear against your proverbial door as often as I can. It is entertaining, enlightening, and sometimes quite moving. It can also be terrifying. There are things far worse than monsters in the deeps.

You might call it clairvoyant or telepathic. I prefer a simpler explanation. I see behind the curtain.

I hear each diver's plunge, raindrops evenly spaced. She enters first so that she may watch the others. She falls lightly and breathes easily. The boy is last. Despite his youth, he is already more finely attuned than his mother. He is a rare find. Every time he enters the water, I feel a surge of hope.

I stay well out of sight, but I remain close enough. I trust the woman and the boy, but if the years teach you one thing, it's not to assume anything. As I said, of all Earth's species yours is the least predictable. Hunger nudges me too, but I control myself. Survival is about control. Taking only what you need.

As they play atop the reef, I drift just beneath the swath of gloaming light.

Below me it is black. I do not look down.

Monsters don't like darkness. Darkness is just as lonely for us.

After the dive, everyone was quiet. The fraternity brothers sat apart in the sunshine with their thoughts.

This was the part Cedar relished. It made her believe in mankind again.

Patience and Blindness

I am not the monster of anyone's nightmares. I possess no razor talons, no yellow eyes, no unbalanced mind or morals. I am capable of short bursts of speed, but as I said, I am rarely quick, and I am far from lithe. From a distance, without the scope of proximity to account for size, my approach might elicit a laugh or a scratch of a temple; though as I grow larger the laugh is likely to clutch in your throat. If there were a red carpet for sea monsters, I would garner accolades for worst dressed. But I am strong, and intelligent enough -- though one should never overestimate one's intelligence -- and, after all these years, though I've discovered many things I wish I could forget, I remain curious. And I am very patient. The importance of patience cannot be overstated.

Although patience cannot be strung out forever.

Cedar knew she watched Justin with a keenness that bordered on obsession. She had watched him today when they were down with the cages. When she had a good group of divers, and the Wisconsin frat brothers had proved to be a good group of divers, she let Justin free dive, descending to the reef with just mask and fins. Should anyone need supplemental air, she could provide it; and really, at forty feet, they could just swim to the surface.

Letting him free dive was selfish in part -- his ease in the water was a joy to behold - but it was practical too. Without a tank, Justin emitted no loud stream of bubbles. He went to the cages first.

Opening them from the top, he gently lifted each nautilus free, handling them for a few moments, gently bumping them up again as they drifted down, acclimating them before the clumsier divers handled them, with their bubble bursts and muffled regulator shouts.

This morning when they had winched up the cages, each cage attached to fifteen hundred feet of line, the chickens were already sorely shredded, courtesy of seven gorged cephalopods. It was a better than average haul. Raised from such depths, the tremendous change in pressure saw most deep sea creatures explode like briny fireworks. Not so the remarkable nautilus. Their chambers released gas as they rose, letting them adjust to the decreasing pressure.

One by one, Justin had presented each Cheesehead with his own nautilus. For thirty minutes the divers had admired them; the brown and white shells ivory smooth, the inner curves white as snowfall. Underwater they possessed the heft of an ephemeral paperweight. When released they wobbled resolutely for the deeps, so that their diver had to gently nudge them upward again. The scene always reminded Cedar of an astronaut volleyball team in sore need of practice.

It was the rarest gift, holding a creature from another epoch. Most divers appreciated this. The Cheeseheads had. But not everyone was smitten. The previous week, the divers back on board eating orange slices in the sun, Cedar heard a man mutter, “What a surprise. A big fucking snail. I could have picked one up in my garden for free.”

She had said nothing. Back at the dock, she had presented the man with his refund, informing him that money can’t buy insight. *That* had surprised him.

They returned to Koror harbor at one in the afternoon, the happy Cheeseheads rumbling down the dock for shade and beers at the White Squall, the thatch-roofed bar that looked out over the lagoon.

Cedar and Justin loaded everyone's gear on two carts, wheeling the carts to the concrete bunker that served as a locker room. They dunked the gear in the rinse tanks, hanging the wetsuits and BCDs on hangers. Justin placed each diver's fins in front of their gear, tucking their mask inside one fin. Full service was what it took to survive.

Cedar left Justin behind when she went to refuel. She didn't ask him, but she knew he would head for the White Squall, where he would order a cream soda and further charm the divers. Had she wanted to condemn him to a life of sun-burnt toil and sleepless nights, she would have made him a business partner in an instant. She knew he would accept in an instant.

Santy was, as always, at the fuel dock. In ten years Cedar had rarely seen him anywhere else. By her best guess, he was well past seventy, but Santy was not a man to divulge personal details, although he was muchly interested in the details of others. A lifetime of equatorial sun had turned him to mahogany. He was equally stoic. She had never heard him laugh, much less seen him smile. On the rare occasion when something amused him tremendously, he tugged an ear. Many thought him a sourpuss.

Santy did not need to be convivial. Owning the island's only fuel dock provided him power and the steadiest income on the island. Even the owners of the big resort hotels kowtowed to him.

Cedar liked Santy. He had two gears, complaint and nosiness, for which he made no apology.

As soon as she stepped down to the rocking dock, Cedar heard the mewling. The two kittens were tucked in the shade of a propped up box. Santy was always taking in strays. He was something of an anomaly on an island that preferred to eat their animals.

"They're even cuter than you," she said, peering under the box.

"They eat too damn much," said Santy.

Something about their needy cries made her stomach feel empty. She tried to push the loneliness away.

"New additions?"

"A coward dropped them here in the middle of the night. Now I have to listen to their squalling even after I fill their stomachs. You want them?"

"You need to refine your sales pitch."

They stood quiet as fuel poured into her tanks and money poured into Santy's pockets.

"Seventh Day Adventists were just here," Santy said. "Holy rollers asked me for free gas for their dinghy."

"Those without, need a lift from us all."

"Those without can take up the oars. Heard the swingers had a party Saturday night. Should have told the holy rollers *that*. A true second coming."

Cedar considered ignoring him, but Santy proved it wouldn't matter.

"Maybe instead I should sell Wesson oil, plastic sheeting and ecstasy," he mused.

"It still won't get you on the guest list."

"You are mistaken. The Nelson woman favors me."

"It could be a wait. She favors everyone."

The Nelsons were ex-pats from Birmingham, Alabama. Although their parties were held in secret, everyone on the island knew about them. The guest list was equally well known. It included some of Koror's most powerful and upstanding citizens. Cedar had heard that, before arriving in Palau, Martine Nelson had served as head of Birmingham's National Charity League chapter.

The tropics changed people. The Nelson's two teenage daughters went to boarding school in New Hampshire and never visited.

"She is a comely woman. No doubt she looks the same, shining in oil."

This time Cedar did ignore him.

Santy spat a glop of betel nut into the water. He gave it single-minded attention as it floated beneath the dock.

"Got an engine needs inexpensive repair," he said. "You interested?"

"Inexpensive repair?"

"Minor."

Santy knew almost as much about engines as Cedar, but he refused to invest in more than the bare minimum of tools. Anything he couldn't permanently solve with creativity and duct tape rapidly went south. The engine on his dinghy was forever quitting, his colorful curses raining down on every ear in the harbor.

"If it's minor, why don't you fix it yourself?"

The water lapped beneath them.

"You are troublesome on every front."

"You've already told me that."

"I am too busy now for repairs."

"I can see."

Santy was very literal. It made him difficult to goad.

"As I said, the repair is inexpensive. Barely worth your while. Let me know. If you are not up to the task, you can send the Filipino."

Santy had known Ernan since she hired him three years ago.

"His name is Ernan."

"That is his parents' concern. You bring the Heidi Klum today?"

Santy always called her that, as if there were imitation Heidi Klums. Cedar had brought the German model to the fuel dock so that she could meet a local character. She had also wanted to see if the presence of Heidi Klum might cause Santy's stoicism to falter. Santy had retained his mahogany visage as Heidi Klum stepped on to the fuel dock, but Cedar had not missed how his hands had fidgeted, picking at his weather-beaten trousers as if pinching himself. He had been so nervous, he had barely talked to her.

Now he never stopped talking about her. She had departed four weeks earlier, back to a life only Heidi Klums know, but Cedar knew she would be the topic of conversation four weeks from now and four years from now.

"She sends her regards."

"Yes. Women are smitten with me."

"Women like the silent type."

"They do."

The old man closed his eyes, opening them again almost immediately. As much as he liked resurrecting Heidi Klum, he liked complaining more.

"Even the Godly try to bilk me," he said, spitting again.

"You shouldn't complain so much. Look at your job. Standing around in the sun all day, shooting the breeze with Heidi Klum, and staring at her breasts from behind those mirror shades."

"They are aviator glasses."

He was looking at her breasts now.

"Fine Charles Lindbergh."

Cedar paid him.

"Tip," she said.

"Tip?"

The slight uptick almost made her smile.

"Push your glasses up on your nose or people will see where you are looking."

"You are a cruel and difficult woman," said Santy, pulling at an ear.

Justin was waiting when Cedar eased the Wendell Holmes into the slip.

He hopped on board.

"Just tie off the bow line," said Cedar. "We're going back out."

Justin looked up to the bridge, disappointment on his face.

"We have an afternoon booking?"

"No." Already she felt badly. "I was just hoping to sleep away."

Cedar saw Issy, standing by the army green dunk tanks outside the locker room. Six feet tall, and most of that legs, she was difficult to miss. She reminded Cedar of those long ago circus performers who marched about on stilts, only they didn't move with a ballerina's grace. The rest of her body matched her legs.

Issy's yoga routines, performed in a bikini at the end of one of the docks, were famous across the island and, no doubt, to shores far beyond. Power yoga on a humid island was sweaty work. That the girl was absolutely oblivious to her charms made her all the more charming.

Not surprisingly, Issy was a profound distraction to her son, but Cedar liked her just the same. The girl was whip smart, and though she was still slightly shy around her boyfriend's mother, Cedar saw how she laughed around Justin, and when he did something stupid she cuffed his temple with the heel of her hand. They'd been dating for six months, if this generation still called it that. She had nice parents. Cedar didn't know them well, they had all met once for dinner, but on Koror they were known as dedicated social workers. Also, Issy always smelled of coconut sunscreen. In Cedar's experience, teenage girls didn't readily apply sunscreen. That Issy's parents kept a close eye on their daughter eased Cedar's mind a little, although the sight of her legs always renewed Cedar's concerns. One heated mistake could ruin a life.

Issy waved and smiled, displaying teeth white as snow. Cedar waved and smiled back, wondering if it was okay to hate her just a little.

"You have plans," she said, looking down at her son.

"There's a new movie."

Koror had one theater that screened one film, usually for about three months at a pop. It was true they were far off the beaten path, but it was also true the theater was owned by a man with little interest in movies.

Justin tied off the bowline in two quick motions.

Cedar kept a small apartment which she used mostly as a rental for tourists. It was empty now. She wanted to say *You can stay*, but you don't put rib roast in front of a starving man.

To firm her resolve, she looked at Issy again.

"Tell Issy I'm really sorry. Really, I am. I'll have you back in time for tomorrow's movie."

"Give me a second," said Justin.

Justin landed soft as a cat. He walked down the dock with an easy bounce.

She hated herself for her selfishness, but she suddenly needed to go. It was often that way. And Justin needed to go with her because his sixteen-year-old girlfriend already had Heidi Klum's legs. He also needed to go because his mother wanted him with her.

Justin stayed below the entire way out. He didn't come up when Cedar cut the engine. She tied the Wendell Holmes to the mooring buoy on her own.

Justin had always possessed a strange sense of fairness. When he was in third grade, the teacher had called everyone to the rug for a discussion. A classmate had stolen a colored pen from one of the other children. How, the teacher asked, did this make them all feel? Justin stood. How, he asked, would they feel if they had to sit and listen to everyone talk about how bad they were? The teacher had called an end to the discussion. She had told Cedar the story at her parent-teacher conference.

This sense of justice had a dark side, though. These days anything that impinged on his magisterial sense of right turned him annoyingly sulky.

When she went below he was reading at the table in the galley. *Of Mice and Men*. Her latest assignment.

"Don't worry. We're tied off."

He didn't look up.

She almost stalked off, but then she recalled she was the adult.

"What do you think of Steinbeck?"

"He's okay. A little slow."

She reached into a cabinet.

"He's a tad short on car chases, CGI and gratuitous skin, but he grows on you." She placed the bag on the counter, but not before giving it a healthy crumpling. "I'll make us a popcorn appetizer."

She waited.

"Popcorn," she said. "My way of saying thanks for coming."

"Did I have a choice?"

"No. Sometimes life is like that."

She popped the popcorn in the microwave and poured the steaming mass into a bowl.

She put the bowl on the table.

"Careful," said Justin. "It's hot."

It was a perfect imitation.

"I won't be around to protect you forever, you know."

His eyes didn't leave the book.

She made tuna casserole for dinner. While she worked at the stove, Justin set the table and returned to reading.

When she sat down, sliding the casserole dish toward him, he said, "It's better already. The book," he added, and she saw the flicker of smile.

"The other, too, shall pass."

Uncorking the rest of the smile, he put Steinbeck down.

"Coming out here doesn't bother you because you're only

interested in one movie." He said it kindly. "I'm sorry. It's just that we were really looking forward to tonight. I can wait until tomorrow." He paused. "You don't deserve to be treated like that."

She looked down into the casserole, allowing for a moment of recovery.

"Summon Kong," she said.

After they cleaned up, restlessness drove Cedar up on deck. She unfolded the director's chair and settled her feet on the railing. The sun was setting, the world assuming a golden hue.

My golden girl Wyatt had called her, back when things were right. It was meant to sound possessive and it rang a little shallow, but in the days when she had loved him with every fiber it had only made her flush.

Alone on the deck, she ran a hand along her thigh and smiled. The skin was the largest organ, always a fun fact, and her skin had always been her showcase. Though at one time she had belonged wholly to Wyatt, she had never belonged to Chicago. Even during Chicago's Viking winters she had somehow absorbed sun from somewhere; in a pasty world she had glowed, a tropical flower (a foreshadowing?) in a snow-blown field. Men had responded like bees. A few women had proposed pollination too, though most simply had a question. *You **must** tell me dear. What **do** you do for your skin?* The honest answer was nothing, and Cedar was honest. Though she had wanted friends, even among the society women (here mostly to please Wyatt), always the women had retreated, angry and stung by her refusal to share.

Although she was careful about the sun, Palau had heightened her glow. In Chicago she had kept her thick hair in bob; a bob dried quickly and so was more conducive to a social schedule that developed on the fly. Now her hair was long. She had no social schedule and she liked the way it tickled the small of her back. Light brown by heredity, salt and sun had lightened it so the tips dissolved against the backdrop of her skin, gold on gold.

Hand still resting on her thigh, she probed with her fingers. As a girl she had been bony and hard-edged, perfect for a tomboy vying for supremacy with Midwestern farm boys. Womanhood had softened and curved the edges, but her fingers told her the underlying firmness was still there, maintained by a life of movement.

Alone on the deck, she allowed these little indulgences in vanity.

Alone on the deck she took her hand off her leg.

She couldn't remember the last time another hand had rested there.

When Justin came up on deck the stars were out. He was wearing boxers and a t-shirt. There was much Chicago in him. His legs fairly glowed in the dark. In a place of blazing sunshine, he was like a mushroom tucked away. It made her want to protect him even more.

"Goodnight," he said.

"Already?"

"It's eleven."

"Hmm. Perhaps it is. Have you been reading all this time?"

"Nope. Watching a movie."

"Oh?"

Justin was looking out at the water.

Sometimes it was like chipping paint.

"What did you watch?"

"Titanic."

Leonardo DiCaprio and Kate Winslet made love in the back of a car.

"Some captains might deem that bad luck," she said.

"Any captain who hits an iceberg out here should be doing something else."

"Point taken."

He was turning to go.

"Justin."

"What?"

"I was young. I had dates. I went to movies. Plural."

She pretended to look out at the water, but she was aware only of her ghostly son. His smile was like the sun rising.

"Is that another apology?"

"Yes."

"You don't need to apologize. I like it out here."

"We'll be home tomorrow in time for popcorn. Movie popcorn. You can eat it at whatever temperature you like."

She tried to smile but she couldn't.

After he left, she sat listening to him moving about below. The porthole window creaked open. She imagined him settling into bed, putting in ear plugs.

She knew why she was restless and sad. Her time was running

out. Now was the time for Issy and the Issys to follow. She now stood in the wings.

This loneliness was far worse than the loneliness that had swept over her on Santy's dock. She wondered if she should take the kittens.

She went below and opened the footlocker.

Up on the deck she sat for a time simply holding the bagpipes. Finally she put the blow pipe to her lips.

A breeze rose. In the dark water, things stirred.

Oil spills, overfishing, rising ocean temperature, ocean acidification, extinction rates 10,000 times the norm; the wanton destruction of our nurseries, our reefs, our worlds. You are, quite literally, killing us. It is almost like war. You force us to fight back. Against you, but for all of us. For as the oceans go, so you go. You are blithely sawing at your own throat.

Why can't you see this? How can a species so intelligent be so blind?

Bull Shark

Cedar was watching the sunrise from the bridge of the Wendell Holmes when her cell phone rang. Rummaging in the pocket of her windbreaker, she found her glasses. It was annoying. She didn't know when they had started making digital readouts so small.

Five-thirty. She pressed the button.

"We want to see the dinosaur freak show."

It was a voice she knew, a voice from her high society Chicago days, a voice of power and quite certain expectations. Men who never heard the word 'no', even when it was spoken, blunt and harsh, followed by a fist to the throat, leaving one of Wyatt's former business partners gawping on the den floor.

Her impulse was to hang up. But yesterday on the fuel dock the dollars had spun away impossibly fast, and in less than two years Justin would be going to college and, though Wyatt had offered to cover everything, she was paying half. To do that, she would have to repair Santy's engine and swallow her pride.

"You mean the nautilus dive."

"Dress it up however you like."

"I'm sorry, but I'm not at the dock."

"How soon can you be there?"

It was a gauzy orange dawn, the smell of brine light on the water. Suddenly she wasn't sure if she wanted to swallow her pride.

"Eight-thirty."

"Are you swimming back? See you at seven."

She imagined bringing her knee up into the speaker's crotch. It gave her some small satisfaction.

"How many in your party?"

"Three."

She had always told Justin to accept people as they are. People didn't always meet your standards, but your standards aren't the only measuring stick. But she hadn't liked this man from his first words and she was growing tired of being open-minded.

"I'm sorry," she said, working to sound like she meant it. "I have a five person minimum. Anything less and it costs me to go out."

"What's a full boat?"

The question wasn't a surprise. Nor was her shame in answering it.

"Ten divers."

"Don't be noble. The other dive boats take at least twenty."

"I'm not the other dive boats."

"That's why we're going with you."

"I still need two more divers."

"We'll pay for ten."

She thought, *I should say that's not necessary. Tomorrow is Tuesday. The weekly flight from Paris will bring in a new batch of divers. Come out tomorrow and save yourself a bucket of cash.*

"If you insist."

"That includes beer."

"I don't allow alcohol on my boat."

"I said I'd pay for ten."

"And I'll say I have rules I won't break."

There was a long silence.

"Safety first," the man said.

"I'm glad we agree. You're experienced divers?"

The man laughed and hung up just as she'd known he would.

She rigged the chickens and sank the cages before waking Justin. She kept a box of whole chickens in the galley freezer. Failing to prepare was preparing to fail. She didn't follow basketball anymore, college or professional - too many paternity suits and selfish egomaniacs - but she still admired UCLA coaching legend John Wooden.

It was odd watching the grease slick spread across dawn waters. It didn't look right. It was a rush job. Already she had a bad feeling.

The men were worse in person, but they were punctual. She saw them as she passed the breakwater, standing at the dock, the tallest man in front.

Justin was sleepily making his way to the bow line when the tall man surprised her by hopping nimbly on board before she bumped against the dock. He had the line in his hand before she could speak.

Justin looked up at her.

“My son does that.”

“Already done.”

She did not miss the easy throw, or how the red-headed man on the dock deftly caught the line but did not fix it to the cleat.

The tall man produced an arctic smile.

“Touch and go,” he said.

“I do my dive briefing here at the dock. Tie us off,” she said to the red-headed man.

The man hesitated and then did as he was told.

The two men on the dock boarded. The men were all in their forties, lean, with faces roughened by wind and sun. The lettering on their dive bags was faded, but the tag on the tall man’s bag showed his name in clear precise letters.

“Coffee part of this rig?” the tall man asked.

Justin was already below.

“My son is fixing it.”

“Boy’s a quick study.”

I want to toss you and that smug smile over the railing. I need the money.

It stung.

She placed the folder on the camera table.

"As you know, there's paperwork to sign," she said.

The red-head laughed.

"What's with the fucking Halloween decoration?" he said.

Jonathan was perched on the closest piling. He leaned forward slightly. She knew what he was doing.

"He's a fruit bat," Cedar said. "Testing the breeze."

"A fucking weather vane."

"In a fashion."

The red-head regarded Jonathan curiously.

"I hear the locals eat them in pies," he said.

"They're a local delicacy," Cedar said. "I haven't tried them."

The man nodded to Jonathan.

"When in Rome. I think I'll eat your sister tonight."

"If they're not prepared correctly, you can die," Cedar said.

The red-haired man had the same white smile as the tall man, attractive until it was set in the face of an asshole.

"Bullshit."

"No, poison. There's a gland in their throat. It contains a digestive enzyme that breaks down the simple carbohydrates in fruit. Good for the bat, deadly for humans." She made it up as she went along, shuffling the dive waivers to keep from looking at the man. Liars knew liars. "If the chef doesn't remove the gland cleanly, gives it the slightest prick," she gave the word *prick* a slight emphasis, "the poison floods the bat's system. It's tasteless. A neurotoxin." She nodded at Jonathan. "A bat that size will kill all three of you. There's some mild discomfort first."

She gave the man her best poker face.

He regarded her.

"Maybe I'll order the meatloaf," he said.

Cedar hoped someone had neglected to shower, but Jonathan stayed where he was, watching the men fill out the paperwork and set up their gear. With the start of the engines, he lifted off with a chaotic whopping. Cedar noted, with satisfaction, that the red head nearly dropped his dive computer.

She watched Jonathan fly toward the jungle. No worthy scent today, but Nature adjusted. She was sure Jonathan had a ready supply of bananas and a harem of smelly beauties waiting for him.

On the way out, Cedar and Justin stayed up on the bridge. Cedar stayed because she piloted the Wendell Holmes. They hadn't planned on a charter. Ernan had the day off.

They didn't speak, warm wind rushing past their ears. Now and again they heard laughter below. The tall man had paid in cash, the fat envelope tucked in the strong box wedged beneath the console. Before accepting the money Cedar had explained there was a better than even chance the cages would be empty. By the time they returned to the reef the cages would have been down for only two hours, and that at the very end of night's feeding.

Handing her the money, the tall man had said, "Who likes a sure thing?"

She had Justin bring the boat up to the reef. She dove in to fix the line to the mooring. She didn't know why, but she wanted to look around. The morning was bleak and overcast. Below her the reef was a dusky blue-gray smear. The three lines affixed to the cages disappeared down into the darkness. The cool water gave her a chill.

She always wore a one-piece Speedo around clients. She saw how the men watched her as she stepped back on board. She slipped her baggy gym shorts on without toweling off and followed Justin to the bow to winch up the lines.

Her son was subdued.

"I hope the catch of the day is strictly chicken," she said, but it didn't sound funny.

"They'll just come out again," said Justin flatly. He stared at the line as it emerged, dripping, from the water. "I know you're doing this for me."

"A half day is gone in a wink. We'll go out to an early dinner before your movie, you, me and Issy."

"I don't like them."

Accept people for who they are.

"I don't either."

Cedar dove with the men, leaving Justin with the boat. She kicked herself for not calling Ernan. He would have come without protest. She was only one set of eyes. She knew the men were more than competent. No one would flood a mask; no one would have trouble with their buoyancy; no one would drift down past the edge of the reef, at least not mistakenly.

She told herself there would be none of the traditional trouble she usually watched for, but it wasn't traditional trouble that worried her. She hadn't trusted the men from the outset. The feeling had only grown stronger.

They handled themselves like the experienced divers they were. There were three nautili, one in each cage. The men waited patiently while Cedar extricated them carefully, demonstrating how to handle them. The men did exactly as they were told, gently prodding the shells up as the nautili tried to make for the bottom. After thirty minutes they hadn't lost interest. When Cedar signaled them for a gauge check, they had more air than she did.

The morning overcast had burned away. Shafts of sunlight slanted prettily through the water, flickering in the foggy blue. Her bubbles made a hypnotic burble. She began to relax. Maybe she had been wrong. Maybe the past had wound her tight.

The bull shark simply appeared. One moment the water column was empty. The next it contained eight feet of shark. A female, like all bulls she was wine cask thick. Her sudden appearance startled Cedar, but there was no cause for alarm. Bulls rarely came to this reef, but when they did the clear waters ensured both sides recognized each other and kept their respective distance. She was relieved the men were experienced. She looked quickly to see if they had seen the shark. The tall man still juggled his nautilus, his head down. He had descended deeper than Cedar liked. She could barely see the shell in his hand.

The bull was beautiful, a rare treat. She swam with casual disinterest, sunlight making wavering ripples along her sides.

The tall man looked up.

Cedar froze while her brain, a stutter-step behind, tried frantically to sort things out. The tall man gave off an explosion of bubbles. In the same instant, he pulled the knife from the strap on his leg and finned directly for the bull.

The bull had jerked slightly with the bubble burst. Now she jerked again. Cedar heard the sharp sound of metal on metal. Turning she saw the red-headed man sprinting for the shark, banging his knife against his dive tank as he went.

The bull convulsed, a dog readying to leap, and was gone.

When Cedar turned back to the tall man, the third man was floating beside him, holding both his arms.

By the time Cedar reached the men, the tall man's bubbles were rising easily. The other man partially blocked her, but the tall man gave her the okay signal and when she turned her thumb up the two men slowly rose together.

Back on the boat no one spoke. The tall man sat staring out at the sea. His friends fiddled with their gear.

"We don't see many bull sharks on this reef," she said. "That was a rare treat."

Something passed across the tall man's face. It wasn't anger, but he was angry.

"Give me another chance and I'll kill that fucking garbage can with my bare hands."

It should have sounded ridiculous, but it didn't sound ridiculous at all.

"Get us the fuck out of here," he said.

She did. By the time they reached the dock, the ringleader had regained his nauseating smile and swagger. His friends disembarked without a word. He stayed on board long enough to make a show of folding the hundred dollar bill and putting it in the tip jar.

He paused before stepping off the Wendell Holmes.

"Busy later?"

"Yes."

"Well then, thanks for the lack of memories."

Scooping up his gear, he stepped off the boat without a backward glance.

Cedar was just relieved it was over. If he had lingered another minute, she would have paid him a hundred dollars to leave.

She saw it as he walked down the dock, a flash of white in his mesh dive bag.

She was on him before he heard her, grabbing his arm and jerking him around with more strength than she knew she had.

"You shit-for-brains prick."

Even in the haze of her rage it sounded silly in her ears, like she was fifteen, but she was so furious it was all she could say. Her head pounded and the world swam around her.

The mocking smile didn't ease her fury

He turned his hands out, palms up.

"Change your mind about tonight?"

She struck his hand with a fist, knocking it down. She was as surprised as he was, but he recovered first.

The words were a monotone.

"Touch me again and I'll ruin your life."

She was shaking with anger and fear. She knew he could smell the difference. The realization made her shake even more.

She remembered how the other man had blocked her view.

"Why?"

The word itself shook.

He stood, relaxed and victorious.

"Well for starters, they're not protected," he said. "I can buy you a shell or crappy pair of earrings on any corner of this third world shithole, but I'm the kind of guy who likes to collect things himself. Plus your poor showing and greedy fee justified a little something extra."

"You don't know anything about the laws here. By law the local people are allowed a limited take. You're not. It's a $10,000 fine, with the good possibility of a jail term. The jail here is not pleasant."

It was another lie, but fury stamped it with credibility.

His eyes said he believed her, but the mocking smile didn't falter.

Reaching into the bag, he removed the nautilus. The tiny tentacles, like pale noodles, sagged, defeated.

He held the nautilus up between them.

"Escargot. Maybe I'll have it with fruit bat soup."

She heard someone running. Ice flooded her veins. The same ice poured into the man's face.

She turned.

Justin held the wrench away from his body.

The world froze.

Softly the man said, "I hope you know how to shit stainless steel."

Now Cedar knew only fear.

She mustered all the authority she had.

"Go back to the boat, Justin. Call the police."

Justin was wise beyond his years. Justin was sixteen.

His white knuckles turned whiter.

"You asshole," he said.

"Strike two. One more and you're out."

"Justin. Give me the wrench. Now."

It seemed to Cedar that she could hear everything; the thudding vein in her temple, her son's raspy breathing, the cry of a bird from the far end of the lagoon, the plea in her voice as all the anger left her.

"Justin. Please."

His hand shook as he handed her the wrench.

"Now go call the police."

To his credit, the man waited until her son left.

"I like strong women. It's sexier when they beg for it."

"You always win, don't you?"

"Sexy *and* smart. The two of us could have some fun. How about a fresh start?"

He threw the shell. It sailed far out over the water, landing with a hollow plunk.

"I didn't know they could fly," he said. "I doubt this backwater has the funds to drag the harbor."

"I'm keeping the tip."

This produced a venomous smile.

"Any whore would."

She nodded to the skiffs lining the dock, nets spread and drying in the sun.

"The island's best fisherman doesn't make a hundred dollars in a week," she said. "They'll scour every inch of this harbor for your tip, although I don't think they'll have to. My guess is five minutes."

"Dumb bitch. Anyone could have dropped it there."

"Ninety."

"What?"

"Tentacles. On average, a nautilus has ninety tentacles."

The phone was in her hand. She bent, taking care to frame the name tag. She took three pictures to be sure.

"Not your average dive bag, lined with tentacle bits."

He stepped so close she could see where he had missed a patch of hair below his lip.

She forced herself to stare up past the quivering patch of hair.

"Is this the part where you make me beg? I'd hoped for some place more private."

The muscles in his jaw worked.

"This is the part you'll wish you could take back," he said.

He was right. Watching him walk away, she wished him dead.

I have only myself to blame. I have grown complacent. I let my guard down. There were only three divers and she was in charge so I stayed deep, though when they first entered the water I rose a bit without thinking, for the tall man's heart beat rapidly, a strange alchemy of anger and fear. Instinct is almost always right, but lassitude is a formidable adversary. The bull shark distracted me too. She was a beauty and bold, though wise enough to keep her distance from me. Sharks are not the mindless cretins you take them for. The tall man's reaction to the shark was equally puzzling; all fury and no fear.

But it is the final moment that weights me with despair. I was already descending, drifting down like an old man settling into an easy chair, when the smallest of all the heartbeats reached out to me, pleading and panicked and -- here my imagination may be running away with me -- crying betrayal. Like a stunned child set adrift. Even then I knew it was too late. Ascending -- to do what I don't know -- I heard the chime of a tank against the swim ladder and the heartbeat was gone.

I stayed down in the dark waters, but my anger continued to rise. I imagined it rising to the surface and vaulting on to the boat. What would anger look like if it took form? I imagined my anger with claws. It buried those claws deep in the man's eyes, slicing cleanly on the entry and not so cleanly in the retrieval.

I made surgical precision my templar when we met later. I wanted him to taste his own panic and despair. I knew he would swim and, when his scent first shot through water, I waited. My will against his, he bent like grass in the wind, though he swam hesitantly away from shore, as if he were just learning how. I should have waited longer; farther out his screams would have reached only indifferent sky. But vengeance makes for oversight. I rushed in, but I allowed him a long, clear look.

Oh yes, he was a different man with his hubris stripped away. I let him scream before I took him carefully apart, as if I might put him together again. He lay upon the sea, conscious of the jigsaw pieces floating about him.

I did not enjoy it after the fact. Revenge does nothing. There is a little sweetness, yes, but that quickly dissipates in the face of things you cannot change.

He tasted foul, as I knew he would.

Cedar was called in. The deceased had been on her boat that morning.

She knew everyone at the station. Behind the front desk Bella waved her through, pointing unnecessarily toward the left of the two back rooms. The door on the right was the unisex bathroom.

The small office reeked of nervous sweat. Half of Koror's police force was inside. Two of the three policemen were standing, gazing glumly at their clasped hands.

Only the man seated at the desk looked at her. Able had terrible acne, a simian brow and a rapier mind. During his twenty year tenure as chief of police he had solved every crime that had crossed his desk, though most of them involved petty crimes like the pilfering of fruit from a neighbor's garden or a bit too much marijuana grown in too obvious a place. This track record kept Koror's smarter criminal element in check. Everyone knew Able's talents were wasted on the island, but only a handful of residents ever left Palau and Able was not among them.

Cedar played poker with Able on Wednesday nights, a group of five men and one woman. When Able drank a little too much, which was rare, they persuaded him to play his ukulele. He played the ukulele well enough, but he had a voice like a mother's lullaby. On several occasions Cedar had sung with him. They sounded a little like Marvin Gaye and Tammi Terrell. Ain't No Mountain High Enough.

Now there was.

Bull and tiger sharks were not uncommon in Palau's waters. Over the years there had been a handful of attacks on local spear fishermen, but this was the first attack on a tourist. Everyone in the room had relatives employed by tourism. If they lost their jobs, those relatives would turn to their relatives who still had paychecks.

Cedar knew most of the details already, provided unsolicited by the dozen people who stopped her as she walked to the station. Inconsequential news spread like the Bubonic Plague and this was not inconsequential news. Cedar knew her client had gone swimming off the hotel beach at dusk. His screams had halted the Polynesian dance show in mid-jiggle. By the time the hotel ski boat made it out to where the man had flogged the water nothing was left but scatterings of flesh and stained water. Tomorrow before dawn locals and tourists would depart the docks to dispatch the killer. The tourists were hungry to avenge their own. The Palauans would set out reluctantly. The shark remained a deity, but money was a now a powerful god. The dead man's friends had offered a reward. It was the biggest news of all. Ten thousand dollars for a shark with a man in its stomach.

Able gestured to the only empty chair. She saw he had taken down the calendar with the women mechanics in unbuttoned overalls.

"Thank you for coming, Ms. Mahoney. I thought it best you be here. We are just beginning our questioning."

His tone was formal. His eyes said *you can help me.*

The red-headed man sat before the desk, slouched and utterly defeated. He had looked at her blankly when she stepped in. She wondered if he even recognized her.

She listened as Able asked questions. The men were from Pensacola, Florida. They were here on an annual fishing and diving getaway. The red head's name was Mark Knowlton. The dead man's name was Ted Marple. With a mild jolt of surprise, Cedar realized she hadn't once used their names. The third man was back at the hotel, ostensibly incapacitated by shock.

Able asked the questions softly but firmly. They needed to know everything they could to possibly prevent a second attack, he said. What he didn't say was a second attack would destroy the island's economy.

The questioning lasted twenty minutes. When it was done, there was silence.

Able stared at the wall as if he wished the calendar was there.

He gave a cough.

"Ms. Mahoney? Do you have any thoughts or questions?"

The red headed man turned to her slowly. *Mark Knowlton.* The pain on his face made him look like a little boy. He sat forward in their chair, fingers gripping the edge.

"I'm so sorry," she said.

Mark Knowlton's face remained blank.

"Jesus," he said. "I can't believe it."

"Mr. Knowlton," the name sounded awkward in her ears, "why did he chase after the bull shark we saw?"

Both of the policemen against the wall straightened. Able did not move.

Mark Knowlton watched her as if he had asked the question.

"I know you didn't like him," he said. "You had good reason not to. I'm sorry he took that thing. It was wrong."

She wondered if Able knew about the nautilus. None of it mattered now.

"He could be a prick."

She recognized her own infantile insult, but she knew the man before her was long past irony.

He seemed to have forgotten the question.

Everyone waited.

Mark Knowlton massaged the edge of the chair. When he looked up, he consulted the cinderblock wall too.

"None of you know him. He was the most loving father I knew. He couldn't stand to be away from his daughter. You wouldn't believe the begging it took to get him to come on these trips. Until it didn't matter."

Cedar saw Able's bland face tic. He was an awful poker player, but an excellent detective.

The man stared at the wall.

"Strange shit," he said.

Politely Able said, "What is strange?"

"No fucking way Ted swims at dusk."

"Why is that?" Able asked.

Mark Knowlton turned to Cedar.

"He wasn't scared of that bull," he said. "He really did want to kill it."

Cedar felt some terrible realization forming just outside her consciousness.

"His little girl was killed by a bull shark. She was swimming right off their dock in Pensacola. He and his wife were on the dock drinking cocktails and watching the sunset. He jumped in the water. The bull kept coming around him, hitting his daughter. She was seven. The shark finally dragged her away." He let out a slow breath. "His only child. Ruined his marriage; ruined his life. I didn't think it could get any worse. There's a fucking joke."

It was more like a cough than a laugh and then Mark Knowlton began to cry.

He has paid, but I am still racked with fury. Your short-sightedness and greed have caused the slights, large and small, to collect until even someone as far-sighted as me struggles to see beyond the moment. I float, trying to extract wisdom from the unbiased darkness, but I want only to lash out. Your wrongs, your self-absorption, your ignorance, they pile insults, one on top of the next, until there remains a great teetering tower ready to be tipped by a breath. What do you call it? Yes. The straw that breaks the camel's back. Fitting that even your aphorisms see animals suffer. The lesser beasts. Ha. Another grand joke.

I must gather myself, remind myself. You lose your head and act on impulse. I do not. That is why I will be here long after you are gone. I'm just not sure it will be a world worth inheriting.

I try, but I cannot contain myself. I send the message, reaching across the seas. It is an easy matter now, as simple as your breaths. It not so much a command as it is a powerful suggestion.

And they are all too ready to take up the cause.

Consequences

Justin was asleep when Cedar returned to the Wendell Holmes. Jonathan hung upside down beneath the towel rack, wings folded like a linty leather coat. He fluttered softly when Cedar taped the note to the door. The attack had shaken her son. Sleep was his escape.

This had not always been the case. When Justin was little she would sit in his cabin and watch him sleep, his lips issuing indecipherable mumblings while his body performed small jerks and tremblings beneath the sheets. Sometimes he would suddenly sit up and shout out, fear clear in his voice, and she would leap from her chair and take her son in her arms, holding him until the jerks and mutterings slowed and finally stilled. He never woke. The next morning he would have no recollection of any of it.

She had tried to write off his tossings as the product of a hyperactive imagination, but she had never forgotten the sound of his cries, frightened, but wretchedly hopeless too, an oddly querulous lament. She wondered what a happy-go-lucky child dreamed that broke his heart. Several times she had asked, but he had only looked at her blankly and she had stopped asking. As he entered his teens she stopped watching him sleep; such behavior might be viewed as psych ward-worthy. But now and again she heard him shout, the familiar wretched cry, and she lay in her berth, her own heart hammering, picturing him slowly quieting until he again became the peaceful boy she knew.

She had her own means of compensating. She made the phone call. A small island had its advantages. It wouldn't take either of them long to get there. Placing her ear against the door of Justin's cabin she listened to his soft snores. Snatching up her windbreaker, she walked up the hill to Shirley's Emporium.

Under normal circumstances the name alone brought a smile, so grand for an establishment with four patio tables and a six-stool bar. Shirley's Emporium had changed ownership three times in the ten years Cedar had lived in Koror, but the name always stayed. Not one of the owners and none of the old-timers could recall the place ever being owned by a Shirley, or even by someone infatuated with a Shirley. Given the number of infatuations men suffer, this alone was surprising.

Cedar favored Shirley's for her view. From any barstool you looked out across the small wood patio and down to the harbor, the uninterrupted sea beyond. Seated at the bar Cedar could see the Wendell Holmes now, a single red Christmas bulb on her stern and bow. Justin had rigged the bulbs when he was ten, running the wiring along the ceiling below decks, so that Jonathan could find their boat. Each evening, when Justin wasn't looking, she had smeared a portion of railing with banana.

Cedar sighed. Justin was too old now for tricks.

"It is indeed a sad state of affairs," said Henry agreeably.

For a moment she was startled that Henry had read her thoughts. Then she remembered why the glum bartender, elbows on the bar, stared out at the night sea with a funeral mien. The bar was empty.

"I was hoping the sad turn of events might draw a few more to the well," he said to the bowl of peanuts in his hand. "Or perhaps bring in the optimists to spend a little advance reward money."

After three years as bartender, Henry had recently assumed part ownership of Shirley's. The weight of responsibility now pressed constantly upon his mind.

"Cheer up, Henry. The All Blacks play the French this Thursday."

Cedar found rugby brutish, but the rest of the island was mad for it.

A smile rose to Henry's face.

"Ah yes," he said, popping a peanut into his mouth. "A grand butting of the heads while the butts wander in a circle." Henry had never grasped the intricacies of the game either. His face went dour again. "Perhaps that will take our minds off this terrible occurrence."

Henry believed he possessed a poet's soul, absorbing the world's sadness as his own. Coming up off his elbows, he sighed again.

"Another?" he asked.

The Red Rooster beer in her hand was nearly full.

"Let me drop it below the neck first."

"I have bought into a bar inhabited by ghosts and teetotalers," bemoaned Henry, moving off to polish glasses.

Marty was right on time. On an island where time mattered to few, Marty Haruo was never early and never late, arriving punctually with nary one curly hair out of place. The island's only home grown pilot, Marty had built his plane, a twin-engine Piper Aztec, from the wheels up. Although he spent most of his time flying over water, he had refused to build a floatplane. On an island of maritime men, Marty never touched the sea. The closest he came was boarding the Wendell Holmes for dinner. He had done this twice, both times crossing himself vigorously as he stepped aboard.

Entering the bar, he bowed slightly.

"Thank you, Miss Cedar, for saving me a seat."

Cedar had ordered his scotch malt. It was an expensive drink, but Marty never drank more than one.

"I took the liberty of ordering."

"As you always do." Marty settled on his stool. "It would go easier on your pocketbook if you weren't always early."

Henry wandered over to give Marty a bowl of peanuts and a mournful nod.

"A fine evening to you too, Henry," said Marty, lifting the scotch and smiling. The man had the whitest teeth Cedar had ever seen. "To tailwinds and following seas."

Marty sipped delicately and put the Scotch down. Half his smile disappeared.

"How are you holding up?"

Henry had sidled off, but not far off. He leaned on the bar, sipping a soda water and pretending to watch TV.

"Worse than I expected," Cedar said. "But problems are relative. I hope your sister's morning sickness has eased."

Henry made a choking noise. Marty's sister was Henry's current amour.

Cedar raised her eyebrows.

"What's the matter with him?" she said to Marty.

"Paternity and a lemon wedged in his throat," said Marty. "Just punishment for nosiness. Although I suppose it would be a dull and uncaring world if we didn't meddle in each other's business."

Henry grimaced.

"A pox on the both of you," he said and disappeared into the kitchen.

"Alone at last," said Marty.

It was their dark joke. She and Marty were always alone. His wife had died eight years earlier of pancreatic cancer. Five days separated diagnosis and death.

The beer was cold. Marty sat beside her. Cedar felt a little better.

"So," Marty said. "Talk and drink. Or just drink. Ladies choice."

Beyond the Wendell Holmes the world was black. The boat suddenly looked very small, a fleck of lint at the edge of a vast carpet.

"Maybe drinking and small talk first," she said.

"I like your hair."

It was a bob cut. Something different. She had done it herself, consulting a cover of Redbook.

It was just small talk, but it still pleased her.

"Thank you. It was getting long. And hot."

"It's quite becoming. You cut off the light hair. It makes you look more like us."

Cedar laughed.

"Well aren't you ethnocentric."

"I did not say dark hair was superior. Only decidedly more attractive."

"For some reason I feel partly responsible," she said.

Marty smiled down at the ice in his glass.

"You have never been much for dawdling. We have moved past small talk?"

"Yes."

"May I be honest?"

"It's what I count on."

"You assume guardian angel-ship for whoever sets foot on your boat. This I understand. But after they leave the boat? While magnanimous, it is impractical. Not to mention ridiculous."

The facts were simple. Ted Marple had died eight hours after leaving her boat. That she was accountable *was* ridiculous, but that didn't stop the thought from nagging her.

"It's more than that," she said.

"I don't understand."

She loved that Marty never pretended. It was the rarest trait in men.

"I don't either."

She'd been trying to frame it into a coherent thought since the news of Ted Marple's death reached her, but she had yet to mold it into anything that made sense.

Marty was the only person she trusted with her incoherent thoughts.

"I can't explain it, Marty. I just *feel* responsible." Even as she said it, it sounded less than sane. She forced herself to finish. "It's not a vague feeling either. If it wasn't so crazy, I'd be certain I played a role."

"Ah." Marty sipped his scotch. "This I would keep to myself."

"I have. I'm not that crazy."

"And Able? What did you learn from our resident Sherlock Holmes?"

Bella the receptionist was Marty's second cousin.

"Not much more than you probably already know. The man's name was Ted Marple. He went swimming at dusk. He was attacked by a shark. People on the beach heard him screaming. Several claim they saw him waving for help. Briefly." She decided to leave out the story of the daughter. It was immeasurably sad, and private, business. “The hotel skiff got there quickly, but they found almost nothing.”

The thought hung between them. Marty didn’t like the sea, but he had spent his life beside it.

“Odd, I’ll admit,” he said. “But we have big sharks and, though an exception to the rule, they don’t salute smartly to Cedar Mahoney.”

Sliding off his stool, he went behind the bar.

The second beer tasted better than the first.

“You’re trying to get me drunk,” Cedar said.

“You would do the same for me.”

“You would never accept.”

“There are always exceptions.”

She smiled.

“Not with you,” she said.

“I should take umbrage.”

“Or be flattered. Do you remember when we met?”

“Of course. The school talent show.”

“And?”

“And what?”

She gave him a wicked look.

“Mr. Haruo. You would make me suffer yet again?”

“And you played the bagpipes.”

For some unknown reason the elementary school talent show had featured children and their parents. It had been the last thing in the world she had wanted to do. But Justin was seven and there no saying no. Virtually the entire island had been in the audience. "Dawning of the Day" the song was called, and it was still the longest five minutes of her life. Even now she could see the pain on people's faces.

"And what did you say to me afterward?"

"That you still needed a little practice."

"And I've trusted you ever since. They found almost no remains. What do you think, Marty?"

Marty smoothed his cocktail napkin.

"A big tiger shark could take everything."

"Maybe. A very big tiger."

She hadn't seen a tiger shark bigger than ten feet in nearly six years. Before that she had seen them regularly, veritable monsters casting ungraspable silhouettes just beneath the surface. Once a tiger shark big around as a Volkswagen had swum casually alongside the Wendell Holmes. Now she saw no big sharks. Sharks of every species were being killed for their fins, their jaws, their meat, their purported aphrodisiac offerings and just plain irrational fear. The biggest ones were killed first. Unfortunately, size does matter.

Outside on the patio the insect zapper crackled.

She felt Marty looking at her.

"I see you are still leaving yourself open to the torment of conjecture," he said.

"There are things that just don't make sense."

"Well then, I have a suggestion. I suggest we go flying."

"What?"

"Good. How's Thursday morning?"

Suddenly, getting as far from the water as possible was all she wanted. She laughed.

"Thursday is perfect."

"Justin is welcome too."

"He can't. He's studying for a history final with Issy."

"Perhaps their generation won't repeat the mistakes we've made." Marty sipped the last of his scotch. "Quite amazing," he said.

"Good Scotch?"

"Passable. Your son's powers of concentration."

Laughing felt good.

"Let's see how they do on the test," Cedar said.

Marty gave great attention to placing his glass on the bar.

"You never just say 'Yes'."

He was right. Maybe it was two quick beers on an empty stomach. Maybe it was fear. Maybe it was drifting without a mooring.

"There are always exceptions." She heard the tinge of desperation in her voice. "Never say never to change."

A cool breeze blew across the patio, picking up her cocktail napkin and depositing it behind the bar.

"The weather is changing along with you," said Marty.

"I hated him."

She wasn't sure why she said it.

"The unofficial police report says he was a bonafide son of a bitch."

She was glad Marty didn't smile.

"I wished him dead."

Now Marty did smile.

"Cedar, it would be a chaotic world if all our desires came true."

Walking back down the hill to the harbor her words still rang in her head. It was as if she *had* sentenced him. As if she were a Mafia don seated before linen, gulping down pasta and red wine, giving only the faintest nod to a cloaked assassin.

They like this very much. Oh yes, they do. Over the next six days, in the Red Sea off the city of Sharm El-sheikh, the Red Sea is indeed red. The sharks, they dedicate themselves to the task, mauling five victims. They unnerve me slightly with their uncontrolled zest. They remind me of what I once was. Or perhaps still am. For neither your species nor mine ever changes completely. We retain our primordial underpinnings

Your scientists proclaim the Sharm El-sheikh attacks an unprecedented mystery. Before this there were only six attacks in the Red Sea over the past ten years. Your theories are amusing. Climate change, a falling off in local fish populations, ships dumping sheep carcasses into the sea, a lone rogue shark who has acquired a taste for human flesh, but no, there has never been proof of a shark acquiring a taste for human flesh before. Yes, opines one shark expert, but there are no absolutes in science either.

Indeed.

In the tourist town, sales of a T-shirt emblazoned with a shark that reads "How 'Bout Lunch?" flourish. I appreciate dark humor as much as you.

My favorite, though, is the scientist who cautions against overanalyzing because sharks are just big predators with small brains.

Might this not be the pot calling the kettle black?

Sharks are not big predators with small brains. They simply indulge in no debate and give no quarter. There are times when I wonder if I would better off being more like the sharks. But then I realize you make them gods. And I do not want to be anyone's god, least of all yours.

I feel a touch of regret when it is done. I try to think of the woman and the boy and the calm that descends to the reef with them.

Two ordinary, extraordinary people, tucked in what you ironically call a backwater, away from the posturing and squawking and self-interest of your politicians and your so-called movers and shakers.

This is our hope. The patient movers of stones. The ones you don't see.

Back at the boat Cedar couldn't sleep. She pulled the newspaper from beneath the sea turtle paperweight Justin had made in fourth grade. The *New York Times* still took four days to reach Koror. She could get breaking news, or for that matter the *Times*, on the internet, but she liked the newspaper. She loved the crackle of the pages and how it smelled of things past, and frankly she wasn't all that interested in breaking news anyway. Most of it broke madly and dissipated with equal speed.

Normally she made coffee, with a touch of cayenne to ward off colds, grabbed a chocolate chip cookie, and nursed paper, coffee and cookie on the loveseat in the galley. Tonight she just took the cookie. She was having a hard enough time sleeping already.

As always, the pages were filled with partisan politics in Washington, and death, riot and mayhem in countries most readers couldn't locate on a map. Far from being jaded, she found the news fascinating. Humanity lurked in the seams of every story and mankind was, without fail, spellbinding and unpredictable. The daily paper trumped anything fiction could imagine.

She turned the pages.

She put the cookie down mid-bite.

She read the headline twice. "Sea Beasts Quietly Attack". Slowly, she read the story. A 375-pound mako shark that plopped into the boat of a stunned fisherman; a woman struck square in the chest by an eight-foot, 300-pound eagle ray, flattening her to the deck; a Pacific blue marlin charging a boat off Hawaii, slamming into the vessel's side with enough force to knock a fisherman to his knees. "I've fished for marlin my whole life," said the vessel's captain. "I've never seen anything like it."

Several weeks earlier she had run into Santy's nephew, Steinman, at the fuel dock. Steinman was fourteen, known across the island for exaggerating everything, even the limp caused by his club foot. His mother had named him Steinman because she thought it was dignified. When he was little, his mother had told him that the gods only gave club feet to those with special courage. Now that he was older, it was Steinman's belief that an exaggerated limp provided him more opportunity with visiting tourist girls. Provided the proper pheromones, Steinman swayed side to side like a windshield wiper.

Steinman was a born storyteller, known for running away with the thinnest thread of truth, but Cedar had believed what he told her that day at the fuel dock.

"I'm divin' out at Lighthouse Reef and I see this big turtle comin', and he's gettin' bigger and bigger. I'm pointin', pointin', pointin', and suddenly I'm thinking, 'He's not stoppin'; he's lookin' to take me out'." The boy had wind-milled his arms slowly, dropping his torso back to perform a nifty limbo. "Maaaaaan, I had to make one of those Matrix moves. This huge loggerhead turtle, his head was bigger than mine, he passes right over the tip of my nose. Yes, man. Everyone wanted to know how I slipped that turtle. Smooth. Like Keanu Reeves."

Cedar scanned the article again, just to be sure.

The incidents, Steinman's included, had all taken place in the past three months.

Sea Beasts Quietly Attack. I like that. Understated. A rarity in today's world of sensationalism.

I am curious how the headline writers will handle the events to come.

Man's Justice

By eight o'clock Thursday morning it was already oven hot. Walking across the runway with Marty, Cedar breathed in salt air and softening macadam.

She waited as Marty walked the Piper from tail to nose and cleaned the windows twice.

Pocketing the rag, he nodded.

"Don't need a pilot's license to see the importance of clean windows."

They flew cocooned in the intimacy of engine-drone and rattle, the sky through Marty's windows filled with the puffy sheep clouds of a child's dreams. Far below, the ocean deeps were blue, the shallows the lightest green, and when they came in low over the islands, creeks, marine lakes, and mudflats flashed back sparkling sun.

They didn't speak until they landed and took off the headsets.

"Better?" asked Marty.

"Better."

"Is that the truth?"

"It's pretty close."

"I'll accept that."

In the cab of his truck, Marty turned and pulled two bottles from a cooler behind the seat.

The homemade lemonade was ice cold, more tart lemon than sweet. Exactly how she liked it.

"Do you forget anything?" she asked.

"Your drinks are like you."

"Very funny."

As they drove Cedar stuck her head out the window, the wind pressing her hair away from her face. It felt like being a kid.

She did feel better. She loved to dive. Marty loved to fly. She was pretty sure it was for the same reasons. Once he had said to her, "Flying is like closing the door on a row."

But you always had to come down. Or up.

Every decision has repercussions. We never walk away entirely untouched. Following my act of vengeance, boats buzzed overhead for four days, crisscross wakes slashing the sea. I gave warning. The older ones listened and vanished, but many of the younger ones stayed. Youth believes itself beyond the rules. I felt each of their deaths; hooked by steel barbs, eviscerated by gaffes, shot with guns. They were so surprised. There is no satisfaction in "I told you so."

When enough sharks were killed - how you measure this, I cannot fathom - the whine of engines ceased. The waters went quiet. I know my retribution temporarily dampened your enthusiasm for the sea. It was nice; the way it once was. Things would not be so bad with you gone.

The boat returns to the reef at the end of the week. I hear her approach like a familiar voice from the far side of a room. I am glad she has returned. I drift up, almost to the top of the reef, a risky maneuver in the light of day, but the light laboring of the engine tells me there is only one person on board. The engine cuts out. The boat drifts down on the mooring, like a leaf settling in an eddy. This gentle touch pleases me every time. There are no chickens. The boat just rocks in the sun.

When night falls she plays the bagpipes. The keening continues deep into the night.

I love bagpipes. They touch me. Their sound is so very old, mournful and endowed with thoughtful meaning. In their time they were played when a country went to war, or a king was laid to rest, or a bride and groom took their lifelong vows among running grasses. Even in these times they remain an instrument of occasion. I believe she employs the bagpipes in the same fashion.

The sound, played only for the stars, is halting and not quite lovely. But it is lovely to me.

Again I feel the flame of hope rise cautiously, a tinder spark, but hope nonetheless. Many have mourned their enemies. It is a sign of respect. But more than that, it is a signal of connection, recognition that, despite our differences, we all share the same pulse, and when a pulse is gone, something irretrievable is lost. The thought that a conceited man, a bully and a taker, is also a loving father, requires you see past your petty inclinations. It requires you see the Big Picture. And the Big Picture is what matters. It is not you alone. It is all of us together. But I fear very few see this.

This woman does. She feels both connection and loss.

At dawn I smell plumeria. Their scent is strong. It reaches me the instant the petals scatter on the water.

The petals float on the surface until, one by one, the reef fish gulp them down.

Hers is a noble action, but I am not blind to her faults. She wished him dead. I heard it clearly, a summons in itself. She is right to torment herself. We were in it together. Collaborators. Accomplices. I was the gun, but she and I pulled the trigger.

Murderess? Righteous judge? Who am I to say? Who are you? You wished him dead too, did you not? You often wish hateful things upon your fellow man. You would place yourself above the animals? Really?

I am not perfect, as you now know. Nor am I all seeing. That's the stuff of your fantasy writers, and maybe your God, if there is one. I know only what I've encountered, though over the years I've encountered a good deal. I've seen good and bad. Mostly I've seen gray and indifferent. Your species is oddly blasé regarding the world you are so fortunate to inhabit and your fleeting moment in it.

Of course, in the beginning I had no inkling of any of this. I was propelled solely by rudimentary need. Food. Procreation. Survival. Proper motivators for the prehistoric life. Believe you me, I had my hands full. The bullfighter in the ring has little time for philosophizing. I was smaller then, and the seas were a lively place. It's true, my kind was once a significant predator, but it is also true there were far bigger fish in the sea. Had I not branched significantly from my family tree, I would not have survived. Even as I grew larger, I remained very much afraid, for those who wished to eat me had jaws and teeth I could only dream of, and not an iota of wobble in their motions. They came like silent arrows on a soundless wind. Though preoccupied with keeping my own blood from clouding the water, I did not miss the beauty of their near perfect design. I don't know if chance, or some Great Hand, is responsible, but in either case I bow my head to such achievement.

As I grew larger still I continued to know fear, but I also came to welcome battle. Youth wants testing, and I received it in spades. There were skirmishes that thundered into the deeps and tore the ocean's surface to blood-flecked froth. Those were the salad days. Tooth and fang, act and react, survival of the fittest, the gladiatorial arena and all that. I won't bore you with my victories. I will only say that if you hold anything close long enough, it will die.

Though size helps, it wasn't size that turned me into, if I may modestly say, an apex warrior in a formidable broth. What set me apart was a slowly growing awareness, so slow growing that for many years I was unaware of it myself. I believed I was acting instinctually, though with quickness and alacrity that surprised me. Gradually I became aware of something more, not just finely honed unthinking reaction, but something concrete. I sensed things beyond the reach of conventional senses. From miles away I felt the frenzied lust of creatures mating. I knew the blood-rage hunger of a Liopleurodon gliding through darkness far from mine. The water whispered hidden secrets. Weaknesses. Fear. Hiding places. Now these rudimentary skills seem laughable, a toddler's first steps, but a toddler is mightily impressed with himself. Now I do not just anticipate the actions of others. I can crawl into their thoughts. I can persuade a man who thinks poorly of swimming at dusk to reconsider.

I confess there are times I feel I have been chosen. But this is a foolish, self-centered outlook, one that, as we have both seen time and time again, leads inevitably to downfall.

More accurate to say that life is full of surprises, and I harbor more than most.

She wished for his end. She is culpable. But revenge didn't sit on the throne long. I feel her sorrow. The feeling is as strong as the scent of the flowers she scatters.

I know she will not wish such a thing again.

We can change. We can become better than ourselves.

You must believe this.

By the fourth evening a dozen sharks hung from the makeshift gallows in front of the police station. The wood structure resembled an enormous swing set, with the sharks, hanging by their tails, as the swings. Half the swings were gray reef sharks. Three were blacktips, not noted man-eaters either. Two were fair size bulls, eight to nine feet. Cedar was surprised to see that the last shark, suspended with extra rope, was a twelve-foot tiger.

Gravity had already seen several sharks drop their innards to the dirt, gray oatmeal puddles thick with flies. The sharks yet to extrude their insides swelled grotesquely, ringed by additional clouds of flies.

Cedar and Able watched an Australian couple pose beside the tiger shark, the man flexing his bicep. The locals did not pose for photos, but Cedar did not absolve them from the blasphemy. She knew which sharks were theirs. The fins were gone. On the Asian market, shark fins fetched a good price.

Able had asked her to look at the sharks. She hadn't wanted to come. She knew what they would look like.

It was worse than she imagined.

Able wore street clothes. He didn't want to answer the tourists' questions.

The evening sun bathed the square in gold haze. They stood at a distance, but the smell was still terrible, like caskets pried open.

Able did not bother with the gray sharks and blacktips.

"The bulls?" he asked.

"Not likely. Too small to leave nothing behind."

They both looked at the tiger.

"And?"

"Possible," she said. "But again not likely."

"Why not likely?"

"Again, no leftovers."

She hated the casual word.

"Shit," said Able. There was real pain in his voice. "Well, what *do* you think then?"

"I don't know what to think."

"You think the shark is still out there?"

"I don't know."

Able sighed.

"You could try harder for a friend."

"I'm trying to be honest. I have no idea. None."

The buzzing flies sounded like mocking applause. Bats veered drunkenly through the gloaming.

"My uncle caught the small one by mistake," Able said quietly. "He didn't want to bring it here, but I asked him to."

Cedar felt sorry for Able. She wished she could tell him what he wanted to hear.

"We both know none of these sharks are big enough, Able. It was something big." Guilt rose unbidden. "It was as if he was inhaled."

Able chuckled.

She looked at him, surprised.

"What?"

"It's just funny."

"What's funny?"

"The one time I want someone to lie to me and they won't do it."

That night she and Justin fought, Jonathan refereeing from his perch on the drying rack beside the sink.

"They killed innocent animals because of that asshole," Justin said.

"Don't use that language and don't talk like that about someone you don't even know. Or someone you do know for that matter."

His hard face made him look older. It unsettled her a little.

"We're all flawed," he said.

He was throwing her words back in her face.

"We are. You were stupid to pick up the wrench. Don't ever do something like that again."

"I could have held my own."

Her son had grown up on an innocent island. He had yet to meet men like Ted Marple.

"No. He would have hurt you, Justin. Badly."

She saw that the words stung, but not as badly as a wrench to the skull. Very soon her son would be out in the world. She only had a few months left to make lessons stick. All men wanted to be the protector, but the world was filled with dangerous men without conscience or morals and, fair or no, dangerous men often won. They were willing, even eager, to go a step farther. She knew these men.

She knew it would make him angrier, but her time was running out.

"You have to be careful, Justin. Just reacting will get you hurt. You have to think."

He was shaking almost as much as he had on the dock, only now he held a half-washed plate in his hand. It would have been funny if her heart wasn't breaking.

"I don't think he was an asshole. I know he was an asshole. I know you hated him."

He flung this at her too.

It made her sick to fight like this, but it didn't weaken her resolve.

"You don't know everything," she said.

She couldn't bring herself to tell Justin what she had learned in Able's office. There was enough death in the story Justin knew.

They stood facing each other, both of them shaking.

Jonathan chirped, as if things were slowing down too much for his taste.

"You stay out of it," she said.

Justin wasn't buying distraction.

"He *took* a nautilus. *He threw it away like a piece of trash.* Were you there?"

It was an argument she couldn't win, because, on most fronts, he was right. It was like fighting with his father. The thought of those arguments made her turn away. She scooped two wet forks from the drying rack and washed them again.

She felt Justin's eyes on her.

"Sometimes I hate who you are," he said.

"Hate is precisely the problem," she said, blinking at the forks.

He slammed his cabin door so hard the glasses rattled in the cabinets.

Jonathan stared at her and shook his wings.

"Big surprise," she said. "You always take his side." She wrung out the dish cloth, draping it over the spigot. "But I'll still let you in on a secret. He *was* an asshole. I wanted to take the wrench and smash his smug face."

It didn't feel good at all.

Jonathan made small scratching noises with his feet, spread his wings, and disappeared up the steps. Maybe he wanted to spare her further embarrassment.

The next night someone cut down the sharks.

Big Noses

Ted Marple's death received viral global exposure, courtesy of several breathless, gruesomely exaggerated accounts from inebriated Polynesian happy hour attendees turned documentarians.

For several months only Germans and Australians came to the island: Germans because Germans are uncanny at sniffing out slashed rates, Aussies because shark attacks are barely news Down Under. By summer the rest of the world had returned too, because Palau has too much tropical glory to offer and the world's attention span is short.

On a squinty bright June morning, Cedar left the dock with a full complement of ten divers.

The divers were a typical mixed bag, two honeymoon couples from Denmark, another group of middle age men connected by some past something, and a man in his mid-forties diving alone. The solitary man's gear was without shine; his dive bag sorely sun-bleached. It brought back uncomfortable memories. But he had given her his undivided attention during the dive briefing and asked for permission to come aboard, and he had smiled amiably at the newlyweds and the sweating men carrying too much gear, and he had rigged his own gear quietly and without fanfare.

He wasn't good-looking -- his nose was too big for his face and his mop of brown hair sorely needed trimming -- but he held himself easily and, though his voice had been deferential, when he had asked permission to come aboard his eyes had held hers. She made it point to never pay anything other than professional attention to the men on her boat, and often they needed it. But this man was capable, and while he was occupied with his gear, she glanced at his ring finger, and when they passed the breakwater and Ernan throttled up and the bow of the Wendell Holmes lifted and planed, she did not go up to the bridge. She joked with the other divers, but even as she talked to them she listened in on his conversation and saw how he turned the other divers' questions into questions of his own.

She decided not to play the game with the album. She thought about mentioning Heidi Klum, but she didn't want to hold herself up to comparison.

When she finally went up to the bridge, Ernan raised an eyebrow.

"What?" she said.

"You are behind schedule."

"Am I so much a creature of habit?"

"Yes."

"Well everything's the same as usual, excluding the fact you're suddenly so nosey. I shouldn't have to explain to you what I'm doing, even if my improving our customer relations puts more money in your pocket."

She had started smiling halfway through the speech.

"Good business practice to charm the customers, even if one comes to it late," said Ernan. "I am honored you finally trust me to man the bridge alone."

"A monkey could do your job," she said, and they both smiled as they looked toward the blue horizon.

When she came down the ladder, he was fixing a regulator. It belonged to one of the newlyweds, a petit, ash blond girl who looked on hapless and charmed. His nose *was* big. She thought of the actor Gerard Depardieu. She had loved Depardieu in Cyrano de Bergerac. He glanced up at Cedar apologetically, but he was already well into the job so he returned to the regulator. He had taken off his shirt. Cedar wasn't disappointed. His waist was trim. When he turned to talk to the girl, the muscles in his back flared. She wondered what those muscles would feel like beneath her hands.

She gave herself a mental slap. She needed to look at the regulator. She couldn't trust a customer's safety with a customer's repair, even if the repairman suddenly made her wish no one else was on board.

Placing the tiny screwdriver in his tool box, the man smiled at the girl whose newlywed beau sported an unmistakable look of agonized inferiority.

"That should do it," he said. "But we should have the captain take a look."

Cedar scrutinized the regulator closely, although in the first instant she could tell the repair was perfect.

"He does good work," she said, smiling at the girl, who looked only a few years older than Justin. "You are now fully prepared for undersea adventure."

The girl flashed her knight in shining armor a flirty look.

"Thank you," she said.

"A monkey could do the job," he said.

When they dove the reef, Cedar let him wander. She knew some of the other men resented it and, swimming past, Justin looked at her with mild surprise, but she was growing tired of unbending rules and this was as good an excuse as any to break one. He was a better diver than she was; herding him was silly.

Back on board he thanked her with his eyes, and she wasn't surprised when he slipped his tip in the jar before Justin even gave the painful spiel they always gave as they approached the dock. *If you liked your service, feel free to leave a little something in the jar... If you didn't like our service, feel free to take a little something out...*

But she was surprised when he approached her on the dock. She was loading empty tanks on the cart, absorbed with a tank that was more weathered than she liked, when a shadow fell across the tank.

He put his dive bag down and brushed the hair from his eyes. His eyes were the same dark brown, as if, in overlapping, the colors had bled into each other.

They did not leave her.

He extended his hand. It was rough and warm.

"Sean Chawkins."

"I know," she said. "The manifest." She felt as if her smile unfolded in segments. "Cedar Mahoney. I'm sorry I didn't introduce myself personally on the boat."

His smile was warm and easy, as if they were old friends. Again her disobedient mind waltzed off on its own, wondering what he did and how many women he had been with.

"It's not the captain's job to glad hand," he said.

"Or apparently check a regulator. Thank you."

"It was my pleasure and, as we both know, an easy repair." He paused. "May I ask you a question?"

She was embarrassingly dry-mouthed. She donned her professional face and added her brightest smile. No foul in compromise.

"As long as you don't ask when I'm going to overhaul my gear," she said.

"We both know that tank has as many good years left as you do."

The smile rose up on either side of the fetching nose.

They were off the boat, she thought. Their working relationship was done. Sometimes it was hard watching Justin and Issy. The hell with it. She could break another rule. She was on a roll. But she was still of the school where the man did the yeoman's share of the courting.

"You did a nice job of fixing the regulator," she said. "Better than I could have done. It's not easy playing second fiddle to a monkey."

He had a boy's uninhibited laugh.

"I meant to apologize for overstepping my bounds," he said. "A captain's word is law."

"I could still have you keel hauled."

"Not much of a threat, to be honest. I'm betting the hull of your vessel is as clean as the rest of your operation."

"Thank you."

"It was an amazing experience. I'd love to come out again."

"You are welcome any time."

They both stood frozen in place. It was awkward at any age.

"You had a question," she said. She wanted it to sound helpful, but it sounded as if she were prodding him. *Christ.*

"Right. I do. How deep is it off the reef?"

She covered her disappointment by pretending to consider the tank.

"Off the edge it pretty much drops straight down to 4,000 feet."

"Any stair steps in the reef?"

"Just one small one on the western edge."

"Right," he nodded, and she knew he had studied the marine chart.

This time she knew what was coming.

"I saw what I thought was bottom," he said. "On the north side of the reef."

"I'm sorry, but that's not possible."

He hesitated and shrugged.

"Well then, mistaken I am," he said, bending to pick up his bag. "Not the first time, and certainly not the last. Thanks again for an unforgettable morning. It was one of the best dives I've ever done."

She nearly chased him down. But what point would it serve? What rational explanation could he offer that she hadn't already considered a thousand times?

He was not mistaken. She had seen it on the depth finder, less than a dozen times, but each time perfectly clear. And there was more. She knew it sounded unbalanced, and equally impossible, which was why she didn't chase him down. There were nights out at Long Drop Off, sitting at the stern watching the stars, the Wendell Holmes moored well off the reef, the waters still, nights when a sudden current ran along the boat's waterline, as if they were passing over shallows, or shallows were passing beneath them.

She lifted the tank.

In a desperate moment, she might share this. But there was something more, and this she would keep to herself. There were nights when she didn't need to look to the waterline, when she didn't need to hear the sudden soft wash of water, cool nights when her skin inexplicably flushed with heat. These moments scared her, and, at the same time, warmed and pleased her. Like soft-spoken men with big noses.

A hand gently took her elbow.

"You put it on the cart, not your foot."

Justin took the tank from her, swinging it easily into place.

"Everything okay?" he asked.

"Fine, now that you've kept my Irish dance career alive."

"What did he say?"

Justin was looking at the tanks on the cart.

By this point, thought Cedar, they had be the most scrutinized tanks ever.

"What did who say?"

"The single man."

She ignored the adjective.

"That it was a beautiful dive."

"That's all?"

"That's all."

"I saw you watching him."

She reached for a tank.

"May I remind you that you are speaking to your mother?"

"That's why I'm asking, Mom."

"Okay. He was nice."

"What?"

"I said he was nice."

"Nice?"

Justin was wearing Ernan's grin.

"Okay. Fine. I found him appealing."

"*Appealing*?"

"Appealing. Attractive. Alluring. Whatever else starts with an A that translates to none of your business. I like big noses. But I don't like overly nosey. What is it with the men I employ?"

"You don't pay me. And?"

"Did I fail to even teach you how to listen?"

"And?"

"And he stopped to thank us for a beautiful dive."

"He didn't thank *me*."

"He knew you wouldn't listen to what he was saying."

Willing herself not to, she glanced toward the White Squall. He was not sitting along the line of barstools that faced toward the harbor. She wasn't surprised. He hadn't looked like a drinker.

She was sorry she looked, but she was sorrier still he was gone.

Justin said, "His name and hotel are on the manifest. Sean Chawkins. He's staying at the Palau Pacific Resort, to save you time."

"That's unprofessional."

"Mom."

"What?"

"I'm leaving in two months. Two months and six days."

She tried to haul herself up with a smile, but she still felt herself slipping beneath the surface.

"It appears you won't need me to help you read your calendar when you're gone."

"Mom. Women ask."

She thought of the good years she'd had with Wyatt. But calendars rifled away, and with them the people you thought you knew.

"Understood," she said. "Next time, I promise I will."

"Next time? Is he diving with us tomorrow?"

"He did say he'd like to come out with us again."

"You don't listen. That wasn't the question."

"Where did you learn interrogation?"

"It's not interrogation if you care."

Where had this boy sprung from?

"Fine. I won't forget what you said. I know I can't spend the rest of my life with a bat. Plus he favors you. I'll bet he flies off as soon as you're gone."

She looked at her watch longer than required.

"If you're finished with your cross-examination, Counselor, we need to get these tanks refilled."

Guiding the Wendell Holmes toward the fuel dock that evening, she could see Santy fussing over a jumble of wood crates. That she couldn't wait to exchange a few jibes with the old man made her realize how lonely she was.

"He's lost his heart to Heidi Klum," she said to the towering thunderclouds. "And his nose is puny and squashed."

Bumping against the dock, she saw the crates were covered with tarps.

She tossed the line to Santy.

Hopping to the dock, she nodded to the crates.

"My Christmas present?"

Santy was in no mood to ease her loneliness. The old man looked tired.

"I am always working," he said irritably. "I don't have time to shop. For you or people I like."

"Not even a sliver of lingerie for the Heidi Klum?"

He didn't tug.

"She is not interested in a decrepit old man."

Santy filled the Wendell Holmes in silence, consulting the mushroom clouds as the setting sun fired their fringes bruised purple and red.

The clouds were beautiful, but Cedar couldn't help noticing that Santy's hands were jumpy.

On the way back to the dock she took a deep breath and called the Palau Pacific Resort.

They agreed on dinner at the hotel. The island was filled with prying eyes and the hotel was no exception, but Cedar thought dinner among tourists would be more comfortable. Still, he insisted on hiring a cab and picking her up. She waited on the deck, jumpy as a middle school prom princess. She thought about a gin and tonic but decided it was bad form to greet a date with liquor on your breath. A date. It made her jumpier still.

She saw him at the far end of the dock, but she hesitated a tick before she waved. He was wearing a white linen shirt and khaki pants that made him look even slimmer. He'd gotten his hair cut. Cut and styled. It ran back to his collar in thick waves. A pale streak ran along the edge of his hairline where the mop had formerly shaded his skin.

She fought to shake the shake from her voice.

"The barber did a nice job, Sean."

Christ. Did they still call them that?

The fetching smile and the shy brown eyes were the same.

"Thank you, Cedar. The hotel brochure promised a new look."

"It would have been a shame to go that far."

She had decided on a simple light green floral dress. The dress stopped conservatively at mid-thigh, but still highlighted her legs nicely and the spaghetti straps showed off her shoulders, descending to just a hint of breast. And, Justin pointed out, the dress matched her eyes.

She liked how the brown eyes took the whole of her in and settled on her face.

"Please give me a moment to remember," he said.

"Of course," she said, though she had no idea what he meant.

"There," he said finally. "Breathe in, breathe out."

They sat on the patio at the table closest to the beach, their faces moving in and out of the light and shadow thrown by the wavering tiki torches.

When the waiter came to take their drink orders, they both saw his face twitch.

"Hello, Gabriel."

"Good evening, Miss Mahoney."

"It was nice of the hotel to provide one of the finest and most circumspect members of their wait staff."

The man stood quivering.

"Yes," he said.

He took their drink orders while staring out at the sea.

After he left, Sean said, "I'm thinking greyhound. I was pretty sure he was going to turn and run."

"I have that effect on people."

"I appreciate you having dinner with me. I suspect it's a small island."

"Slightly larger than this patio."

"Is your friend Gabriel truly circumspect?"

"Better than most. But I know he'll tell at least one person, and therein lies our downfall."

"E News?"

"The Paluan version. His auntie."

When Gabriel returned to the table with their appetizers, the tray also bore iced champagne.

The brown eyes smiled.

They watched silently as Gabriel filled their glasses. The flickering torchlight performed alchemy, turning the champagne gold.

After Gabriel left, Sean raised his glass.

"I loved that you said barber. Stylist seems too hip, and maybe even a little effeminate." He kept his glass against hers. "I also loved that you checked my repair. Most of all, I love that you called. "

"I'm afraid I've watched my professionalism wholly unravel. Dinner with a customer is a first."

His smile had a lovely way of drifting to every corner of his face.

"To firsts," he said.

"To firsts."

They sipped the champagne.

"Do you like it?" he asked.

"It's lovely."

It was.

She laughed.

"What?"

"I don't think I've had a glass of champagne in ten years. Part of its circumstances, but to be honest, I'm more of a beer drinker."

When he really smiled, the tips of his ears pushed up through hair.

"Praise the Lord. Me too. I was just trying to impress. Since I have an expert at hand, tell me, what's the best local beer?"

"Red Rooster."

"Voiced with conviction."

She laughed again.

"I hope I'm not impressing you as a beer swilling, lackadaisical dive outfitter who lets any monkey with a screw driver have at a customer's gear."

"You are and I am. Impressed. By your honesty. For that I like you even more."

It felt as if someone had dipped one of the tiki lamps close to her face. She hadn't flushed like this in years either.

When Gabriel returned to the table, Sean whispered in his ear. Cedar was surprised to see Gabriel smile.

He returned to the table carrying an ice bucket filled with Red Rooster.

"Very classy," Cedar said.

"A compromise," said Sean.

He reached for two beers, but she raised a hand.

"Please," she said. "Allow me."

Gabriel had attached a bottle opener to the ice bucket with a silver chain. She opened a beer for each of them, watching Sean's tan throat bob as he drank. She wondered if there was a part of him she didn't like.

"Should we send it back?"

"Not a chance," he said. "It's lovely."

It *was* lovely. The flickering torches made his eyes darker, more mysterious. Unreadable. Like an animal. She decided she liked that. Over his shoulder the moon ladled molten silver on the water.

"The perfect cap to the perfect day."

For a moment she wondered if she'd spoken her thoughts aloud.

"I was thinking the same thing," she said.

He put down his beer and regarded her seriously.

"You know it wasn't a line, what I said about the dive. I meant it. It was fantastic. I've been fortunate to dive some beautiful spots, but today's dive ran off with the prize. It wasn't just that the nautilus were impossibly beautiful. I thought about it all afternoon, and I'm still trying to figure it out. I can't put my finger on it. There was something hypnotic about the experience, something that burrowed inside me. But I still can't place it." He gave a self-effacing smile. "I hope you don't think I'm a closet obsessive bereft of imagination."

"You stepped into another world."

She watched him absorb this.

"Maybe a better world," she added.

She leaned toward him. Softly she said, "This is the ship of pearl, which, poets feign, sails the unshadowed main..."

"Oliver Wendell Holmes."

She nearly cried out.

"You know the poem."

"Honestly? I know a verse or two, and then I'm a goner. But I did see you named your boat after him."

"Cheater. You sure I didn't name it after the barrister?"

"Who names their boat after a lawyer?"

"The perfect closing argument. You know what's really nice?"

"What?"

"For once Oliver Wendell Holmes isn't a conversation stopper."

Dinner was delicious. The Palau Pacific had a new chef, lured away from a five star resort in Tahiti. They both had spiced prawns, perfectly seasoned and garnished with mango and lemon.

Cedar had Gabriel bring them pichi pichi for dessert; the cassava and coconut were the perfect counter to a spicy meal.

Maybe it was the champagne and beer, maybe it was the silver night and torchlight, but while they ate, she told Sean about Wyatt and leaving Chicago and how Justin was now going, kicking and screaming, back. Maybe she was also a trifle nervous, but she couldn't seem to stop talking. It didn't help that he kept asking questions, leaning forward with the same attentive look she had seen during the dive briefing. Finally she wrestled her tongue into submission and directed the questions at him. She learned that he was an engineer with an international firm in New York. His firm was currently overseeing construction of a dam southwest of Beijing. He wasn't the best engineer, he said, but unlike the best engineers he was able to communicate the engineering gobbledygook to clients who didn't know basicity from a bimetallic couple. He also spoke a touch of Mandarin and Cantonese.

"A touch?"

"I know the words for basicity and bimetallic couple. The dam's at least two years from completion so I split my time between New York and Beijing, with side trips to the South China and Philippine Sea for diving. All play and no work."

"I have to ask."

"Anything's fair game."

"What's a bimetallic couple?"

"It's a union of two dissimilar metals."

"It sounds a little illicit."

"I suppose it does. But if it's done right, the union is permanent."

They conversed as well-behaved adults, but they each caught the other's gaze straying. She saw how Sean's eyes absorbed the smooth slope of her shoulders, then slipped along the spaghetti straps to where they met the rise of her breasts She was not terrifically well-endowed but her breasts were large enough and still youthfully firm. Wyatt had always fondled them like an amazed little boy bestowed a prized Christmas gift. She took good care of herself for herself, but it had also earned her the figure of a woman half her age. She saw how, when she picked Justin up at school, the clumps of boys fidgeted and laughed too loud, and their fathers stared until forced to quickly looked away.

Sean's stolen glances were only slightly more refined. She managed her own surreptitious glances and she knew they lingered longer as the ice bucket emptied. White linen suited a tan, and the shirt was just tight enough so that when he moved it pressed against the chest she had seen on the boat, smooth, broad and taut. She wished she could trade places with the linen. She told herself to behave. The champagne and beer had gone to her head, but it was fun so why fight it? The heat of the torches caressed her bare shoulders. She imagined it sliding down inside her dress.

Just before dessert arrived she said, "Confession."

"Ah. These are always fun."

"I like big noses."

"Happy coincidence. The hotel does not offer plastic surgery."

"You shouldn't change a thing," she said, maybe a little too quickly. Slowing slightly she said, "When I first saw you, I thought of Gerard Depardieu. I have a thing for him. Adrien Brody too."

It was silly and girlish, but she didn't care. She hadn't had this much fun in a long time.

"Hmmmm," said Sean. "I'm trying to make the connection."

He held up his hand, making her wait a dramatic beat.

"Confession," he said.

"It's only fair."

"You don't look like anybody's mother and I'm hypnotized by green eyes."

"Which is it? Hypnotic eyes or hypnotic dive? If everything's hypnotic, then we're just not ourselves."

Sean didn't smile.

"I've never been more spellbound in one day," he said.

By the time they rose from the table, most of the wait staff, including Gabriel, had gone home. A young Indian boy cleared their table. Another waiter started snuffing out the torches.

Sean held out his hand.

"The beach is still open," he said. "I know a walk on the beach is kind of a busman's holiday for you."

She took his hand.

"For you, I'll make another exception."

They walked without talking. The sky was cloudless, the bright moon turning night to near day. The barest hint of swell washed against the beach, the sound like lovers moving beneath the sheets.

"More spellbound," Sean said.

She was pretty certain she was the one who stopped and turned, but it was Sean who drew her close so that she finally felt the muscular press of chest against her breasts.

His hands caressed the small of her back, while his tongue moved delicately in her mouth, sending currents of pleasure everywhere. She tasted him, beer, spice and the faintest tinge of seawater salt.

They finally separated.

"Breathe," she said, and they were kissing again.

The elevator ride to the eleventh floor took an eternity. They kissed and giggled and reached for each other, and when the doors suddenly opened and another couple stepped in, they put on their adult masks, although Sean's hair looked as if he had just exited a tornado.

Inside the room, they fell into each other. Now Sean's hands, impossibly hot, were doing some serious reaching. She spread her legs, pushing forward to meet him. Gently, a strange hand touched her for the first time in years and the shock and familiar pleasure saw her cry out.

She felt herself lift off the ground. They bumped and stumbled across the room, oblivious to their awkwardness, hearing nothing but their own pleas and pants. Out of the corner of her eye, she saw a single lilac on his pillow.

He entered her as they fell to the bed and it seemed to Cedar that they just kept falling.

As I said, I have seen the best and the worst. I prefer to focus on the bright spots, the near misses, the moments when the flame stops wavering and flares straight and tall. If not hope, what remains?

Perhaps the brightest moment unspooled in a sea of oil slick and acrid flame, though you might not consider it hope at first glance. Someone's submarine encountered someone's ship. I don't know who was who. Why keep a scorecard when everyone loses? In this instance I suppose you could say the ship came out on the short end. The explosions shattered coral twenty miles away. Even back then, your talent for destruction was impressive.

By that point I was pretty much inured to the violence. Your war had already waged for two years. But I was curious.

It was night. The men in the water called for God, for their wives, for their lovers, for their children. They cursed their superiors. They cursed the Japanese. They cursed God.

I drifted in the dark water, basking in their cries, the flailings above me like a thousand strokings. Bloodlust never leaves. Once a primordial being, always a primordial being. And then a man cried apology.

It was as if I had been slapped across the face. Everything stopped -- the screaming, the ragged toothed forms sliding through the dark all about me, the jarring concussions of cartilage against flesh.

I was so overwhelmed, for a moment I lost my bearings. I thought our time had come.

The man shouted out again as if hailing me.

I surfaced, approaching through a litter of burning debris.

He was sitting on top of a toilet, bobbing clear of the water. The toilet swayed slightly back and forth. By some miracle he kept his place.

I felt the night breeze on my face.

He regarded me with childish delight, face charred black so that his eyes appeared huge.

"I'm on the crapper," he said.

I saw the ragged hole at his left shoulder where his arm had been. He wore a formerly white apron. Another chance, bleeding away.

"I'm from Sebeka. Sebeka, Minnesota. There's nothing like this in Sebeka." He looked about. "I'm truly sorry for this mess."

Of course I had no way of answering. But he felt what I felt and he was nearly past caring.

His ship was called the USS Indianapolis. You may know it.

"I know," he said. "It really is an awful mess." He rubbed his scorched forehead with the hand he had, the skin crumbling away in hunks. "I just wanted to be a chef at a fancy summer resort. Maybe fall in love with a nice waitress. And here I am on the crapper."

Things blazed. The air was thick with the smell of diesel and smoldering metal. Choking smoke ran low across the water, past his shins.

He looked at me as if he were the teacher. His face held impossible sadness.

"I can't tell you why we do it," he said. "Now here we are giving the sharks indigestion. I don't want to be eaten."

For a moment he faltered, and then he gave an apologetic smile.

"I've been drinking salt water. I know that's wrong. But the kitchen isn't open."

I flared my wings and he calmed.

"I'm so sorry for all we've done. It's terrible."

You hadn't yet dropped the atomic bombs. You are always one-upping yourselves. In this, you are truly remarkable.

I felt the passing beneath me, like water scooped away. It left a slight boil on the surface.

The man saw the boil. He looked out at the sea of blazing fires, but not before I saw his fear.

"It's like a kitchen," he said.

Big sharks are made impudent by their size. This one rose almost directly into my tentacles. I clamped down hard, moving off a short distance until it was over. I did not want the shark's thrashing to tip the man from his pedestal.

When I returned, he was contemplating the fires. I don't think he even saw me move off and return.

"It won't end here," he said. "We'll keep plugging away. Bang, bang. You're dead, and you're dead, and you're dead. Did you see all the fish?"

I had. Wide-eyed fish floated everywhere.

"We can't just go alone. The whole damn ship has to go down."

He smiled at his joke. The water lapped softly.

"There's not always tomorrow. Not tonight. Not always."

Someone screamed. Their screaming lasted a long time and then it turned to shouted prayer.

"A kitchen," he said, although he did not sound convinced.

I lifted him gently. He shuddered slightly at my touch, but made no protest. I finished him quickly. I ate because I did not want the sharks to have him. He was sweet as candy.

I drifted briefly among the flaming debris, beneath the ceiling of stars. For some reason the screaming bothered me now. I sank away, but I have never forgotten this man. Rocking on a toilet in an earthly version of hell, he was like a window to a sunny day. You have it in you.

Not long after that, the fighting stopped. But it would start up again. Oh yes, it would.

Ships litter the bottom in the waters I currently call home. They're a playground now, divers swimming in and out of them like children in a maze. But they weren't always a playground. There's nothing playful about a man sinking into the depths holding his severed leg.

A man can cry underwater. But what makes me sad is that other men see this as victory.

We take what we need. You kill and kill and kill, and then kill some more. It is nonsensical. Like a man dying of thirst in the desert, drinking sand.

I do not sway the special ones. I find them as they are and I let them be. Some of them have long shelf lives, some don't. Some perish just as we meet, the flames of foolhardy self-interest laughing all about them.

Water Whispers

They took Tuesdays off. Even now, with the cost of college keeping her awake at night, she refused to relinquish the day. Tuesdays were theirs. She'd take out an extra loan or pick up more repair jobs. She still had a year. She knew Wyatt thought she should be running trips seven days a week, but he never said anything. There were times when she wondered if she should have left him.

Some days she and Justin went back out to Long Drop Off. If there was no one there they stayed, wiling the day away free diving, playing poker, and drinking orange soda in the shade. More and more often though, boats were moored at Long Drop Off, and they waved at the captains and motored on.

Today there were four boats on the reef, rolling easily and throwing off flashes of sun. Chrisman saw her and waved. She liked Chrisman, an energetic fireplug of a Kiwi, and she tried to muster an enthusiastic wave, but the sight of all the boats made her feel soiled. She had been the first to do the nautilus dives. She had even taken a dive magazine writer out on one of the early trips, rationalizing that if she didn't do it someone else would; rationalizing because she knew the publicity would be a boon for business. Regarding that she had been right in spades, and now there was no turning back. She often thought of Pandora's Box. In Greek mythology, Pandora was the first woman on earth. The first time she came upon Long Drop Off, she had felt like Pandora.

Once they were beyond the boats, she nodded to Justin and he opened up the throttle. The wind pushed his hair back, exposing his fine-boned features. The sun lit up the downy hairs along his jaw line. Shaving cream and razor had appeared in their shared bathroom six months earlier.

Her boy-man. Just watching him produced an upwelling of joy. Did mothers always fall in love with their sons? She wanted to find something to dislike, it would make things easier, but he only continued to charm her in newfound ways.

She stepped up beside him.

"Where to, Captain?" he shouted.

His teeth were straight and white. Braces had never been part of their life. The Wendell Holmes leapt forward like a puppy.

"Bring me the horizon," she shouted back.

"What about fuel?"

"What about it?" she said, and laughed.

Justin banked the boat left, then right, then left again.

"Second star to the right and straight on til' morning!"

Her son *was* Peter Pan. Beneath them the hull of the Wendell Holmes chattered happily.

The eastern seas were the windward seas. They almost never came this way with divers; rough seas and distance were things few divers fancied. Even the fishermen kept to the inner reefs. With no landfall between here and California, wind and waves had plenty of fetch to work up a head of steam. But today was windless. The ocean lay inert, rippled only by smooth swells.

Sheer luck saw them find the reef. One minute 3,000 feet of water; the next, forty, though neither of them needed a depth gauge to note the change. Beneath the blue water they could see the top of the sea mount clearly.

Justin throttled back. The Wendell Holmes settled in the water, her wake running around to the bow.

Beneath them spread a madcap garden of brain, plate, and lettuce leaf corals.

Justin hooted.

"Neverland!"

The reef was big. It took nearly ten minutes to putter around the perimeter.

There were no moorings. Justin positioned the Wendell Holmes above a patch of sand and Cedar carefully winched down the anchor.

The world went to lapping silence.

"Pursuing the horizon has its rewards."

She looked up toward her son's voice. Justin stood, balanced on the bridge railing two stories up and then he whooped and fell to the sea, a lovely dive that sent up the barest raindrop patter. He was still whooping as he swam back to the boat.

There is a heaven.

They geared up. They spent the first thirty minutes combing the top of the reef. Cedar had never seen healthier coral. The brain corals were the size of small cars, the sinuous folds of lettuce coral as thick as her hand. Tropical fish swarmed like confused commuters. She heard Justin laughing through his regulator.

They nearly missed the two openings, side by side like unblinking blue eyes. Cool water rose from each opening, causing the water above the openings to waver milkily. Cedar floated hesitantly above the left eye. Turning she watched Justin pump his fists overhead and then disappear into the other opening. For an instant she was irked that he hadn't consulted her first. Then she laughed, unclipped her dive light and finned into the opening.

The passage was roughly two arm lengths wide. It descended virtually straight down, a chute of dark rippled wall. It was like swimming down a throat. Cedar made a slow, hypnotic fall, checking her depth gauge. At seventy feet, the chute yawned wide and she drifted out into the cavern.

Cedar was relieved to see Justin floating upright in the cavern's half-light, pumping his fists wildly again. As she watched, he turned a somersault and spread his arms wide. Half-conscious of her movements, she sank to the cavern floor some thirty feet below, going to her knees with a soft bump on the white sand.

Kneeling was appropriate. When she was a girl, her father had taken her to see Winchester Cathedral. They had arrived late. The cathedral had just closed. Her father had charmed the dour caretaker. She had never forgotten how it was, standing alone in the vast nave, daunting yet uplifting at the same time. Her father had died in a car accident two years later.

Slowly she turned. Her father would be pleased to know there were two Winchester Cathedrals.

She didn't need the dive light. Although they appeared wholly enclosed inside the sea mount, light came from everywhere. Cedar saw now the thin fissures in the basalt. Light wormed through the cracks, gracing the cavern with a deep purple hue, sunset's last toehold before dark. The water was clear as sky. Even in the dusky light, Cedar could see the cavern's far reaches.

A cold draft touched her hands. Halfway through her pirouette she spotted the enormous arc of opening just off the sandy floor, the dark basalt walls nearly blending with the indigo sea beyond.

Above her Justin finned easily along the cavern wall. She was rising up off her knees when she heard the clanging. Justin stopped banging on his tank. Sheathing the knife, he flicked on his dive light and swung it back and forth.

Cedar swam up to where her son hung, suspended some twenty

feet below the ceiling. Placing both his hands to his forehead, Justin gave a muffled hoot and fell back so she could press close.

The rock shelf was recessed, disappearing into total darkness. She trained her light on the interior.

They resembled Chinese lanterns, white, with a liberal dusting of gold. There were eight of them, each roughly the size of a football. It was the most pointless reaction in the book, but Cedar pinched her eyes shut and looked again. They were still there, resting like ancient artwork in a flooded museum. Her heart raced and her mind whirled. Justin tapped her shoulder. She was almost surprised to see him there. His hands were pressed together in prayer. Their private dive signal. *Beautiful.*

Back on top of the reef, they were accorded a final treat. They heard the sound first, a muted pop, like a fist smacking into a palm, the massive bait ball displacing water as the tiny fish jerked as one. The enormous tornado funnel of silversides was at least twenty feet wide and forty feet tall, though it was hard to measure as its shape changed from instant to instant as muscled bluefin tuna slashed through, gulping as they went, the thousands of silver shards swirling and pulsing like a living rainstorm, a glistening world of predation. She did not need to look at Justin to know his hands were pressed together again.

On board the Wendell Holmes she made lunch. They ate peanut butter and jelly sandwiches and drank lemonade in silence, Justin staring out at the ocean like a happy village idiot.

Her mind still raced. She was virtually certain, but she was also certain she couldn't be right. It was not possible. Her imagination was duping common sense. A sleight of hand, a card trick. Perhaps a tincture of narcosis. She needed time to think.

She closed her eyes, tried to forget for a moment as her tired thighs dissolved into the warm deck.

"We should name it," Justin said.

She opened her eyes.

"Name it?"

Justin looked at her, eyes radiant, sandwich tumbling inside his mouth.

"Hello? Were you here today? The reef, Mom."

She smiled back.

"*You* should name it," she said. "But not with your mouth full."

She loved watching him think. He took his time.

"Did you hear the sound the water made?" he asked.

"The slap?"

"Not the bait ball. The sound just above the openings. Just before we went in."

She saw herself hovering over the milky opening. She remembered no sound.

"I didn't hear anything."

"You could barely hear it. That was the coolest part. The water whispered." He took a bite of sandwich, chewing with satisfaction. When he smiled there was peanut butter on his teeth. "Water whispers," he said.

"It's perfect."

He gave an odd nod of confirmation.

"It *is* perfect," he said.

The look on his face was the same one he used to get when he finally solved a particularly troubling math problem.

"What are you thinking?"

Her son gave the universal dismissive teenage shrug.

"Nothing much. Maybe how great this lemonade tastes. A little tart. I like it."

"It's Marty's recipe. More tart, less sweet. He says it's like me."

"He knows you," Justin said, but his eyes were already wandering back over the water, the bright armor surface turning back the noon sun. "What do you think those things are?"

"I don't know," she lied. "Some kind of shell probably."

"Mm." He got up and poured them both more lemonade. "You know something?" he said, handing her her glass.

"What?"

"It felt good just being down there."

He was right. It had. The realization surprised her.

He stuffed a last half of sandwich into his mouth.

"I really wanted to touch them," he mumbled.

They had been too far back to touch. But had they been able to reach them, Cedar knew they wouldn't have felt like a shell.

Eggs cases were slightly soft to the touch.

They stayed the night. She asked Justin to wear his earplugs.

The bagpipes made her feel better. Again, she wasn't sure why.

When they returned to the harbor early the next morning, they went directly to the fuel dock. Cedar doubted they had a leftover drop.

Today Santy was his jovial self. He hailed them as they swung toward the dock.

"Ah! The pirate queen *and* the crown prince. Tell me you have the smelly bat and my day is complete." He tugged his ear. "It's possible I have let my bananas go rotten."

Justin jumped to the dock and gave the old man a playful jab.

"Hi Santy. Jonathan's off in the jungle. Mom says you have kittens."

The bump of the Wendell Holmes had already set off a mewling.

"You want them? I'll give you a good price."

"He does not, and you will not," Cedar said from the bridge.

"Queens become too accustomed to having their way. Maybe that is why they are so short-tempered and difficult," said Santy. "No matter. It would be impossible even if you decreed differently. Like most females, the kittens have eyes only for me."

Justin crouched close to the box.

The mewling stopped.

He held out a hand, making soft cooing noises.

"Two problems, crown prince," Santy said. "The hand is empty and it does not belong to Santy."

The first kitten, a calico, stutter-stepped cautiously into the sunshine. The second tottered forward, a midnight black puffball.

Justin cupped his hands. The black kitten stepped into his palm, followed by the calico. They circled, executing small stampings before sprawling atop each other.

Gently Justin brought his hand to his chest and stood.

The kittens purred.

Cedar almost forgot her troubles.

"Apparently, in this rare case, you have competition as a suitor," she said.

"I'll be goddamned," said Santy. "Keep this boy away from the Heidi Klum."

That night Cedar turned on the laptop in bed. She didn't want Justin coming up behind her.

She typed in the words and clicked.

Identical egg cases, infinitely smaller, appeared on the screen.

She sat back against the pillow, impossibilities swirling. Her mind snatched at them, a child grabbing at bubbles, but the breeze lifted them and they moved out of reach, impossible to absorb.

Mostly she thought of the flayed chickens. A jungle of tentacles peppered with sharp radula, a crushing beak.

Given the right circumstances a grown man could disappear entirely.

You wonder if we have memory. I believe I have already answered this question, but our memory is not yours; and so you struggle to define us within your narrow parameters. Recently your scientists conducted rudimentary experiments that again provided surprise. They fed Chambered Nautilus after setting off a flash of light. Several hours later the scientists flashed the light again. The nautilus, and I quote, "appeared to show interest in the flash of light." After twenty-four hours no one, with the exception of the scientists, responded to the light. Although the experiment was officially complete, three days later the youngest scientist, prodded by his own forgotten lunch, flashed the light at the Nautilus again. This set off a waving of tentacles and discussion of potential study flaws. In the end the scientists published only the 24-hour study. Still, they were floored to find even short term memory. Our brain, by your again narrow definition, lacks the requisite regions dedicated to learning.

I propose an alternative. Perhaps science should design an experiment to determine a region of the Nautilus brain dedicated to humor. Maybe we are conducting experiments on your scientists.

I also raise a related, more sobering, suggestion. Perhaps we are not the ones who should be tested for forgetfulness.

Blank Spots on the Map

There was no rational way to tell Marty her theory, so she told him straight out. They sat in his tidy cinderblock office just back from the air strip. It wasn't something you broached in public, even to someone as circumspect as Marty.

She called it a theory because this left her with a toehold in sanity.

It was ninety-eight degrees outside, sixty-five degrees within, courtesy of an air conditioner that, for ten years now, had issued arctic blasts and a last death rattle. Model airplanes, suspended from the ceiling with monofilament fishing line, spun slowly in the not-insubstantial eddies. Behind Marty's desk a framed document proclaimed "OAOO". Besides Marty, Cedar was the only one on the island who knew what it meant. One and only oasis.

To his credit, Marty absorbed her lunacy soberly. But she did not miss how he avoided her eyes and how he chose his words carefully, as if the merest whiff of agreement would land him in the same lunatic ward.

"So," he said, tapping a broken-nailed finger down a regimental line of pencils, "something is out there. Not something. A snail, actually. A snail that might be the size of a bus, or possibly larger, big enough to be mistaken for a patch of reef on a depth finder." She knew he wasn't mocking her. He was trying to make it easier to digest. "An animal capable of ingesting a man completely." He trailed off. One of the pencils rolled away from its brethren. Marty let it roll.

She placed the pencil back in line.

"Let me help you along," she said. "Not a snail. A cephalopod. And even in its conventional size, a ruthlessly efficient predator. If you ever came out on my boat, you'd see what they can do."

"Only that would be stranger than this."

She gave him a look.

He raised his hands.

"I'm sorry," he said. "I know you're serious, so I'll be serious too. Even if you're right, I wouldn't share your theory with anyone else just yet. Here's the short version. You have no visible proof. Without visible proof you'll lose your reputation, your business and everything you've worked for. And not at a good time. If there is a good time for such things."

Cedar knew what he was thinking.

"I haven't said anything to Justin yet."

This, at least, was true.

"Good. You still cling to a thread of reason."

"And what if I'm right?"

Marty ran a hand over his close-cropped curls. Nothing budged.

"I already said that's possible. But there's another possibility. What if you're not? I am afraid of the ocean, but that does not mean it doesn't interest me. I have read that ninety-five percent of the ocean's depths are unexplored. Surely such a sprawling blank spot on the map might sequester inhabitants we have never seen. Please note the last word. We see, we believe. I'm not saying that's science, but it is the way our science works. Not to mention our friends and neighbors."

The air conditioner rattled. Above Marty's head a Grumman Hellcat dipped its nose to the floor.

He looked at her beseechingly.

"Do you have *anything*, Cedar? Anything other than your theory and a depth-finder that might possibly be on the fritz?"

She had made up her mind before she came.

"No."

Marty's kind face watched her. For a moment her resolve wavered.

"You are willing to risk everything?" he asked softly.

He was right. Everything he said made absolute sense. He was the yin to her yang.

"It's really irritating, you know," she said.

"What's really irritating?"

"You."

"Me?"

"You. You don't even realize we've had ten years of arguments and I've never won one. *One.* You could at least throw me a bone."

"Mmm. That *is* quite an impressive record." His smile disappeared. "Here's your bone. I said don't go public. I didn't say you were wrong."

She actually leaned forward.

"You believe me?"

She knew she sounded desperate but she didn't care.

"I respect you. As much as anyone I've ever known."

"There's a difference."

"There is. Respect forces me to be honest with you."

She stood. Marty stopped pushing the pencils and looked up at her.

"One more thing," he said. "If you *are* right, do you think it wise to be taking divers out to the reef?"

That very question had kept her up most of the night.

"I think the attack was a solitary incident. I'm almost certain of it."

She didn't say *planned*. She didn't say vengeance and retribution. She was not ready to give voice to all her beliefs just yet. She knew Marty wasn't willing to shimmy out on that fragile branch with her. It was too early to lose her only ally.

Marty counted the eraser heads as if he didn't know how many were there.

"And if you're wrong?" he asked.

"It will be my responsibility."

"I fear you already ferry an unbearable weight of responsibility."

It swept over her. It was what she had wanted all along, the reason she had come to Marty. She spoke before she could stop herself.

"Then help me when I ask for help. Please."

"Anytime. Anywhere."

At the door she turned back to him.

"Have you ever seen anything unusual when you fly?"

"Such as?"

"I don't know. Maybe a shadow where it shouldn't be?"

"Look around," said Marty. "Shadows are everywhere."

For once his smile was forced.

Outside the heat rushed over her in a volcanic belch. She hesitated on the bristly doormat. She wondered what Marty was thinking on the other side of the door. She wondered if he had sensed her lie.

It made complete and utter sense to tell him about the eggs. They were more than a small shred of evidence. They were an exact replica, albeit thirty times the size. We see, we believe. But she hadn't told him, and in this matter, too, she was equally adrift. She had never shied from decision before. She had left her husband and her comfortable life and moved halfway around the world to raise a son. Every day she made decisions; about weather, about divers, about fuel, about life. But now her mind foundered for purchase as if it were no longer her own, cut loose and adrift upon a sea of indecisiveness.

Eggs.

As she walked across the shimmering air strip, a frigate bird rode a thermal, making ever tightening circles as it rose. The tourists loved frigate birds, but they always reminded her of vultures and death.

She wondered if she really was insane.

Your scientists denigrate, ridicule, and pooh pooh each other. It is part of your nature and your process. Skepticism is healthy, but sometimes it blinds you.

A paleontologist from Massachusetts has broached an interesting theory, based on numerous ichthyosaur bones found in the Berlin-Ichthyosaur State Park in Nevada. The bones, he notes, are arranged strangely, piled as if collected. Some bones are marked, the marks strongly resembling sucker marks made by members of the Coleoidea, which includes octopuses, squids, cuttlefish and their relatives. The ichthyosaur, I should point out, was, or so it was believed, the apex predator of its time, and not inclined to being stacked.

The theory of the paleontologist, a Mr. McMenamin, is straightforward. A giant squid, like nothing man has seen, crushed and splintered the ichthyosaurs, then hauled them to its lair to feed. This kraken, opines Mr. McMenamin, would have been a beast of otherworldly power and size nearly 100 feet long.

The problem to those outside paleontology may not be obvious. Cephalopods are primarily soft-bodied; with the exception of a sharp beak, they leave no fossil record. You require hard evidence. In weigh the other scientists. Impossible. Ridiculous. A case of reading the bones as if they were tea leaves scattered to tell a fortune. Too many nights watching the Science Fiction channel. Without evidence, there is only conjecture.

I put forward my own theory. Perhaps Mr. McMenamin is only partly right.

Yet another scientific discovery, this one by biologists in Indonesia. Observing veined octopuses in the wild, the biologists watched as the creatures carried a halved coconut shell with them across the exposed muddy bottom. When the octopus stopped, it placed the shell over its head for protection. This was not a case of a hermit crab selecting a shell. This was an example of advance planning before crossing hostile territory.

Your scientists were again astonished. Chimpanzees use tools, but not even chimps use natural materials to create shelters over their heads. "This is evolution in action," opines a scientist. "In fact, this may be happening in species beyond the octopi."

You don't say?

Changes are afoot. We have always been full of surprises. Now we are evolving quickly. We have to. You are changing the rules of the game.

You must adjust your mindset to keep up.

Soft Rabbits and Hollow Hopelessness

Monday was a school holiday. When Justin asked if Issy could come along on the charter, Cedar hadn't hesitated. She didn't take the girl as a favor. Simply put, Issy lit up the world around her. Perhaps because her parents were missionaries, she lived each day like it was a heavenly gift. The girl also knew how to work. She had been out on the boat before and put everyone to shame. By the end of the day, even Cedar couldn't keep up. If she hadn't been too much, too close, Cedar would have hired her to come out with them weekends and summers.

When Cedar, arranging Danishes on a tray on deck, heard someone singing James Taylor's "Fire and Rain", she looked to the dock. Issy was pushing the cart of tanks. Justin carried a cooler behind her.

Cedar whispered to the Danishes.

"Good God almighty."

Issy wore a string bikini. Head to toe, the girl was skin and smooth curve without blemish. Cedar glanced down at her own legs and said a silent curse. No Danishes for her this morning.

Issy swung one unnerving leg and a tank on to the Wendell Holmes.

"Top o' the morning, Mrs. Mahoney! Thanks for having me!"

How could it be anything but? The girl looked like a fawn. Justin looked like a buck in the headlights.

My son is a ruin and so is my breakfast.

"The pleasure is always ours, Issy. I made Danishes."

To fatten you up.

She couldn't even insult the girl in her subconscious.

Issy eyed the gooey pastries as she eyed everything else, with unconcealed delight

"I could eat the whole tray," she said.

"You could," Cedar said, "but we have our customers to consider." She gestured to the paper bag beside the tray. "There are napkins, cups and forks in the bag. If you don't mind arranging everything so it looks pretty, I'd be obliged. Justin can get the tanks."

Issy started before she finished asking.

Cedar looked to her son. Now was not the time for a lesson. She doubted he was even aware of his mother's presence.

"Issy?"

She did not look up.

"Yes, Mrs. Mahoney?"

"Might you put on a tank top and shorts before the divers arrive?"

"No problem."

The tank top and shorts only accentuated her figure. There was just no winning.

They had a full boat of ten but it felt like half that because the divers, all men, were polite and organized, and they clung to Issy's every suggestion like unabashed clams. Not one to put pride ahead of a tight ship, Cedar had Issy do the pre-dive briefing.

It was the kind of day dive operators dream of; no one left anything at the dock, no one got seasick, no one drifted off for Hawaii. First they dove a wreck and then, after a pleasant surface interval, a nearby reef pass on the outgoing tide. Both wreck and reef were fat with color and life. At the wreck, a Japanese destroyer, a school of barracuda some forty strong hovered in the water column, their chain mail forms glistening in the sunlight.

Back at the dock the tip jar swung madly, but what Cedar liked most was the sound of laughter disappearing down the dock.

Even on perfect days everything had to be washed down and stowed away, but they finished the job in half the time. Issy worked in an efficient flurry. One day, thought Cedar, she would have many someones snapping to. She wondered how the girl handled Justin, who drifted from moment to moment as easily as a leaf.

When they finished rinsing the boat and the gear, Cedar pulled an envelope from her file folder and held it out to Issy.

"A day's wage, plus one-fourth of the tips," she said.

"No thanks, Mrs. Mahoney."

"I insist."

"Nope. You saved me from getting sunburn."

Justin smiled.

"Mother to one and all," he said.

Issy waved a finger at Justin.

"It was nice of your Mom to look out for me. *You* didn't tell me to cover up."

No you didn't.

Their teeth were white, their faces smooth; their eyes fairly glowed. It almost hurt to look at them.

"I can't let you work for free, Issy," Cedar said.

"I can't work for anything else. I got to dive for free."

Missionaries don't give in and neither do their offspring.

"Fine then. Refuse dinner and you'll never set foot on this boat again."

"You're a tough negotiator, Mrs. Mahoney. Thanks. Dinner would be nice."

Poised too. Was there any reason she should like this girl?

Dinner *was* nice. She took them to the Thai restaurant she knew Issy favored. They talked and laughed and drank sweet tea, and Cedar ordered a second glass, even though she knew it would go right to her thighs. Mr. Na Songkhla, the owner, a jolly man shaped like a jelly bean, came over and sat with them for a few minutes until the restaurant began to fill up.

When they finished, he brought three bowls of green tea ice cream.

"Compliments of the house."

Cedar started to protest, but he raised a plump hand.

"Stop," he said. Leaning in, he whispered. "Everyone, they hear your laughter from the street. Look how full my restaurant is. Who can resist an establishment filled with bliss?"

Late that night, passing Justin's cabin on her way to bed, Cedar saw light under the door.

When she knocked and poked her head in, her son was in bed reading "Of Mice and Men."

"The perfect cap to my perfect day," she said.

Justin's eyes didn't leave the book.

"I'm near the end."

She shut the door softly.

She was drifting off to sleep when Justin knocked.

"I'm going to get Jonathan a banana," he said. "Want anything?"

That the rest of my days repeat this one.

"No thanks. Thanks for a great day."

"Thanks for bringing Issy."

"I'd hire her if she wasn't such a distraction to you."

The way he blushed made her want to rescue him.

"What did you think?" she asked.

"About what?"

"The book."

"Kind of slow in the beginning, but it turned out to be really good. The ending was incredibly sad."

It was on her mind every breathing moment.

"Sometimes you have to let go," she said.

"Sometimes." He had a way of studying her that melted her heart. "You know I love it here. You know I'm coming back." His smile broke slowly, like dawn. "Meanwhile, wherever I am, you'll manage to lecture me."

Cedar turned to settle her pillow, hoping he would take it as a signal to leave.

"You know you can bank on it," she said.

Lying in bed she thought of Steinbeck's sadly beautiful ending; George lifting the pistol from his jacket, speaking softly as Lennie looked out to the river, soft rabbits hopping in his mind.

A farm, a friend, a first love, a son. So many things we would like to go one way, so easily go another.

Her sleep was restless and troubled.

She woke in the middle of the night, her heart galloping. Beneath the hull the faint scratching was rhythmic, like a stroking. Pulling a t-shirt over her head, she went up on deck. There was nothing, only still water and floating trash.

Back in bed, she dreamt. In her dream she and Wyatt were still lovers. They were young, her body sleek as Issy's. She ran her hands over Wyatt's nakedness, every inch hard as teak. She thrilled to the tropical night against her bare thighs as Wyatt's urgent hands pushed her skirt up. She shimmied up his calves as two fingers pulled her panties aside. Her intensely private husband, made different by tropical madness, slid inside her, the two of them hidden in foliage a stone's throw from the crowded hotel patio. They both gasped in pleasure and surprise, rocking, holding their breath, nearly laughing and nearly crying, the Polynesian drumbeat taking up their own rhythm. Chills swept her body like schizophrenic breezes.

Back in the room they laughed at their daring and made love again, quietly this time, but with equal effect. They fell asleep entwined, Wyatt's breath slightly sweet from the fruity drinks that in her dream smelled more like flowers.

Even in the dream Cedar noticed how Wyatt's caresses were strangely gentle and oh-so-right, his touch like a woman's.

Yes, I now come to the harbor. It is irrational, foolish, dangerous, and more. But there I am. There are times I feel as if my will is not my own. I do this rarely. Some might see this as weakness - I do - but I allow myself this indulgence. It is quite pleasant being guided by something outside of intellect. I find it comforting, and, honestly, more than a little stimulating. It is stepping beyond the rules of convention. Maybe this is part of the attraction of what you call love.

Reaching out I gently clasp the hull, smooth like a shell. We lay together in the darkness. I do not try to influence her thoughts. With this one I do not want to overly interfere. In these midnight moments I don't know if I could. Her loneliness is a tremendous weight requiring great effort to push aside, a Sisyphean boulder that keeps rolling back into place. Instead I insinuate the seed of something pleasant, but beyond that I have little control. She dreams her own dreams. A curious thing, but I have found my powers have their limits in the face of good things. Wicked people and wicked thoughts are easily manipulated. But the pure few, they are a far tougher shell to crack. I do not know why this is. I have existed for millennia, but the unknowable permeates my life too. Mystery is part of all our lives

Life. A cup full of surprises to the last drop.

Yes, I had a mate. He is responsible, in part, for my current spate of irrational behavior. And, of course, the eggs. He lives still in the eggs.

What happened, you ask? I prefer not to talk about it.

I know her loneliness. It is far worse than hunger. Beyond hollow and hopeless.

It is what you feel when you know there are no more chances.

She woke wet and mildly embarrassed. She lay in the dark, still tingling. Wyatt had never accomplished anything of the sort during their marriage. When it came to lovemaking, he was no sure-of-hand gunslinger. He was more of a lustful farmer.

She let the pleasure continue to course through her body, and then she listened. Jonathan fluttered. In the ensuing silence she strained for sounds, but she heard nothing.

It was strange. She was no longer dreaming, but she still smelled it. It wasn't fruit, or her own muskiness.

It was plumeria.

She drifted back to sleep, remembering how her body had jerked.

I am back on the reef by dawn. If you'll pardon the pun, I often rise at dawn, lifting from the deeps to float just above the reef. No matter how many dawns I witness, the magic never wanes. I am touched by the way the light creeps slowly over the stalks of staghorn and the wave-smoothed plates. Every dawn is the unveiling of a fresh painting. After all these years, it still moves me.

Before you slip into meditative bliss, let me tell you I have seen dawn on other reefs, broken and bleached, the colors gone. These reefs are not like a lovely painting. They are like a splintered ichthyosaur carcass, like Hiroshima, like smoking rubble and burning flesh that, a moment ago, was a pre-school.

There are more and more ruined reefs. And, with tough love in mind, you're doing a stellar job on terra firma, too. Great swaths of forest slashed and burned. Rivers reduced to curdled brown eddying. Skies of filth and soot. Outside of epoch ending comet strikes, our world has never witnessed cataclysm like this. Never before have such terrible changes been wrought by a single species. You are making history.

We are racing to the end, but even I cannot say what the end will be. You speak of mankind's will to survive. Wholesale redirection and recovery are one thing; survival another. Imagine a world of fire and ash and hot, sour oceans, where your phlegmy, emaciated child may or may not last the day on pickings. There are no discards.

Not a pretty picture. No fable either. Already terrible fires are burning on your continents. Already dead zones carpet vast swaths of sea floor. Already ocean temperatures are rising.

The average species lasts a few million years. You're probably not even going to make the average.

Just because you have an opposable thumb, doesn't stop you from sticking it in your eye.

Departure

Wyatt's e-mail was brief and to the point, though not without heart. He knew what this meant.

He'd bought the plane ticket. Justin would leave in a month. Wyatt pointed out that mid-August was already pushing things. In Chicago the private high schools started in late August. Their son needed to arrive for his senior year on time. No wandering into third period with saltwater dripping out his nose. Ha ha.

When she and Wyatt were in graduate school - Wyatt at the University of Chicago for business; she at Purdue for ocean sciences -- they had written each other every day, old fashion letters where the ink smudged and she doodled hearts and smiley faces in the margins. Wyatt hadn't been much for things beyond the margins, but he had written beautiful letters, pages long, telling her how he missed her every breath and movement, the way she unfolded drowsily from bed, waking as she rose, the light growing in her eyes as if someone were ladling it in, turning them greener and greener still, like those time lapse films of blooming flowers.

Was a time she would have told him about her wet dream, even coached him along, hoping he might make dreams come true.

But that time, like so many, was gone.

Cedar stared at the life-changing e-mail, four paragraphs in all.

Cedar waited until Justin came home from school. She waited

until she fueled up the Wendell Holmes, Santy oddly evasive. She waited until Justin came back from listening to music with Issy (was that a euphemism?). She waited until he finished doing his homework on the foredeck, the soft evening light turning his rapt face even younger.

She waited until she stood at the kitchen counter scooping brown rice on to their plates, Jonathan balanced hopefully a few feet away.

"I heard from your father."

Justin was at the table. He stopped, salad dressing tipped just short of pour.

"When?"

"Your flight leaves August fifteenth."

It was a face you saw at funerals; lost and hopeless and stamped full with dull resignation. It would be so easy to make him happy, but making him happy was not her job.

"It's time to go home," she said.

"This is home."

"We've been over this before."

He put the salad dressing down harder than required.

"I left when I was six. Other than Dad, I don't know the place. Since when is that a home?"

"Since it has good schools with enough tennis players to field more than one doubles team." She hated this. She pretended to stir the rice, the steam warm on her face. "We can talk about it again and again, but it the answer is simple. You can't live your life here."

"It's simple for you because it's not your life."

Jonathan chirped.

She felt herself growing angry. How much was she supposed to take?

"You want to run a dive boat for the rest of your life? Really? Maybe Jonathan could be your first mate. You can bartend at The White Squall at night. Listen to your divers tell you what you saw that day and every day for the past ten years. Tell the same jokes during the dive briefings and when it's time for tips."

"I didn't say I wanted to run a dive boat." It was meant to sting, and it did. "I said I want to run my own life."

"A good education gives you a better chance of doing that. You need to spend your senior year at a good high school to better your chances of getting into a good college."

Just like that her anger died, but Justin's didn't.

"I don't want to spend my senior year in Chicago. I want to spend it here. Then I'll go to college."

She placed the plastic serving spoon in the sink. It seemed like yesterday that she had bathed him in this sink. How did that happen? She tried to keep the thought from rising into her face.

"I want you to go back. Your father wants you to go back. It's what's best for all of us."

"*You* decided to leave Chicago. *You* decided to leave Dad. No one else decided that."

"That's completely different. And unfair."

She didn't know how much longer she could hold on. It was like the pushups her high school lacrosse coach used to make them do. *Okay, ten more. Okay, now ten more because you know you can.* One by one everyone on the team had eventually collapsed. Not once had she quit. She had thought it was the hardest thing she'd ever do.

"Mom, I appreciate what you're both trying to do. I want to go college. I appreciate the opportunity you're giving me. I just want to finish high school here. I work hard in school. I do all the extra credit work I can and then some. You're not in class with me. I'm getting a good education here."

Okay, ten more.

"How many members of last year's graduating class went to college?"

"*That's* unfair. They'd rather fish. They'd rather stay with their families."

She ignored the second statement.

"You want to be a fisherman?"

"Why not?"

Because we are wiping out the oceans. First the great whales, then the cod. Now Chilean sea bass, orange roughy, walleye pollock and salmon. Even here in their little world, ostensibly tucked far away, nets came up empty. Ninety percent of large wild fish, already gone.

Both she and Justin had read a recent United Nations report forecasting the possibility of a fishless sea by the year 2050.

She didn't say any of this. Justin knew.

Her hands shook. It was too hard. She wanted to quit.

"There's nothing here for you, Justin. It's a dead end. No future you would want. And yes, no future I would want for you." She hesitated. "Issy's going to leave eventually, too."

"She leaves in five weeks. Her whole family's leaving."

This blindsided her.

"Where?"

"They're moving to Ocala, Florida. It's where her mom's from."

Cedar had been to Ocala once. It was filled with hard-partying, sun-wrecked Conchs who had fled the Florida Keys after the Keys got too expensive. She tried to imagine Issy's parents in Ocala. Plenty of empty pew space to fill on Sunday mornings.

Jonathan had shuffled to the lip of the kitchen sink. He leaned forward like a slow toppling bowling pin, pink tongue tapping a water droplet suspended from the spigot. Rising, his eyes bored into Cedar.

Judgmental bat.

"I didn't know they were leaving," she said.

"There's a lot you don't know."

There comes a time in a parent's life when they can stop acting. If she knew everything she wouldn't be in the galley of a dive boat in a remote jungle outpost, facing a dubious future and losing a staring contest with a fruit bat in the present.

Her own failings firmed her resolve. This, she thought wryly, is what parenting often boiled down to. *Don't be like me.*

"You can argue all you want, but it's decided. You can decide how you'll handle it."

She came around the counter with the plates. She put Justin's plate in front of him and then moved to her chair.

Justin always pulled out her chair.

She sat and picked up her napkin.

"See?" she said. "I'm already learning how to be self-sufficient."

She was surprised to find herself fighting back tears. Finally, one push-up too many.

A chair scraped.

Justin bent and kissed her cheek.

"I'm a jerk and an ingrate. You've done everything for me. I know how lucky I am."

Goddammit. Now she was crying.

She hiccupped, her smile gummy.

"You *are* a jerk, but you're my jerk."

The boat rocked. Her son stayed bent, his arms around her neck. She wanted it to last forever.

After dinner she stayed at the table while Justin washed the dishes, surreptitiously passing Jonathan scraps.

"What say tomorrow we go for a dive, just you and me?" she said. "We can even bring your garbage disposal."

Jonathan loved being on the boat but he rarely came along. Being on the boat excited him and excitement stirred his bowels. Fruit bats made a mess that was hell to clean up.

She didn't care if Jonathan shat his way from bow to stern and back again.

Justin gave her a sly look.

"Sloppy Joes for lunch?" he asked.

Sloppy Joes were Justin's favorite, and Jonathan's too. This ran counter to a fruit bat, but there it was.

"You're taking advantage. Sloppy Joes too."

"And we dive Water Whispers."

Her stomach dropped.

"Never one to stop pushing your luck," she said, trying a smile. "Why do you want to go there?"

"There's something about the place. It's not just that it's beautiful. I can't really put it into words. The closest thing I can say is it feels comfortable. Like home."

"It's almost as far as Chicago," Cedar said.

"If I got a good job I could help you pay for fuel. If I got a really good job I could buy Santy out and he could retire with Heidi Klum." He placed the last dish in the rack. "Chicago isn't home. But I guess I could learn to make it home for a little while."

"You're manipulating me."

"It's possible."

"Fine. Water Whispers."

"Great!"

Justin held out his forearm and Jonathan hopped nimbly aboard. Boy and bat started walking away.

"Wait a minute."

"What?"

"You know that was a sucker punch," she said.

"Maybe. But I threw it for both of us."

She tried to look indignant.

"I hope you suffer children one day."

She smiled at him.

"You see, don't you?" she asked.

"See what?"

"Sometimes you do get to choose."

After they left she sat at the table, unwilling or unable to get up.

Water Whispers.

Just the words sent cold creeping through her limbs.

That night she walked up the hill to Shirley's. She was late. Marty sat on his prescribed stool. Two tourist couples sat at one of the patio tables drinking pina colodas. Their faces were redder than their straws.

A Red Rooster rested on the bar.

"One day you'll do something that surprises me," she said, sliding on to the stool.

"That seat is taken."

"You're right."

A steady breeze was blowing. A napkin flopped off a table. Marty went out to the patio. Retrieving the napkin, he carefully situated the silverware on the remainder of the napkins.

He walked back to the bar. She loved to watch him walk. He

moved like a dancer, his steps graceful and light.

A pretty girl stood behind the bar near the kitchen door, wringing her hands. Cedar didn't recognize her.

"Did Henry hire a shy bartender?" she whispered.

"Not exactly. At present, Henry has difficulties."

"Ah. Damsel difficulties?"

Marty carefully folded the napkin and placed it on the bar, leaning close as he did.

"A former flame. She arrived on the mail boat this afternoon. I believe Henry is in the back, trying to flush himself down the loo."

"Just like a man to take the sensible approach. Is your sister aware of this newcomer?"

"I sincerely doubt it."

The girl walked down the bar, stopping opposite the small television affixed to the ceiling beneath the row of rugby banners. Pretending to watch TV, she kept glancing back toward the kitchen. When Henry finally came through the door, she lit up like a roman candle. The pleasure on her face made Cedar a little sad.

"Apparently Henry has not yet acquired the gumption to inform her of his current relationship status," Marty said.

Henry, carrying a bowl, passed by the girl quickly, giving her a sickly smile.

Placing the peanuts on the bar, he whispered, "Help me."

Cedar saw the girl making her way back toward the kitchen. When she disappeared through the door, Cedar said, "Be sweet, but be honest."

"Lord," groaned Henry.

"He won't help you," said Cedar, "but we can get our own drinks."

Henry groaned again and slouched off slowly toward the kitchen.

She turned to Marty. She wondered if he had ever slouched.

"I can't let go of him," she said.

"Henry has enough female problems already."

"Stop it."

"Ah. I'm sorry. You heard from your husband?"

Marty always spoke as if she was still married. It irritated her, but she ignored it this time.

"Yes. He booked the flight. Justin leaves in a month. I've lost a piece of my heart already."

"It is a good thing you are so well endowed."

Her grip on the bottle relaxed a little.

"Do you ever say the wrong thing?"

Marty spun the ice in his glass.

"No need to waste my breath," he said.

"What am I going to do?"

"Have you considered other interests?"

"Other interests?"

"Beyond your son."

He delivered it gently, as kindly as a priest, as expertly as a tuxedoed waiter.

She looked out across the patio. The world was dark sky and

sea, but all she could see was the pinprick of light in the cabin far below.

"In one year I'll be putting that son through college. I don't have time for hobbies."

"There is always time if you wish to find it."

"Fine. I'll stop before I lose this argument too."

"It is not an argument."

"And?"

Marty raised an eyebrow.

"And?" he said.

"You already have a proposal in mind."

"Correct. I propose you learn to fly."

"I can't afford to go stateside to find a competent pilot."

"Only one port in this particular storm."

It just popped into her head.

"Fine. And you learn to dive."

Apparently Marty could slouch.

Something smashed in the kitchen. Followed by several somethings in quick succession. Next came high pitched screaming.

Marty turned to the startled tourists.

"The dishware is insured," he said. "Did you know that my best friend here is going to learn to fly?"

Walking back to the harbor, Cedar saw a limping figure approaching in the dark. As the figure drew close, the limping stopped and Santy's nephew veered off into the brush.

Maybe a small place made everyone queer.

Jonathan

Cedar recognized the perch as soon as she climbed the ladder to the bridge, the world gray in the early morning light. Justin had made the perch in sixth grade, tunneling a hole through the center of a cylindrical block of wood and then twisting a longer section of rebar through the hole to weigh down the perch. Now rusted rebar ends jutted from both sides of the wood cylinder, making the perch look like a tooth-breaking corn dog. Justin's woodworking skills had improved considerably, but Jonathan had taken a fierce liking to this first rendition and there was no arguing with Jonathan.

The perch was tucked behind the plexiglass windshield, affixed to the console with zip ties. Cedar noted, approvingly, that Justin had placed one towel on the console and another beneath the perch.

Justin had fashioned a leather tether. Similar to the kind falconers used, it was tethered to Jonathan's left leg. Jonathan suffered sudden bouts of wanderlust. They hated tethering him, but it would be far worse if he indulged his wanderlust miles out to sea.

He actually looked a bit like a falcon.

"Well don't you look regal this morning," she said, plotting in the coordinates to Water Whispers.

Jonathan ignored her, staring off toward the breakwater at the harbor entrance, where winged creatures of some sort milled in the sky.

"You know, you could cozy up just a little. Pretty soon it's just going to be you, me and the bananas."

He continued to stare bulbous eyed at the breakwater.

"Blink if you love me," she said.

When Justin came up the bat pivoted and made several short ineffective hops.

"No shoulder today," said Justin, stroking the velvety wings. "But wait until you see what's for lunch."

Justin pulled a blackened banana from his windbreaker. He scratched Jonathan's ears while Jonathan slopped breakfast on to both towels.

Cedar laughed.

"Most boys have dogs," she said.

"Most boys aren't half as lucky as me."

For the entire trip Jonathan leaned out around the windscreen, the wind sculpting back the hair on his face so that his enormous eyes looked even bigger.

When Cedar finally eased off the throttle and the Wendell Holmes settled into the water, a terrible stench rose to greet her.

She leaned out, shouting down to Justin on the bow.

"I hope you brought a bin of towels. Next time I drop the anchor and *you* come up here."

She tried to sound amused, but in her ears her nervousness made her banter sound like the bad acting it was.

Justin didn't notice.

Grinning up at her he said, "Maybe your driving upsets him."

The gentle sway of the Wendell Holmes ran up her legs. It was a perfect day for diving, the waters calm as shadows.

Cedar looked out at the empty ocean, not a boat in sight. It should have thrilled her.

Jonathan fluttered and looked at her.

Cedar watched her son swam directly into the cavern, but not before putting his ear to the opening and folding his hands in prayer. Then he performed a flip and disappeared.

Justin's joy didn't make her feel any better. On the boat ride out she had tried to convince herself that maybe this was a good thing. Maybe a second look would prove her wrong. Maybe her imagination had run off with her. Maybe she had too much motherhood on her mind. Maybe they weren't egg cases. Every day the ocean unveiled new mysteries.

Even as she told herself these things, she knew them as lies. From the moment she had known they were coming here, she had felt edgy, weighted with a growing apprehension. While Justin lay by the opening she had scanned the waters, looking out to a ring of fall-away blue. Divers fantasized about days like this.

She felt like an intruder.

Yet she wasn't afraid, and this was the oddest feeling of all. If she was right about the eggs and the attack, they were dealing with a creature any rational person would regard as highly dangerous. A ruthlessly efficient predator, she had told Marty. But in her heart she was almost certain about what she hadn't told Marty. It was not a mindless predator that concerned her, but something beyond her, or anyone's, ken.

Which drove a different fear into her bones.

Listening to herself debate, she wondered if she might really be insane. Maybe, in certain unhinged cases, water actually did whisper.

By the time she entered the cavern, Justin was already floating up at the shelf, flashlight trained on the opening. Her eyes went to a section of wall twenty yards to his left. Here light insinuated itself through a series of narrow, horizontal fissures. The light bathed the cavern in understated ethereal glow. She gazed at her son, yellow mask pressed against the shelf. He barely moved.

The light in the cavern dimmed for an instant, a cloud passing across the sun.

Cedar finned up beside her son. He moved aside, playing his beam across the perfectly arranged eggs. They were eggs. She had no doubt.

They came on board to silence. Jonathan always produced a cacophony of high-pitched squeaking when Justin came out of the water. Only the sight of Justin shut him up.

"Asleep at the wheel," said Justin, prying his mask strap free of a knot of sun-bleached hair. "I don't think it'll make much difference if we threaten to fire him."

Something was wrong. She wanted to stop Justin, but in the time it took her to find a reason, his bare feet were slapping up the rungs.

His choked cry was both affirmation and condemnation.

She did not recall ascending the ladder. Somehow Justin had torn the perch from the console. He gripped it, his mouth making rapid sucking noises, as if he were drowning on the bridge. The dangling tether held a dark branch.

Unable to bite through the leather, Jonathan had chewed off his leg. There was shit everywhere and blood, too. She had never seen so much blood.

He must have been nearly dead when he lifted off, adrenalin alone seeing him into the sky.

She bent, adding her breakfast to the mess.

I was puzzled, though not threatened, by their return. But, as I recently learned yet again (perhaps your forgetfulness is contagious), I cannot be too careful. I watched them descend through the openings. Hovering off the wall of the sea mount, I listened; to the looping currents, to the wind making its gentle passage across the surface, to the one heart beating confusion and apprehension and the other tom-tomming excitement like a song. When the boy stopped swimming, I knew without seeing, that he hung suspended before the eggs. I was not concerned. In truth, I was a little proud.

But her fear, I confess, is mildly troubling. She knows what she has found. More accurately, she thinks she knows what she has found, but she pushes the realization away, as she tries to adapt to this new world far beyond the strictures of the old. She is evolving. I know she will adjust and accept. She is a quick study.

The bat could not absorb reality. The vehemence of the creature's protest surprised me. I knew the bat would react to my presence, but I did not expect him to react as he did. Animals have souls, too, and the bat's soul, like the boy's, was serene. Or so I thought. Fear can make us wholly unlike ourselves, leading us astray.

I am deeply sorry, but now that she has discovered the eggs I have concerns beyond a fruit bat. I do not know what she will do next. I know her soul. I fear no direct harm from her. But anything else is possible. The eye of a storm is calm, but unpredictable chaos swirls beyond.

I hover before the shelf. To enter the cavern I must leave my shell, but this is not an overly difficult endeavor. Watching our offspring, I tremble. I do not possess maternal instincts, nor do I require them. They will care quite ably for themselves when they hatch. What I feel is a rising anticipation.

They are exquisite, if I may say so myself, their gold flecked edges like the hem of an Empress's gown. In the dim water they exude an iridescence that throws light far beyond refraction's conventional dictates.

Chinese lanterns must be very lovely.

For a moment, I allow myself to succumb. I float in the blue cavern, buoyed by feelings you might call gratitude and pride. And then, always, rising sorrow. Eggs are a product of two. Again, hollowness digs its maudlin hole inside me, ruining the moment.

Enough. It is the facts that matter now. They are better than the sum of their seeds. It is the math of Darwin. They are endowed with powers beyond mine. Communicators even you cannot ignore. Each generation should improve on the next, though this is not always the case.

In ten months they will hatch and all our odds of survival will increase. The odds may even teeter toward recovery and, hope beyond hope, rebirth. It's possible. This planet we share is resilient. Not indestructible, oh no, but tough enough to bounce back from some sore kicks in the teeth.

I am trembling again.

That night Marty called from his cell phone. Marty almost always called her from his home phone. The island had a party line. He was single. She was single. Letting everyone eavesdrop on their conversations stopped rumors in their tracks.

There was no preamble.

"I saw something today," Marty said. "At least I think I did."

She was replacing an o-ring on one of the tanks, working on the back deck of the Wendell Holmes beneath a sorry puddle of fluorescent light. Her eyes burned from fatigue.

She settled the o-ring carefully and sat back.

"Where?"

"A half mile off the northeast end of the island, just before dusk. The falling light made it harder to see."

"You don't sound sure."

Was she trying to dissuade him?

"I'm not sure. The water was already going dark. I only got a quick look. I had a passenger. I couldn't drop the nose and put a client through the window. I rely on repeat business."

"What did you think you saw?"

"A shadow. Twice the size of your boat at least. Maybe bigger. I don't know how deep it was. It was moving. Not fast, but fast enough to see steady movement."

"Cloud shadow?"

"It was moving opposite the wind."

Maybe, she sighed.

"It's not proof, you know," said Marty.

She almost laughed.

"You sound like my 8th grade science teacher."

"One more thing," said Marty.

"What?"

"Draw a straight line and it was headed for the harbor."

After she hung up Cedar leaned out over the railing. Dark water moved along the hull toward the sea, the tide going out.

Just before midnight, at slack tide, the current ran briefly again.

I have told you I do not feel love as you know it. What I feel is more an actual physical attachment. This physical attachment is no less powerful than your lovelorn emotional trappings. When a child pries a sea star from a rock, it does not go unnoticed by those left behind. But the survivors do not feel an absent pining; they feel a measurable shock through every appendage. It is not phantom pain at all. My mate met a terrible end. Does the pain recede? Perhaps with time, but the pain I still feel is as real as a bat gnawing off its leg.

I believe, over millennia, my evolution has brought me closer to the love of which your poets speak. Part of me relishes this. Part of me wishes it away. You understand this. I don't have to preach to you about the heights and depths of love. Wasted breath. I will only say this. I am beginning to feel the whisperings of things that are not physical, things I cannot label or pin down. Maybe this is the point. Love, you say, is a many-splendored thing. Perhaps this is your way of absolving definition. I like the indefinable. Life is meant to hold mystery. Love, God, peace, heaven, hell, Satan, terror, fury, war, hatred. It would not be life if there were no questions without answers. No spice, without a little confusion.

If I may use the word, the love I feel when I clasp the hull of the boat is not the passion I transmit to the woman, but it is no less powerful. Even as she writhes in the arms of perfect dream lovers, beset by blood poundings and flushings, I am there on her periphery, with her, too. Females understand each other's needs. It pleases me to please her. But how to explain our connection in terms you might grasp? Perhaps two women who have each lived long enough to know life, sharing hidden sorrows and secrets in a late night kitchen, one reaching out to gently caress the other's brow, taking some sadness for her own.

Who is soothing who is a matter of debate. I come here to the harbor as much for me as her.

I need reassurance too.

Given the inclinations of your species, it is so easy to doubt.

A Special Guest

Two weeks later Cedar received an unusual request.

The e-mail was exceedingly detailed, not one stone left unturned. There were, the writer explained, five men and two women in their group. Both women and four of the men were comfortable on boats. The fifth man would spend the first day at sea retching violently and then put it behind him. Two in the party were vegetarian; two were gay (so that there would be no whispering among the crew). Cedar liked how the writer did not identify any of the parties; she would figure it out by the first meal and the first night. She appreciated this forthright airing. The matter of sexual preference was an individual's private business, but when you were spending a week on a 45-foot vessel with strangers it was best to know certain things up front.

They were free divers who spear fished. They were interested only in trophy fish - big tuna, possibly a sailfish if they were undeservedly lucky - though now and again they would spear something smaller for dinner. They all had a soft spot for fresh sashimi, which she and her deckhands were more than welcome to enjoy. They wished to charter the Wendell Holmes for a week. They would pay the going rate and two thousand dollars extra since she would not be able to charge for tanks and air. The fee would go up if they asked to be taken to remoter waters. The price of fuel these days, the man wrote, was an abomination. The oil companies were today's pirates. He preferred the pirates of old, because you knew when they were running you through.

Cedar sat back in her chair and smiled. Maybe she would print up the e-mail and deliver it to Santy.

The writer did not identify himself until the end of the e-mail, and then only by signing his name.

She picked up her desk calendar. Her eyes walked along the days. She went to the bookshelf.

When Justin came aboard that afternoon, she stood there grinning.

"What?" he said.

She didn't miss how his hand went, like a divining rod, to the small red mark on his neck. She wondered if there were marks out of sight.

"You'll have to be more specific," she said.

"Okay. What's making you smile like I just told you I'll obey your every word?"

"This is better."

She gave him a long head to toe look, pausing at his neck. It was wrong to make him squirm, but she was running out of chances.

His eyes went to the book in her hand.

"What are you doing with Jimmy Maas's book?"

"Figuring out the best place for him to sign it."

"What?"

"He just hired us for a week's charter."

"What?"

"When you keep asking the same question the conversation goes nowhere."

"I don't believe it."

"Trust me, it will."

He hugged her before she could react, giving her a spine-altering squeeze. He broke away just as fast.

"Jimmy Maas!" he shouted.

He performed a short jig, long arms and legs everywhere.

"I should have gotten you dance lessons," she said.

She waited, savoring the moment. *One last going away gift.*

"It's a long trip. We'll need help. Issy can come if it's okay with her parents." She wanted to look at the hickey for emphasis but he had suffered enough. "You sleep on deck. She sleeps with me. The charter starts Thursday. Dawn. I have no doubt they'll be on time. I'll need help getting supplies."

"I'll obey your every word."

"I'd like that in writing."

"Yea," said Justin, and she knew he hadn't heard. He was pulling his phone from the pocket of his shorts, no doubt to tell Issy they'd be sharing a boat if not a berth, but he stopped. "Why do you think he picked us?"

Blue water hunting was a small world. Now and again she won a local spearfishing contest, much to the chagrin of the local males, but that was no reason for Jimmy Maas and his friends to travel halfway around the world.

"I can't say," she said.

Cedar would have smiled, but more and more this applied to the world around her.

Jimmy Maas was surprisingly tall in real life. Only as he walked down the dock did Cedar realize she'd always seen him photographed together with some otherworldly fish.

He was older, too. Except for a dark streak at his left temple, his curly hair was sugar white. The outstretched hand had age spots, along with liberal nicks and scars.

"Thank you for having us."

Milky blue eyes acknowledged her briefly before performing a slow bow to stern appraisal.

She tried not to sound too apologetic.

"She needs a little work."

"Working boats do."

Jimmy Maas made quick introductions. Cedar conducted her own bow to stern appraisal. Each diver carried several spear guns, a dive bag and a single small duffel. She made a mental note to ask for packing tips. They ranged in age from mid-twenties to Maas, who Cedar knew to be just past sixty. All were lean and fit. Several faces looked familiar, no doubt from magazine photos.

"A ragtag bunch with slipshod manners and habits, but we know those habits, which is important when you travel together," said Maas. "I'm also a man of habit. I'm the one who gets sick." His face puckered and unpuckered. He did not follow it with a smile. "Real sick and fairly quick."

Man of his word, Maas started puking as soon as they passed beyond the breakwater and into the first rolling swells. Cedar had seen her share of *mal de mer*, but the retchings of Jimmy Maas were in a league of their own.

"He's saved thousands of dollars skipping breakfast," remarked one of the men. He scowled. "I think I'll skip breakfast, too."

It was piteous the way his whole body heaved.

"Is there anything we can do?" Cedar asked.

"Push him overboard."

By lunch Maas was fine. He inhaled Cedar's butter and cucumber sandwiches like he had skipped breakfast. He was also one of the vegetarians.

At Maas' request they had stopped to investigate a string of kelp paddies. In the open-ocean small fish used them to hide. Small fish often drew bigger fish.

Maas wanted to dive the patties. It was already clear he made the decisions. Maas worked a bolus of bread and cucumber and stared over the side.

The other divers tinkered with their gear while they ate.

Justin held the tray and stared.

One of the men glanced up from his spear gun.

"He puts his pant legs on one at a time, when he remembers where he put his pants," the man said in a clipped South African accent. Cedar remembered now. Away from diving, Jimmy Maas was famously absent-minded. "And, as he's already ably displayed, he'd also do well to keep tabs on his bib."

The man grinned at Justin, extending a hand.

"Hello, Justin. Murray's the name. Pretoria's home, although I could get used to this."

Balancing the tray, Justin shook Murray's hand.

"You're all friends?"

Murray was nearly square, with an outthrust jaw that would have threatened confrontation had his eyes not resonated constant amusement.

"Most of the time," he said.

Though he stood only a few feet away, Maas did not appear to hear them. Staring into the water, he stuffed the last half of his sandwich in his mouth.

Cedar nearly laughed out loud.

"Opted out of finishing school," observed Murray.

Pulling his t-shirt over his head, Murray folded it neatly and placed it on the bench beside him.

Cedar tried not to stare. Murray's entire torso, waist to neck, was covered with tattoos. Cedar had seen tattoos before; she had one of her own, a tiny leaping dolphin on her left ankle. But these tattoos were enormous, sweeping, artistic swirls that melded one into the next so that a mermaid's hair became jellyfish tentacles and the body of the jellyfish, turned slightly, became a crescent moon. Or possibly a breast.

As his muscles moved, so did the tattoos.

There was something about the tattoos, but Cedar couldn't quite figure it out.

Issy came up on deck with a pitcher of lemonade. Cedar was glad she had opted for a windbreaker over her bikini, although she could already see the men weren't easily distracted.

"Wow," whispered Issy.

"A living piece of scrimshaw," a voice said. "Murray's his own Sistine Chapel."

The blond woman smiled at Cedar and Issy. She had freckles and big ears that would have been easily covered by something other than a bob. Cedar ticked through her memory, marching down Maas' introductions.

"I've seen my share of tattoos, Mary Jayne, but I've never seen anything like that," Cedar said. "They're beautiful."

"Thank you," Murray said. "Bit of an ink addict. I get them to commemorate special occasions. It's been a lucky life."

"Oh my God," said Issy.

Cedar turned, surprised. She had never heard the girl use God's name, except when she said a mealtime prayer.

Issy flushed.

"I'm sorry," she said, but Murray was already laughing.

"No need to apologize for being keen-eyed, young lady. Twenty percent of tattoos are cover-ups. Though I skew the percentage."

Cedar saw them now, lines that wavered where they shouldn't, as if, at points, the tattoo artist had handed the needle gun to a three-year-old.

"Murray is also our resident chew toy," Mary Jayne said, and Cedar knew they had used this joke a thousand times before. "Swallowed to the shoulders by a white shark off Cape Town. Alerted to his change in circumstances by sudden darkness and an odd grinding noise. That was the shark working on his head. Bad luck for the shark, sampling the only meatless part."

"Talk me up," said Murray.

"Your diving does the talking," said Mary Jayne.

This time, Cedar knew she wasn't joking.

By the end of the first day, they had adopted Justin and Issy as their own. Cedar let Justin dive the kelp patties with them. She told him he was supervising, but that was ridiculous. Justin spent the day unabashedly orbiting Jimmy Maas. Each time Maas bobbed to the surface, Justin surfaced not far away.

"I didn't think I'd lose him to another man," Issy said.

Cedar and Issy stood on the stern, watching the watery slick where Maas and Justin had just disappeared.

"You could start doing yoga."

"Even that won't work."

The girl looked genuinely downcast.

Cedar touched her elbow.

"Men are always infatuated with something. If not themselves."

"Justin's different."

It wasn't a compliment. It was a statement of fact.

"Not this time," Cedar said.

That night Justin was so exhausted he barely offered half a hand with dinner and an eighth of a hand with cleanup. At one point Cedar was fairly certain he was sleeping on his feet.

It didn't matter. Everyone pitched in. Murray had speared a good-size wahoo. One of the men made an improvisational paste - the most noticeable ingredient was ginger - that transformed the fish into something just short of heaven. Another man made baklava that attained equivalent heights.

"Tony and Allen own separate restaurants on the same block in Healdsburg, California," Murray confided to Cedar when he brought his dishes to the sink. "They only take vacations if the other one does. Four Michelin stars are not built on blind trust."

Ernan ate with them. He usually ate by himself, but to Cedar's pleasant surprise at lunch he had asked if he could join everyone at dinner.

Reading her face, he had said, "This is not your average group. I can learn from them."

At dinner Ernan learned that four members of the group had been to Manila, and that everyone was curious about the place. Cedar learned things about Manila, and Ernan, that she had never known. He discoursed eloquently on the history and economy of the Philippines. He spoke of the gated communities along Roxas Boulevard overlooking Manila Bay as if he had lived in them; and the slums as if he had written a graduate thesis on Manila's economic extremes.

After dinner and clean up was done, Cedar followed him up to the bridge.

She stood quietly while he reached for his chewing tobacco and then checked the GPS.

When he turned, she smiled.

"What was that?"

"Checking our positioning."

"Very funny. I meant at dinner."

"That was too much talking," he said, and spat into the paper cup.

"You were the life of the party."

"They are good people and genuinely curious."

"And you should be the Philippine ambassador."

Ernan turned and looked out over the water.

"I prefer the view from here."

That first night Issy changed in the bathroom. The bathroom was half the size of a small shower stall. Cedar lay in bed, smiling as Issy banged about. The girl's sudden decorum was endearing.

She came out nursing an elbow and smoothing a football jersey down past her knees.

"I've never seen that before," Cedar said.

"Neither has Justin." Issy smiled. "It belonged to an infatuation."

"Ah."

Women, thought Cedar, were a surprise even to women.

Cedar woke before dawn. The radio in the galley was on and so was the coffee.

She went up on deck, stopping to look down at her softly snoring son.

Jimmy Maas sat by himself, legs dangling off the bow.

An orange scrim scratched the horizon. It was warm already, the warmth like a comforting blanket.

She loved it here.

She prodded her son with a toe. His eyes were clear the instant they opened.

"Good morning, Mom."

Putting a finger to her lips she nodded toward the bow and whispered, "It certainly is."

Justin wormed silently from the sleeping bag, his salt-stiff hair shooting off in one direction as if he inhabited his own quadrant of howling wind.

Down in the galley, Cedar said, "You might consider a comb."

"We're just going back in the water."

She tried to sound casual.

"Hear anything last night?"

Justin pushed down his hair. It sprung right back up.

"Nope. Slept like I was dead."

They were just words, but Cedar hated them just the same.

Swordfish

Each day the routine was the same. Maas woke everyone, including Cedar, by turning on the radio and the coffee at precisely 5am. When she offered to get up earlier and fix the coffee, Maas had simply said, “If you do, I’ll just get up at four-thirty.” He was in the water by six. Everyone else went in between seven and eight. Though unspoken, Maas’ time alone was honorary. He was the legend. Legend earned him first shot.

Everyone exited the water at eleven-thirty for a brief lunch - sometimes sashimi from a freshly speared yellowfin, more often Cedar’s finger sandwiches - everyone except Maas, who went up and down all day like an Eveready cork, with rare breaks for grape juice swigged while he rested his elbows on the swim step. Even Justin couldn’t keep up with him.

Maas stayed focused even during his swim step rejuvenation, but once, when Cedar handed him his grape juice, he smiled up at her.

“Boy’s got lungs,” he said. “Makes me feel my age.”

Cedar spent most of the day on the bridge. The bridge afforded a 360-degree view of her charges, who wandered much farther from the boat than she liked. But she said nothing. As Ernan aptly put it, “Their skill is as visible as their complete disregard for the rules.”

On the fourth day Cedar took them far to the east, to an isolated sea mount she had discovered accidentally almost a decade earlier. The mount was a free diver’s dream. It rose like a spire, 5,000 feet from the ocean floor. Smaller fish used it as protection on an otherwise empty plain. Bigger fish knew it as a buffet. It was a locus of life, but she never brought clients here. It was distant and dangerous. Currents were unpredictable; the water was often murky and big fish were on the hunt, although often you never saw them. It was stark and beautiful. But mostly it was a world that was not theirs -- powerful, primal and wholly uncaring.

She had a first aid kit on board, the best money could buy. She knew Maas had brought his own; more than likely, the other divers were prepared too. But if something serious happened, all the first aid kits in the world would not be enough.

It was part of the thrill.

Everyone reacted to the sea mount as if they had just been goosed, even Maas, who to Cedar had always looked as dour as an undertaker in his magazine pictures. Without exception the writers gushed about the man, claiming he had a supernatural affinity for the sea, a photographic memory that allowed him to recite conditions that made for a successful hunt - tides, currents, bait fish activity - twenty years earlier, and the stamina of a honeymooner. But the photographers captured only the undertaker.

When they pulled up on the mount, Maas did a jig, his gangly form all shadowy knees and elbows against the setting sun.

That night at dinner Murray told her, and the rest of the table, that Maas had arrived in Palau with a better-than-rough fix on the sea mount.

"Got it from whispered rumors and the diligent application of Google Earth," Murray said, forking up a potato. "He was hoping you might take us here. Kind of you to save him the agony of asking."

"It's the perfect spot for your group," Cedar said. She gave Maas a playful look. “But I didn’t know you were such a big fan of technology.”

Maas returned a sheepish grin.

“I dislike technology but I’d be a fool to ignore it.”

“Whatever it takes to make dreams come true,” said Murray.

Finishing his beer in two enormous swallows, he gave a happy belch.

“To dreams come true,” he said.

“Men are pigs,” said Mary Jayne, belching.

Maas said, “Tell me why I travel with unrefined heathen?” and then he burped.

For the rest of dinner, everyone carried on like ten-year-olds.

Cedar was glad she had brought them here.

That night, although she was already fairly certain, the gay couple revealed themselves. The women’s cabin was next to hers. No doubt, they tried to be discrete, but if she listened she heard their sighs and rustlings, and something that sounded like prayer.

She glanced at Issy. The girl snored softly, sleeping with the ease of the young.

The murmurings continued, rising, falling away and rising again. Cedar tried to think of something else, but it was no use. She felt herself begin to tingle. She had an inkling of what it was like to be with a woman.

These divers are different. They hunt as we do, with stealth and cunning and selectivity. None of your kind is meant for our world, all flailing limbs and awkward jerks, but these divers come close. The one in particular. He fins deep into the fuzzy blue and drifts upright, legs crossed, fins pointed down, turning ever so slowly. His stills his heart so that even I can barely detect it. The stupider fish nearly bump into him. But while his heart stills, his mind crackles, absorbing barely perceptible intangibles. It is quite impressive, though when he is finished diving he still swims to the boat as if he is pithed. You are all fish out of water.

They could learn a thing or two, but I must confess they all exhibit a degree of skill. They are hunters. If I wore a hat, I would tip it to them.

In the afternoon, the other divers taking a break and warming in the sun, Cedar went to the stern where her son sat on the swim step, pale legs dangling in the water.

"You should get out of the sun," she said.

"He's been under for two minutes and thirteen seconds."

She gazed at the choppy green waters, a paltry mirror of the currents below.

"It's amazing."

She meant every syllable.

Justin's eyes didn't leave the water.

"I'm wrecked," he said. "He's been diving since five-thirty and still going strong."

"Don't try this at home."

She said it as a joke, but not entirely. Every year free divers died of shallow water blackout. Shallow water blackout was precisely what it spelled out, although it occurred as readily in deep water as shallow. Stay down too long and one second conscious, the next drifting and dead. Or sinking and dead. Dead either way. Tired divers made more mistakes, pushed already fatigued limits, took foolish chances. She had personally known two free divers who died of shallow water blackout. One was a twenty-four-year old girl.

She felt she needed to say something without outright telling her son Jimmy Maas was unsafe. That would only make Justin mad.

"He's spent years doing this, Justin. I've also heard he's a physiological freak."

"I could do it. With practice." He turned back to her with that smile she couldn't resist. "I know what you're thinking, Mom. It's not a risk if you're prepared and careful. I'm not naive."

No, but you are sixteen.

"No one is beyond physiology" she said softly.

Justin was watching the water again, lost to her.

"No," he said, "but you can come close."

Thirty minutes later Maas swam to the swim step. Justin had his water bottle of grape juice ready. Maas pulled off his mask to drink. His face was swollen.

He drank. Justin handed him a banana. He ate it solemnly. Swaying with the waves, he got a large portion of banana on his face.

Cedar thought of Jonathan. The day chilled a little.

Maas handed the bottle back to Justin.

"Thanks. Just saw a good-size bluefin swimming around with its stomach gone."

To Maas and the rest of the free divers, the presence of big predators was happy news.

He was already treading water, settling the mask on his face.

Behind Cedar, Mary Jayne said, "Didn't your mother tell you to wait twenty minutes before you go back in the water?"

"Nope," said Maas, his voice made slightly whiny by a pinched nose. "Nothing to lose but a banana."

Placing the snorkel in his mouth, Maas gave a honk and finned away.

Nothing to lose except an appendage, thought Cedar. *What is the matter with me?*

The other divers were pulling their camouflage wetsuits back on.

Justin reached for his mask in the rinse bucket.

"No," Cedar said.

He turned, hand still in the bucket.

"No?"

"The swell's picking up. I need you on the bridge to keep an eye on them."

Justin started to protest.

"I shouldn't need to remind you that you're part of the crew," she said.

She saw his jaw clench but she didn't care. A mother did what a mother needed to do.

The screaming turned Cedar cold.

She went up the ladder to the bridge without realizing it, mind racing through the emergency checklist.

Shit, shit, shit, shit.

The screaming stopped.

"Over there!"

Justin and Ernan were pointing southwest, directly into the sun. She couldn't see a damn thing. She squinted, saw Maas a football field away, waving his arms frantically overhead amidst the bobbing swells. The universal distress signal.

Shit, shit, shit. How in the hell had she let him drift so far away? He was still screaming, the sound waxing and waning. The swell had risen. Maas disappeared, reappeared, disappeared, thrashing the water. Shit. She could barely see him.

Stay calm. Push everything else away. Calm saves the day.

It was a stupid little ditty she had learned in a long ago Coast Guard Reserve class.

It took her a moment to realize only Ernan stood beside her. Her eyes jerked away from Maas - *cardinal rule number one, never take your eyes off the victim* -- sweeping the deck. Justin was at the starboard railing, fins and torpedo buoy in his hand.

"No!"

One foot went to the railing.

"It's our only choice!" he shouted.

Even in her panic she noticed he didn't take his eyes of Maas.

He was right. The other divers were in the water and she didn't know where. Plunging ahead full throttle wasn't an option. If she ran over a diver she'd have a certified nightmare on her hands.

"One of the other divers might be close to him," said Ernan.

Please, please. Someone surface.

She summoned every ounce of authority.

"Justin! Wait!"

A hand took her wrist, squeezing once, firmly but gently.

"Good advice," said Mary Jayne.

The woman spoke as if she were complimenting an entrée suggestion.

Cedar thought it ridiculous to voice the obvious, but she did.

"He's in trouble," she said.

"No, he's not. He's a little boy who loses all control when he gets stupendously excited. I wonder what he's seen," she said with genuine curiosity.

Cedar felt her jaw go slack.

"What?"

"I said he's absolutely, perfectly fine. Awfully loud, but perfectly fine."

Cedar felt the air leave her.

"Jesus Christ."

It didn't seem possible, but Jimmy Maas yelled louder. The words rode clearly over the swells.

"Holy fucking shit!" Maas shouted. "Murray!"

They could see Murray now. He had surfaced twenty yards from Maas, a second dark silhouette on the sun-dashed surface.

"Apologies again," said Mary Jayne. "When he's really excited, he also suffers from severe potty mouth."

Cedar didn't smile. The way Maas spun in quick circles made the nape of her neck prickle.

"What?!"

There was an edge in Murray's shout.

Maas yelled.

"Fuck! Didn't you see it?"

See what, God damn it.

"See what, God damn it!" yelled Murray.

"Huge swordfish! Swimming right at you. It just disappeared. Bang! Gone. Fuck!"

Cedar saw the other divers now. They were scattered far off the stern. Everyone was casually treading water like it was a Fourth of July pool party.

"Hang on!"

Mary Jayne and Ernan snatched for the captain's chair as Cedar shoved the throttle forward. Cedar was on the two men in seconds. For an awful moment she thought she might actually run over Maas. He was now waving his arms with genuine alarm.

As the Wendell Holmes sank back down into the water, Mary Jayne whispered, "Whoa."

"Get out! Now!"

She heard her panic, the words lurching between her rapid breaths.

Maas shot her a puzzled look but he was already swimming. Still, he looked around for Murray as he swam. Cedar looked too. Murray was gone.

Maas stopped swimming. He hesitated, started to turn back, then put his head down and sprinted for the boat.

She heard the swim step bang.

Maas was by her side, scanning the water. His voice was flat.

"You didn't say what it was."

She didn't give two shits that he was angry.

"It took the swordfish," she said. "That should be enough."

Some of the flatness left his voice.

"What takes a swordfish like that?"

She didn't answer.

They waited. Maas looked at his watch.

"Murray doesn't have two minutes in him. Something's wrong."

He turned for the ladder.

"No," said Cedar. "You're not going in." Her mind was working, churning through what she thought she knew. The other divers were now 150 yards off the stern. If she was wrong she would not be able to get to them in time.

Dispenser of justice. Arbiter of vengeance.

Please be right.

"You don't go anywhere. You're on my boat."

Maas swung on to the ladder.

"Your boat, my friend."

The screaming came from far away. The cold flooded back.

Maas was beside her again.

"Seven o'clock," he said.

She was throwing the throttle forward, hands spinning the wheel. They were moving fast, Maas shouting out the decreasing distance. Murray was clearly visible, thrashing wildly on the surface. He was three hundred yards from where he had been. No one swam that far underwater. He had been dragged there. The way he jerked about on the surface made Cedar sick.

Only when they were on him did Cedar see the beatific smile.

"Take your sweet fucking time!" Murray yelled, arms and legs egg beating the water to a foamy froth. "I'll just wait here treading water until Elvis is president, holding the biggest fucking swordfish you'll ever see."

They all stood silent, gathered around the black form stretching the length of the stern deck. Only a man as strong as Murray could have stayed afloat.

But it wasn't the size of the swordfish that earned their silence.

They had all changed and showered, except for Murray, who had gone straight for the cooler of beer. Now, on some unspoken agreement, they had all wandered back to the stern.

A cool breeze ran across the water. The sea mount jutted from the water like a halved thumb. The low sun turned the exposed rock deep amber.

Maas crouched. For a long moment he simply looked, and then he ran his fingers lightly over the lacerations.

Murray tipped back his beer, wiping his mouth with the back of his hand.

Cedar had already seen Murray crumple at least four cans.

"Like a cat-o-nine tails," Murray said. "I thought I was fucked when it started to run after I speared it. Fucking autobahn to the bottom. Then the line just went slack. Maybe its heart burst." Murray tipped the can to the setting sun. "Here's to Lady Luck. This is much better than the bottom."

The eyes bulged unnaturally. Cedar knew what Maas was feeling with his fingers, doing it again even though he was already sure. The bulges and compressions rolled like waves across the body of the great fish. The sword had snapped off, leaving a ragged stump. Coagulated blood nearly filled the open mouth.

"Always a bigger fish," slurred Murray.

Maas did not take his eyes off the swordfish.

"She should have been dead when you speared her," he said quietly. "I don't know how she made that last run."

"I do. At warp speed." Alcohol and uncertainty turned Murray's smile loopy. "Still a bitch hauling the line up. Like a fucking Volkswagen filled with cement."

Maas looked up at Cedar.

Unable to hold his gaze, she looked away.

The swordfish was a cocky mistake. It is true I have few matches, but swordfish are quick and strong. There is also the matter of the bill. I was lax as I pulled her close. Her bones were already splintering. I heard a lung rupture and felt her heart racing toward its last beat. Foolishly, I relaxed. She wrenched free and drove her spear forward. Had I not instinctually twisted, the spear would have pierced my eye. My opportune twist saw the bill snap off against my shell. In my moment of frozen surprise, the man finned down from the surface and released his spear. I was already backing away, and we were already deep. At nearly 80 feet it was very dim. And the man had eyes only for the billfish.

I would have known if he had seen me.

There is some small humor in this. Had the swordfish succeeded in her attempt, she would have written the theme for our pageant.

The blind leading the blind.

But my amusement dissipates quickly. It was a foolhardy mistake. If I am wholly honest with myself, it was an act of conceit. I was showing off for the hunters. Here's how it's done.

I wonder if I am not the only one doing the influencing.

Back at the dock Maas said, “I don’t know what to tell you.”

It was so unlike a man not to have advice. She was grateful he had waited until they were alone. The others were still on board, gathering the last of their gear and saying goodbye to Justin, Issy and Ernan.

Standing in the sunshine, the water sighing around the pilings, she had told Maas what she had told Marty. Marty was right. It was too much responsibility. Maas had spent his life around the ocean. He might be able to help. He might tell her she was wrong.

He didn’t.

“You didn’t report any of this?” he asked.

“No.”

“Do you think you should?”

“I don’t know. I’m not sure anyone would believe me. The last time they went on a shark killing spree. Who knows what they might kill this time around. They’ll have to kill something. Even if I do tell them, I know they won’t find it.”

“You knew this thing was out there,” he said.

“Yes.”

“But you don’t think you put us at risk.”

“No.”

“How can you know that?”

She had known him before he came here. She had watched him all week. She knew he would think it through, applying cold logic. She decided.

She spoke before she could stop herself.

"I think we communicate in some way. I think it reads my thoughts. I think, to a small degree, I feel what it feels. I don't think it's dangerous. At least not to most of us. I think it's selective in what it kills."

For some reason she couldn't say "who."

Maas stood quietly, digesting this new puzzle.

"Do you think there's more than one?" he asked.

The thought had troubled her since she found the eggs.

"I don't know."

"Does anyone else know?"

"A friend. That's it."

"Mm."

One of the sea's most formidable predators crushed as easily as a sponge. They had all worked together, cutting the swordfish into fillets. The fillets were on ice in the hold. She planned on passing them out to the needier families on the island. *Aiding and abetting. Erasing the tracks.*

I think I can feel it. I think I know it. I think we communicate in some impossible fashion. I think it comforts me, and then some.

I think you should put me away.

It was like gathering water in a strainer.

She felt the weight of it, pressing down on her.

"I know I sound crazy."

Maas gave a half smile.

"You do."

She wanted to hug him.

"Are you going to say anything to your friends?"

"Do you want me to?"

"No."

"Fair enough. But I have to tell you, I'm not sure I'm right in this."

"Neither am I."

They stood looking at each other.

"I let my son go in."

"That's the reason I believe you."

Maas tossed his dive bag over his shoulder.

"It's a mysterious world, isn't it?" he said.

"It is."

"I don't envy your position." He settled the strap on his shoulder. "Well, one thing's certain."

"What's that?"

"Murray's getting another tattoo."

That night, sitting on the deck beneath the stars, she felt the wind caress her like a tentative hand, offering apology.

She had another erotic dream. It wasn't quite Wyatt, it wasn't quite Sean. She was embarrassed to recall there might have been a bit of Jimmy Maas, and maybe even Marty, too. Whoever they were, they did a masterful job. Her body jerked and bucked as if it wasn't her own.

She woke up sweaty, exhausted and smelling of sex.

Blackout

Two days later, cumulus clouds piling into the heavens, she called Marty on his cell phone.

Marty always answered the same way, no matter who was calling.

"Good morning. What a fine way to start my day."

"You can start it by packing," she said.

"Packing?"

"Bathing suit. Hat. Sunscreen. Any other knickknacks you like to have close to you. I'll supply lunch."

"I love a beach picnic." She heard a chair scrape. She could picture him moving around his kitchen table to the plantation shutters in the living room. An abacus clacking followed. "But it looks like rain."

"Where we're going, rain won't matter."

"Oh Lordy," said Marty.

Cedar went over the basics, the two of them sitting at the picnic table in the shade of the dive shop awning. That Marty was a good listener and a quick study was no surprise. She knew he would consult his dive computer, with its digital gauges for depth and air consumption, as if it were the Oracle at Delphi. He absorbed the hand signals - thumb up for ascending, thumb down for descending, a quick slash across the throat for out of air, the universal okay signal, the universal distress signal (here she thought of Mass) - somberly practicing each in turn, and then running through them again. Like windows. He asked questions and asked them again. He was the model student.

She pulled the instruction sheet from under his hands before it was thoroughly soaked.

"I didn't know it was possible for one person to sweat so much," she said.

"It occurs when I focus," Marty said, a trifle indignant.

"I'm going to have to find the squeegee for your forehead." She gave him an encouraging smile. "Diving is easy as walking and you've absorbed everything." She patted his hand as she stood. "Now it's time for a cooling swim."

Behind the dive shop, she picked out a wetsuit from the rental rack. When they came through the back door, the matronly shop manager was bending at the waist and breathing fast, a large paw sweeping helplessly just above the floor.

Marty crouched.

"Please, Miss Irma Mae. Let me get your phone for you."

As they walked down the dock, Ernan waved and started up the engines.

"No doubt she already knows my wetsuit size," said Marty.

"No doubt."

"She's in the doorway, you know."

"Of course."

When Marty reached for her hand, she was so startled she nearly jerked it away.

"Let's give them something to talk about."

"Oh Lordy," she said.

Justin helped Marty get his gear on board.

He gave Marty a broad smile.

"You're lucky," he said. "You're in for an amazing treat."

"Yes. I am. Lucky," said Marty.

She stood grinning, equally proud of her son's kindness and her friend's game effort.

Justin held the box out to Marty.

"Danish?"

"Thank you, no. My stomach seems a trifle uneasy."

"You'll be okay," said Justin. "The worst part is right now, with the engines idling at the dock. I'll get your gear stowed away and then we'll be off and you'll be good."

"Good."

Cedar left Ernan alone on the bridge. She pretended to tinker with a camera as they idled from the slip.

Marty started putting on his gear as they passed the breakwater. Justin moved to stop him, it was thirty minutes to the dive site she had picked, but Cedar waved him off.

She sat on the bench beside Marty, watching him perform each action - clip in the integrated weights, tighten the straps of the BCD, check that his air was on, purge the first and second stage -- as meticulously as he checked the instruments on his plane.

When he finished, she reached around and turned off his air.

His eyes widened.

She bent close.

"You breathe this air on the way out. You'll turn your air on right before you go in. I'll double check. Plenty of people forget to turn it on. Ten years, I've only forgotten to double check once. Fussy guy, asked so many questions I forgot what I was doing. Fussy customers throw me off."

"Very funny."

She watched him for a long moment, his smooth face so serious.

"I'm going up to the bridge. Do you need anything?"

"Terra firma."

She touched his cheek, surprising them both.

"I'm doing you a favor," she said. "It's a very special place I'm introducing you to."

When she glanced down five minutes later, Marty was sitting stiffly upright, taking deep breaths and staring solemnly out to sea. He looked like an overdressed yoga pupil.

She had chosen a shallow reef patched with large spreads of white sand bottom. Reef and sand ran flat for nearly 800 yards before finally starting a gradual slope toward deeper water. A popular beginner's spot, the reef rarely had any current. The maximum depth, should you burrow into the sand, was forty feet.

An imaginative dive instructor had named the reef "Forty Feet Max."

Justin tied them to the mooring buoy.

Ernan bounced down the ladder. Pouring himself a water, he toasted Marty.

"To new beginnings," he said.

"They told you to gang up on me," said Marty.

"Since I am only doing as I am told, you can leave me the tip," Ernan said.

Cedar shrugged into her gear and sat down on the bench beside Marty.

He was cleaning his mask with baby shampoo.

"Questions are still fair game," she said.

"Who would do this to a friend?"

She got up and brought him a paper cup of water.

"Here."

She watched him fondly. The man even drank with dignity.

"Relax, Marty. It's fun. It's like flying."

"And you clean the windows first," said Marty, tapping a finger to his mask.

"That a boy. Up you go."

She held his elbow as he staggered to his feet. Still holding his elbow, she walked him slowly to the stern.

Standing beside him on the swim step, she conducted a last head to toe check. Each piece of gear was perfectly situated, although his eyes bulged.

"Mask a little tight?"

He shook his head. The regulator was already in his mouth.

She reached behind him and turned the tank valve just to be sure.

"Didn't think you'd miss that one." She patted him on the back. "You look like a pro. Not a strap out of place. Really. Now all you have to do is remember to breathe."

"Uhhhhhn."

"Having fun?"

Marty nodded soberly.

"Well then, you absorbed the most important lesson of all." She squeezed his arm. For some reason she thought of Miss Irma Mae. "I'll be right next to you the whole time. Hand on your mask, big stride," she said and they both stepped into space.

Marty was an awful diver. Instead of tucking his arms against his side and finning easily, he clawed at the water with his arms, in the manner of a man frantically separating thick brush. The clawing of his arms was accompanied by a wholly out of sync and equally spastic kicking of his legs. It was as if he had left every shred of grace on the boat.

Although it didn't seem possible, his buoyancy was worse. He rose toward the surface, plummeted toward the bottom, then rose toward the surface again. Finally Cedar took his hand.

Justin free dove nearby. Since the trip with Maas, Justin had eschewed tanks at every opportunity. The only time he wore a tank was when they dove with clients and he was the safety diver. But on this dive she could handle Marty, barely, alone.

Maybe it was Marty's flailings, but on this morning Justin seemed to swim more beautifully than ever. He moved through the water like a pale dancer, his hair flowing back in waves, his fins performing a languorous, sleepy beat as he made for the sandy bottom. He didn't so much swim through the water as meld with it, a human current.

As she escorted Marty back and forth over the reef, she kept only half an eye on her son. He moved from surface to sand with the ease of a drifting leaf, sitting lotus-legged on the sand, arms folded across his chest. She knew his eyes were shut. Maas performed the same drill. Once she glanced at her watch. When she looked again it had been two minutes. Just as her own chest started to tighten, Justin opened his eyes and rose easily off the sand. He hung suspended, smiling at her, and spread his arms wide. She waited. Nodding once, Justin finned for the surface, silver bubbles dripping from his mouth, sunlight moving across his smooth muscles.

It was a joy to behold.

Marty saw this, too. Grinning madly through his face plate, he gave her the thumbs up, quickly folding his thumb into a fist when he realized he had given the signal for going up.

She scowled at him and laughed.

Soon enough he did have to go up.

Back on the boat, Marty couldn't stop talking. He'd been terrible in the water - he harangued himself for this - but he had been transformed. Cedar had seen this transformation in beginning divers hundreds of times, the way they went in mute and frightened, agitated hands plucking at their gear, and then, like the newly baptized, they were back on board, waving their hands now, futilely trying to pantomime the wonders they had seen.

It was the greatest joy of her job, made greater still because this was her closest friend.

She listened attentively as Marty gushed without pause; about the Hobbit forest coral, and how the schools of fish moved as one, and how the gnawing noises came from everywhere, and how the flickering sunlight was like God's own hypnotic trick, and how he was worried about squeezing the blood right out of Cedar's hand, and how he dove like a rubber ball.

She got him water, but he only held the cup in his hand and kept talking.

Ernan came down the ladder. He stood smiling behind his shades, waiting for Marty to take a breath.

Finally Cedar put her hand over Marty's mouth.

"The captain has something to say."

Ernan said, "We should go. We have afternoon divers. Where is Justin?"

She stood so suddenly her mask dropped on the deck.

She was turning to look where she had last seen him on the surface - *how long had it been, she had only looked once when they first got out of the water* -- when she heard a small cough. She spun and her stomach fell. Justin floated, forearms resting on the swim step, mask on top of his head, the picture no different than thousands of times before, only now the green eyes were unfocused, the expression dazed, the confident creature of the sea gone.

He looked up at her, his expression frightened and mildly surprised, like someone who has just quit in the middle of a long race they knew they would win. Like the little boy she would never let go.

She was rushing across the deck.

"Justin!"

He waved and gave a feeble grin.

"It's okay. I'm okay," he said, and he began to cry.

Only after she had helped him on board, removing his fins while he sat with his head down, wrapping him in a towel to stop the shivering she knew she couldn't stop, did she ask him what had happened.

The apology on his face broke her heart yet again.

"I'm so sorry. I pushed too far. I blacked out." He was crying noiselessly, big, single tears sliding down his cheeks. "I'm so sorry. You were right."

"Oh God."

She thought it was her voice, but she wasn't sure. She was crying now, too. She felt a hand on her shoulder.

You should have died. How could you be on this boat? You slip instantly into unconsciousness while your mother pays you no mind and a procession of lives shatter.

She touched his cheek, thanking God for its warmth.

"I hit my head on the bottom of the boat." He said it slowly, more like a question. "If I hadn't hit my head, I would have drowned."

She wanted to take him in her arms and hold him there forever, but he was already standing and looking over the side. Ripples of sunlight ran across the sandy bottom.

"I hit my head on the hull," he said softly.

She already knew, but she played the last useless card anyway.

"You must have blacked out under the boat and floated up the last few feet."

The sea softly batted the Wendell Holmes.

"No. I was away from the boat. The last thing I remember I was sitting on the bottom. I'm sure of it."

His face had lost its dazed expression. His eyes narrowed.

"How did I get under the boat?"

That night she stood in the doorway for a long time, watching her sleeping son, and then she went up on the deck.

She stood staring at the dark homes scattered on the jungled hillside. Palau was an island of early risers. A single light held back the dark; a valiant wisp of civilization.

The light winked out.

Turning to the water, she went to her knees. She hadn't been to church since she was a girl. She didn't pray anymore. Prayer seemed a passive, fruitless exercise.

She wasn't praying now.

Swaying slightly, she spoke.

"Thank you."

It was no symbolic gesture. She knew it heard. Just as she knew it clung to the bottom of the boat, sharing her thoughts and trying to ease her loneliness.

I brought him to just beneath the boat, at the last, nudging him gently so the impact wasn't damaging. It had to be done, and there was no real risk that I could perceive - no other boats, just the woman and the man who swims like a tumble weed -- but if there was any question in my mind, it was answered as soon as I lifted the limp form from the sand. The boy ferries an impossible airiness. Let me explain. Holding your kind I feel a weight that does not correlate with size. The man on whom I performed my pleasant vivisection, I wrestled him about as if he were an anvil. The man on the toilet, dying in my arms, I had to look twice to ascertain his presence. I don't know what makes the difference. Maybe evil is accumulated baggage. Maybe purity is holding few things close, only the things that truly matter. I don't know. I'll leave it to your disciples and philosophers.

I do know the boy weighed almost nothing. He was lighter than anyone I have ever encountered.

I lifted him toward the sun as if he was an offering, my own heart running light-footed with joy.

Little Boys and Dragonflies

For a time, I travel. In days gone by, my journeys were undertaken for hunting or hiding, for as I have said, there were bigger fish in the sea. These days my travels are mostly a matter of reconnaissance, an inspection if you will, and, to a small degree, a checking in with the troops, though, unlike your leaders, I do little to sway the opinions of my fellows. They know where they stand individually; they know where we stand collectively. With a few exceptions - the opportunists who can make use of changing circumstances -- these positions are one in the same. Just a few feet back from the precipice. And moving rapidly forward as we speak.

Long ago, these journeys set me brimming with joy and excitement. Oh, but the sea was a lively place, a kaleidoscope of beauty, a pageant of beginnings and endings beyond number. Now the pageant has grown darker, and many of the endings look the same. I wish you would spend less time nitpicking over the length of a cephalopod's memory and more time looking at the bigger picture.

Perhaps if you saw with your own eyes what I see, it would light a fire under your backside. Let me sink my hand into the top hat of ills, rummage around, draw something out. There is so much to choose from. How about this? In the Pacific, halfway between California and Hawaii, there is a trash pile. You have dubbed it the Eastern Pacific Garbage Patch. Assembled by converging currents, it is not just any trash pile. It is its own vast, oozing ocean. In protest, a man sailed a ship made of plastic bottles. He named it the Plastiki. Another trio, also imaginatively, built a raft out of junk. It seems to me effort would be better directed at the problem itself. But your strength is drawing attention to matters, not addressing them. I would tell you how big this garbage patch is, but it grows overnight. By the time you finish this story, whatever I tell you now will be obsolete. Oh, right. The Atlantic

Ocean has one, too. Some of your scientists think the Atlantic Ocean garbage patch might stretch from shore to shore.

Drifting in the night I watch lantern fish rise from the deeps to feast on the plastic bits that mimic the plankton they eat in more pristine seas. The lantern fish nibble and nibble. Even plankton, the mainstay of the ocean menu, rarely assembles in so impressive a mass. It is pretty in a fashion, the way the moonlight sparkles off the plastic, a glittering jeweled sea.

But, if you will pardon the turned-on-its-head pun, these garbage swaths pale in comparison to your Dead Zones. In science-speak, these are areas of the ocean with oxygen levels so low that most life cannot survive. These Dead Zones are caused by nitrogen-rich runoff - your farms, your sewers, your street waste, your dish detergent, finding its way to the sea. No surprise, there's a whopper of a Dead Zone off the mouth of your Mississippi River. Dead Zones, you'd think, would be black, but they're more like dirty snowfields; a boneyard of sea creatures smothered beneath a white mat of opportunistic bacteria. For those who are not scavengers, these are terrible places. Off Namibia, I watched waves of rock lobsters crawl ashore to escape poisonous gases released by rotting algae. Closer to my heart, I have watched baby octopi inching their way up crab trap lines to escape oxygen barren waters on the seafloor.

Take the town you live in. Smother it bridge-of-the-nose-deep in excrement, leaving everyone a single nostril to breathe from. Fatten the air with gravy-thick soot. Quickly the old and the infirm, then the middle-aged and not-yet-infirm, they die. The last elders that remain watch the young haul themselves free and leave for another world. Hope springs eternal until their rent bodies return, drifting down to rejoin the excrement from which you watch. Do you think the crabbers gently peel each octopus from the line?

The Dead Zones, they are a real show stopper.

"Runoff from Modern Life Foments a Tide of Toxins." "Growing Seawater Acidity Threaten to Wipe Out Coral." "Algae Blooms

Invade Coastal Waters." These individual headlines you idly scan over coffee will one day reach a sum that will not allow for subtraction.

So many important matters that you ignore.

Did Nero really play the fiddle as Rome burned?

I don't know, but I wouldn't doubt it.

Justin left on a Tuesday evening, the United Airlines flight from Guam touching down, refueling, replacing its crew and lifting off again.

Koror, Guam, Houston, Chicago. Dragonflies flitting above the mangroves after a rain; snarled commuters above the Chicago River on the Well Street Bridge. The miracle of modern travel.

They stood staring at the runway through streaked glass. On the tarmac a baggage handler looked their way and waved. Justin hadn't wanted a grand sendoff and she hadn't either. They'd had a small going away party on the Wendell Holmes. Here at the airport it was the two of them and the laughter of tourists heading home.

Her chest clutched, making it hard to speak, but she did.

"I've got something for you."

It was a hardback, with hand drawn illustrations and gold gilt page edges. She had bought it online from a collector in Massachusetts.

Justin lifted Oliver Wendell Holmes' words from her hands.

She saw how his hands shook.

He kept his eyes on the cover.

"Printed in 1890," he said.

"With poems beyond time."

"I know. I learned about him from my mother."

He'd find the check later.

After he left, she stood by the glass. A teenage girl closed the restaurant's mock bamboo doors. The gate attendants whispered to each other and left. When the security guard passed, he looked away.

Outside by the curb, a single taxi driver slept.

Cedar walked past.

When she stepped aboard the Wendell Holmes, flowers rested on the camera table. The flowers were in a bamboo vase, orchids from Marty's garden. A small envelope was wedged in the flowers, her name, in Marty's flowing script, on the front.

Cedar looked at the flowers and then she went down to her cabin. It wasn't quite dark, but she slipped out of her clothes and into a nightshirt.

When she reached up to shut the porthole, there were two photos on the small bedside stand. The new frame was simple dark wood. The photo did not curl at the edges. She was playing the bagpipes. Justin stood beside her grinning. She remembered the evening he had taken the photo, setting the camera on a rung of the ladder and trotting back to stick his fingers in his ears.

There was another envelope. She opened this one and read the note.

She fell asleep with the seashell frame on her chest, Justin, ear to the shell, smiling his dreamy smile at the ceiling.

She dreamt of little boys and dragonflies.

Darkness

Thirty miles off your Galapagos Islands, once an Eden, now tourist-trammeled, I am swept with panic and white-hot pain. It is not my suffering, I do not feel it, but I know it as surely as you are aware of your fingers at the end of your hand. Fury bursts inside me.

I swim as quickly as I can, but I am not quick enough. When I arrive, it is done. I see them on the bottom in the half light, dark squirming apostrophes, beating haplessly against the rock. The sharks make no sound that you would hear, but the water around me reverberates with agonies that would give your Spanish Inquisitioners pause.

The fishing boat bobs on the darkening sea. The three men stack the fins they have hacked away.

How appropriate that the sun is setting.

I approach on the surface so that they may see. One man runs below deck - really, where to? - another jumps into the water - again, where to? The man in the water is easily retrieved, gently wrapped and held high like an anticipated present. Little rabbit, his heart races oh-so-fast. The third man goes to his knees and prays. If God created man and beast, why would He listen to the prayers of a man who has just maimed His creations?

I am not interested in God's approval. I hold the little rabbit high above the water so that the praying man can witness earthly reality. I remove his limbs - he loves me, he loves me not - one at a time, twisting ever so slowly. You can make an atrocious amount of noise. The screams are absorbed by the empty sky and sea, but I know they reach the man below decks, for I feel his heart hammering like a piston. Below me the sharks thrash. Above me the man, bereft of appendages, thrashes.

Poetic justice, don't you think?

I reach for the praying man next. Blood falls like rain.

I pull the last man from under his berth; his trumpeting heart gives him away. I bring him gently up the ladder so as not to brain him. I want him to be wholly with me during our moments together. He is fat, with flesh like butter. His spirit is flabby, too. I peel him like a carrot. Exercising great delicacy, I keep him alive the longest. Before he dies, I push him to the bottom so that, at the last, he writhes alongside the sharks.

I crush the sharks quickly. Finished with this sad chore, I destroy the boat. The shark fins sway as they descend, like a swing, back and forth. They remind me of something.

Flower petals.

You kill some 70 million sharks a year. Ah, but the sharks may have the last laugh. Recently one of your researchers discovered a neurotoxin with links to Parkinson's, Alzheimer's and Lou Gehrig's disease in the fins of seven shark species. The neurotoxin is produced by blue-green algae, which, passed through the food chain, is eventually ingested by sharks. Blue-green algae bloom when you pollute the sea.

Stick that in your soup.

You are foisting diseases as slow and painful as finning upon yourself.

A little black humor there.

I swim without rest for three days, accompanied by dark funk. I am hurrying home. To seek what? Comfort? Solace? The familiarity of hearth and home?

Companionship?

When I return, I know in an instant I will receive no good cheer. I know this well before I embrace the hull. I feel it, enfolding me like a cold current. But it is not a current. It is without substance. It is a blank spot. An empty hole. As black as the deeps I know.

The boy is gone.

One heart beats on the boat.

I wish I could play the bagpipes.

During the day she tried to busy herself with charters and the myriad tasks accompanying them, but at night she was alone in tomb quiet. Often she found herself standing still, with no clear idea of what she was doing. She kept the door to Justin's cabin closed. She rested her hand on the handle more than once.

Each day when the work was finished, the first thing she did was check e-mail, scrolling through the junk to find the address that mattered.

Justin wrote several times a week. His e-mails weren't long but she made them so. He hated the weather, that was a given, but he liked the school and his classmates and Dad kept his nose out of his business (also, thought Cedar, a given). He was adjusting to Chicago but it wasn't home. He read one of Oliver Wendell Holmes' poems each night before bed. He was actually starting to like poetry.

Tonight's e-mail was longer. The sentences were short, with a glaring number of typos. Staring at the screen she smiled. She could imagine his excited fingers crashing across the keyboard. He had joined the high school swim team. He was already the second best distance freestyler on the team. The longer he swam, the stronger he got. The team trained two hours a day in a disgusting indoor pool that reeked of chemicals, but he liked the workouts and his teammates. After practice, in the locker room, they snapped towels at each other, and if he wasn't paying attention his best friend, Tim Malloy, reached out and yanked out a fistful of chest hairs, smiling and asking, "Odd or even?" When the high school season was over, he was going to keep swimming. The high school coach coached at a private club. The coach said he was a natural. If his times kept dropping the way they were, he had a good chance at a scholarship at a Division III college, and maybe even something better.

Justin wrote that he liked the hard work and the discipline, but his real reason for swimming was his -- and her -- secret.

Swimming will make me a better free diver. After college, I'm coming home.

Youth. So certain of what will unfold.

Turning off the computer, she sat in the dark.

She wondered when he had started growing chest hair.

Plate-size sea spiders, carnivorous sponges covered with glass-like needles, six-gilled sharks. Your scientists are astonished by what they are discovering in the ocean deeps. In and out of the sea, you are discovering new species at the rate of about fifty a day.

It is amusing, like watching an infant discover its hands. Oh my. Look-ee here.

Don't congratulate yourselves. Ninety-five percent of the ocean deeps remain unknown to you. Oh, the surprises that await.

You are a small child ladling from the surface of a pond.

The nights were too long.

At first she turned to books -- they had distracted her from sadness in the past -- but now her anxious mind jumped about, unable to focus for more than a few pages. She began reading on the computer. Internet news suited her reduced attention span. To her embarrassment, she also devoured items about celebrity divorces, furniture that moved around a house on its own accord, top ten love mistakes (you had to have a lover to make them) and aliens sculpting messages in Missouri cornfields (If they were sophisticated enough to travel to Earth, why wouldn't they just use the radio?). After Justin had been away for three weeks, she took a Chicago news quiz and missed only one question.

Most nights she never saw the passage of dusk to dark. Looking up from the hypnotic screen, she would note with mild surprise that the galley was black.

On Friday nights she pulled a bag of Doritos from the pantry and watched King Kong. She knew this was a tad strange, too. She wondered if loneliness made you lose your mind.

I am reaching out to others. I am not so foolish as to put all my eggs in one basket. The stakes are too great. Some of the others are famous and powerful, able to use fame and power to make things happen. It's why I choose them, though frankly your politics seem to accomplish only stalemate and gridlock. Cooperation, compromise, acceding to the needs of the whole, these traits are feeble fires waning on a vast dark plain. Your Congress, your Politburo, your Parliament (pray, don't forget the capitals), they have become infants beating each other over the head with blocks. I have little faith in these particular channels, but it can't hurt to try.

"Fifty years ago, we could not see limits to what we could put into the ocean or what we could take out," writes one of your well-known scientists. "Fifty years into the future, it will be too late to do what is possible now. We are in a sweet spot in time."

A nugget of wisdom. Delay is not an option.

Your difficulties - our difficulties - they can be solved. But you need to stop whining and blaming. You need to pull yourself up by your bootstraps. Who said this?

Somebody's grandfather, I think.

The ones I reach out to, they are unaware. The midnight lightning strikes of inspiration, the sudden obvious option for compromise, an innovative act of conservation, the timely calls to action; they believe these coups are the product of their own fruitful mind. Only she knows I am here. The woman with the boat named for a poet. The woman who plays the bagpipes so badly. The woman whose son just might change the world. Her offspring. My offspring. Hope. The faintest tincture of fresh dawn.

Would you like to be saved? Of course you would. Survival dictates your every move.

Are you willing to do what it takes? I am not so sure.

But we will certainly see.

Marty

Marty's proposal was simple. Once a week, come hell or rough water, they would fly or dive. She could pick the day, but once the day was set there was no backing out. She'd had to look away when he made his proposal, the two of them watching the sunset from deck chairs on the dock. Despite his enthusiasm, she knew he was still afraid of the water.

She picked Tuesdays. Twice a month, Marty dove. Twice a month, she flew. She progressed quickly. She liked the orderly step-by-step process of flying, the cozy cockpit and the instrument panel with its strange numbers she could now decipher. Marty did not progress as she did. He sucked down his tanks so fast Cedar wondered if she had filled them, and he bounced up and down in the water column like a skittish EKG.

"Perhaps I was a cork in another life," he offered.

His ineptitude didn't embarrass him. He tried his hardest, but as the weeks passed Cedar still found herself grabbing him as he shot up and sank down. Each time he shrugged and grinned through his face plate. It always made her laugh. It was the rare man who admitted to his shortcomings, much less saw the humor in them. But slowly he improved, until one day, finning along the edge of an atoll that dropped away into blue-black darkness, Marty swam the length of the reef without an egregious bob. When they reached the end of the reef, he floated, perfectly suspended, regarding her soberly before breaking into a mile wide smile.

Back on board he kissed her with equal soberness, the kiss so gentle, Cedar actually wondered if it had happened. But he had been eating peanut butter crackers and she tasted peanut butter on her lips.

"Thank you," he said, "for making me a better person. Although I am still a crummy diver and you are already a fine pilot."

She was not surprised when she leaned forward and kissed him back.

"Yours was a near flawless flight," she said.

Two weeks later when they returned to the dock from diving, Marty did not leave the boat. That night they re-learned a timeless skill.

The next morning Santy hand-delivered her weekly newspaper. Usually she picked it up in her mailbox at the dive shop. Cedar was alerted to Santy's presence by coughing up on the dock. Slipping on a bathrobe she went up on deck.

The old man blinked uncomfortably. His embarrassment was amusing.

Just for fun, she waited.

Santy almost never spoke first.

"I am a busy man. I need to go." He thrust the paper out over the water. "Take this."

Cedar ignored his outstretched hand.

"When did I start paying for newspaper delivery?"

"Mock a man for his attempt at neighborly kindness."

No doubt, they had drawn straws and he had lost. Cedar almost felt sorry for him. His eyes strayed to Marty's dive bag on the camera table, and flicked quickly back to her face.

"I hope you're also coming back with coffee for two," she said, taking the paper.

The old man actually blushed. It was mildly endearing.

"Miss Irma put me up to it," Santy growled. He scuffed at the dock with the toe of a weathered boot. "That damn woman is a witch."

"Since when have you been afraid of women?"

"It is nearly seven. Since when have you lolled about?"

"You're an adult. You figure it out."

She meant it as a joke, but it sounded harsh.

She had never seen Santy lack for a retort. His shoulders slumped as he turned away.

"Santy?" she said gently. "What's the matter?"

"I am old."

"It's still you I pine for."

"Too bad. I have lost my heart to Miss Klum."

He almost sounded serious.

Watching him walk away, something nagged at her. Lately she had heard his engine idling out of the harbor late at night, and when she came to the fuel dock she saw how he moved away, occupying himself with another chore. There was a shiny new lock on the shed on his dock.

She wished that instead of always making jokes with him, she had asked him how he was doing.

When she returned to the cabin, Marty was propped up against a pillow.

She held up the paper.

"Courtesy of Santy."

"Ah." Marty smiled. "It would be interesting to hear his report.

Perhaps he thinks I stayed to clean your windows."

She looked at him. His chest was smooth, the muscles defined. Last night, her hands running the length of him, every inch had been hard.

The sheet rose to his waist.

She felt stirrings. She let her eyes linger.

She saw he was stirring, too.

"You're intoxicatingly beautiful," he said. "Even with silk in the way."

With a nudge, the robe slid away.

When they finished they stayed entwined, breathing hard in each other's ears.

Marty smiled.

"I'm glad Santy didn't come back with coffee."

"I felt sorry for him. I know he didn't want to bring the paper."

"The price of living on this island. I love my home, but I confess there are times when I grow tired of prying eyes and ears." He traced the bridge of her nose. "It is not easy holding my breath in your loving presence."

"I have a solution."

It took thirty minutes to reach the spot. It was a tiny islet, smothered in jungle and graced with an equally tiny inlet big enough for one boat. Raucous birds rested in the trees like white fruit.

She anchored the Wendell Holmes so that they faced out to sea.

She had slipped on jeans and a t-shirt to guide them out of the harbor. Bending to make sure the anchor line was set, she felt trickling sweat.

Fingers deftly unsnapped her jeans.

As she turned Marty's hands slid everything down to her ankles and pushed her up against the railing.

"Too hot for jeans," someone mumbled.

Still on his knees, he kissed around her, ignoring her encouraging moans when he glanced close. Finally she made sure his lips were where she wanted them. Her head rolled back to blue sky, and when she wanted all of him, she spun around so that she now looked down into blue. The sun flared against her nakedness.

That there could be so much heat and pleasure was too much to ask.

Lovers and birds cried out in joy.

That night Cedar crowned their altered standing by sliding "King Kong" from the bookshelf.

"Justin and I watched it," she said. *Every Friday. Date night.* "It was his favorite movie."

She did not miss the tense. It made her a little sad.

"Then I know I will like it."

"You've *never* seen King Kong?"

"I confess I see few movies. Actually, any movies."

"Well that's going to change."

They sat close, picking popcorn out of each other's lap.

She cried again at the end, but this time she couldn't stop.

Marty pulled her close and kissed her slowly.

"It was beauty who gave herself to the beast," he said.

All but a hint of hollowness is gone. This is evolution of a sort. I should draw hope from her adaptation. I have been unable to accomplish this in my own life. My own darkness continues to yaw and ache without end in sight.

I have reconsidered. I will tell you what became of my mate. I tell you not because I am past the pain of remembering, but because, when I work to look at it objectively, I see the lesson in it, a lesson for the both of us.

In the time we shared, my mate and I were often apart. In the early going, it was simply impractical for two apex predators to share the same territory. Overharvesting as it were: the tragedy of the commons instinctually averted. My mate would disappear for long weeks to hunt and feed. Later, as we evolved and our motives became more complex and less self-absorbed, he again disappeared for long periods to monitor our world's progress and, slowly, its decline. There came a time when his absence stretched far beyond the conventional. I went looking for him.

He was long dead when I found him, impossibly tangled, a riddle without answer, in a mesh of netting on the sea floor. He had left his shell in a futile attempt at escape. The ropes had cut deep into him. I know he died slowly. Feeding began before he died. Many were feeding when I arrived. I did not go close. I could not bear it. But from where I drifted I could still see giant isopods (think crab, but nearly three feet from head to tail) crawling over his ravaged form, tearing and gorging, plucking at folds of white skin waving like listless flags of surrender.

Did this make me angry? As I said, we do not blame. But it did make me infinitely sad, a sadness that nearly sees me forget my point.

The takeaway lesson? My mate and I, we ate giant isopods like jellybeans.

Remember. A throne atop the food chain guarantees nothing.

I drift in the night water, away from the boat.

She no longer needs my dreams.

She has pulled herself up by her bootstraps.

I wish I could follow her example, but I have no one to rescue me.

He and I. Together in the eggs.

The thought lifts me just a little.

The Poet

On the nights when Marty didn't stay, she returned to the computer. Now she skipped the celebrity shenanigans and alien sightings. The trend had risen slowly to her consciousness; first one news story, then another and another, gathering raindrops buried deep within the Sisyphean heap of words. Now she found the items virtually every night, short news bytes that most readers likely still didn't see, buried in the trivia.

Altered migrations. Strange feeding frenzies. Never before seen behaviors. Unprovoked attacks. Shocking mutations.

She told herself the stories were simply the result of more reporting. Random stories with no possible connection. Filler in infinite internet space. But in the dark galley of the gently rocking Wendell Holmes, they felt like something more. Like scratchings. Like whispers. Like clues.

They fit like puzzle pieces.

And there were more and more.

She waited until Marty had logged fifty dives before she took him on the nautilus dive. The dive was easy. They strayed no deeper than fifty feet, but with Justin gone she was alone in monitoring the divers underwater. Ernan had to stay with the boat, and with college on the horizon she couldn't afford to hire another crew member. On the paying trips she couldn't babysit Marty.

But Marty now had his buoyancy under control, although he still insisted on stroking through the water with his arms, no matter how many times she told him how much easier it was to just kick with his legs.

"I allow you to fly with your arms and your legs," replied Marty, who somehow managed to look regal even when defending the indefensible.

Marty's first nautilus dive took place on an unusually windy day in early June. The wind was unexpected. It started to build as they left the harbor. By the time they were halfway to Long Drop Off, it was blowing hard, scouring the tops off the waves, increasing Cedar's worries. Novice divers do not like floating on the surface in choppy waters. It slaps at their faces, obscures their view, pushes into their mouths. More than once she had seen beginners panic in chop.

Cedar had a full boat, a group of Japanese divers from Nagasaki who had chartered the boat. Language was a bit of a problem, but the Japanese visited Palau in droves and Cedar, with a small gift for languages, had picked up enough Japanese to manage. Plus these Japanese were, as always, unfailingly polite, and when they dove they clustered together like preschoolers in a haunted house.

Six nautili had come up in the cages, the divers handling them as if they were 3rd century vases. Cedar couldn't help but smile.

Occupied with her responsibilities, she had virtually ignored Marty, although she had noted proudly how he had helped one diver get into his gear, and replaced the broken fin strap of a smitten thirty-something.

That he was attractive made her proud. That he was good with his hands gave her other pleasures.

That night after they made love, they lay quietly, the smell of brine drifted through the porthole. A sliver of moon hung just off the porthole's center, a fish hook, waiting.

Marty stared up at the ceiling.

"Well?" she asked.

"Well what?"

"What did you think?"

"Passable."

She was so surprised she sat up and stared down at him.

"*Passable?*'

"We're discussing the lovemaking, correct?"

She jabbed a muscled rib.

"You know what we're discussing, smart ass."

The word made her think of Ted Marple and her happiness dimmed.

"They were absolutely beautiful," said Marty softly. "Like time in a shell."

She watched his eyes search the ceiling an arm's length above them.

"How can this one be so much bigger?" he asked.

For a time, the subject had gone away. Cedar hadn't known whether to feel relieved or abandoned.

"I don't know. My simple guess is it's much older. Much, much older." For some reason this didn't frighten her. It made her feel secure. "Even the," she searched for the right word, "conventional ones keep growing. They secrete new chambers as they grow."

Marty still looked at the ceiling.

"The chickens were torn to pieces."

"That's what nautili do."

"Do you think it was there while we dove?"

It was the question that was always on her mind.

"I honestly don't know," she said.

Marty rolled to face her.

"It's a big leap of faith you're taking," he said. "Maybe it's riskier than you think."

"No."

"No?"

"Nothing has happened. Nothing will happen."

They both heard the anger in her voice. Was she lying to Marty? To herself? The nautilus dive was her breadwinner. College loomed. She knew it was what Marty was thinking, but he knew it wasn't necessary to say it out loud.

Delicately tracing her spine, he said, "End of interrogation. I'm sorry."

"I worry about it, too."

"Well, you worry too much."

Gently he pulled her back down.

They lay facing each other.

The finger, graceful as the man, traced her chin and trailed a crooked tingle down her neck. It continued making pleasant circles down.

"I love your touch," she said, her voice already husky.

"I love to touch."

The finger stopped just short of where it had performed its earlier magic.

"Please," she said.

The berth creaked as Marty repositioned himself.

He kissed her navel, his lips now performing the slow, excruciating downward spiral.

She spoke to the ceiling.

"Build thee more stately mansions, O my soul, as the swift seasons roll. Leave thy low-vaulted past. Let each new temple, nobler than the last, shut thee from heaven with a dome more vast, till thou at length art free, leaving thine outgrown shell by life's unresting sea."

"It's beautiful," he said, his warm breath making her quiver. "Who wrote it?"

"Oliver Wendell Holmes."

"Your poet."

The chill that ran through her was not from his kisses.

She sat up.

"What's wrong?"

She didn't hear him.

The words rang in her head.

Thanks for the heavenly message brought by thee, child of the wandering sea...

Yes, I knew this man Oliver Wendell Holmes and he knew of me, but no one, not even his loving wife, knew of our connection, at least not directly. Poets are sensitive souls, but they are not fools. In Mr. Holmes' day, sanatoriums were particularly unpleasant places.

The Chambered Nautilus, you might say, was a collaboration.

Mr. Holmes and I also knew Emerson, Longfellow and Hawthorne. He (and I) outlived them all. This led him to comment, "I feel like my own survivor... We were on deck together as we began the voyage of life... Then the craft which held us began going to pieces."

These were his words alone, but they are endowed with appreciable foresight, wouldn't you say?

Let me be clear, so that you may understand. They speak their own minds, but unconsciously they speak mine, too. You know these people. Ralph Waldo Emerson. Henry Wadsworth Longfellow. Nathaniel Hawthorne. Henry David Thoreau. Jules Verne. Moving closer to your time, Theodore Roosevelt, Rachel Carson, Jacques Cousteau, Sylvia Earle. These days even a few television actors turned environmentalists. The latter are no Oliver Wendell Holmes, but your television is quite the bully pulpit. And at this point, every bully pulpit must be utilized.

"The globe began with the sea so to speak; and who knows if it will not end with it," penned Mr. Verne.

A little ghost writing.

I did watch them as they dove. As always, she was bewitching. He was a mess.

Three days later, Marty delivered a ham radio and medical supplies to one of the remote islands. He stayed overnight, showing the younger villagers how to work the radio.

Cedar slept alone. She dreamed of Chinese lanterns. Inside them, the flames danced.

Breath and Blood

She hunts as she always has. I influence her in no fashion. They are simply on a collision course. A random lightning strike. Small good fortune for one, terrible misfortune for the other. Such is life.

Had I been orchestrating, I would not have chosen this man. He is a dedicated school teacher, a good husband and father. But he is diving for lobster at the wrong time. He sees her first as a gray-white cloud in the water far above him. His soul chills. He is an experienced diver. Pressed against the bottom, he waits.

She disappears. Shadow into shadow. A living poem.

Rightly, he waits a very long time. When he cautiously surfaces, waves slapping against his mask, he sees nothing. Relief is like fatigue. As he turns, looking for the boat, his mask dips to the water. The pink mouth is yawing improbably wide, the serrated teeth God's own scalpels.

The impact snaps his jaw shut. The first items he parts with are his tongue and a goodly portion of his left thigh. Spinning in the water he sees pretty rose bubbles. He can only gurgle for help. A second sledgehammer impact. Again there are terrible sounds; the crunching is the bones in his arm. She takes him under. Imbued by the vision of his three-year-old son, he pulls his arm free. He is halfway to the surface, swimming queerly, when she hits him again, driving breath and blood into the water.

Weighted by his diving gear, he sinks to the ocean floor. He lies there - what, precisely, he sees, I can't say - the exposed bone of his right hand clawing pointlessly for the surface. Sometimes your will to live is strong. Briefly, love trumps agony. Finally the hand relaxes and the arm turns listless, wafting a conscienceless good bye before settling to the bottom.

For some reason this shakes me. I remind myself that his demise is fate alone, and fate takes good as readily as bad. But always there is opportunity for lesson. I plant the thought. She surfaces and nudges the zodiac. The two men, searching vainly for something beyond a dissipating patch of blood, draw back with shouts.

Her nudge - my nudge - is simply a reminder. You are not apart from these seas. They are only two men, but one dismantles monumental ignorance and hubris stone by stone.

You are seven billion and counting. It took only a dozen years to add the last billion. Your future population forecasts are not heartening. Nine billion by 2050; ten billion by the end of the century.

Sharm el-Sheik was my doing, a child's petulant tantrum. But most of these encounters between man and purported beast are a simple matter of numbers.

More of you everywhere, a tide that refuses to retreat.

And our hunting could turn more purposeful. Your United Nations warns of the possibility of fishless oceans by the year 2050. One billion people, you estimate, rely on fish as the mainstay of their diet. What will they eat, you ask, if the fish are gone?

Recall, it's not just about you. Recently one of your scientists observed whale sharks feeding on plankton off Belize. Their feeding behavior, your scientist noted, was oddly frantic, "like the whale sharks just couldn't wait to get food." They couldn't. Thanks to pollution, ocean temperature change, and ocean acidification, plankton levels are plummeting. Even the docile whale shark grows desperate.

Imagine the carnivores of the seas, with little to nothing on their plate.

By 2050 there could be serious impetus to skip the swim.

Silent Stars

Selling petrol, even at inflated prices, wasn't enough. Loading the boxes, Santy felt his back seize with each heft. Beside him, his nephew grunted in the darkness. They both sweated profusely. Puffs of breeze tossed mangrove mud smell and body odor into Santy's face.

"You stink, boy. I would rather plunge my head into a buffalo dropping."

"You smell worse than the White Squall's shithole."

"You are lucky I don't add sting to your stink."

Santy had never insulted his elders like children did today. But in his nephew's defense, they were both on edge. No matter how many times they went out, the entire operation always seemed a stomach-churning eternity. They had started going out at night six months ago. They could stop anytime. But the envelopes of bills the German gave him were impossible to resist, and Santy saw how Steinman's breathing quickened when he accepted his share. The boy was not greedy; they lived on a poor island. Santy himself didn't really care for the extra money, but he had a plan and it was costly and so they kept going out.

He always took the long way out of the harbor to avoid passing too close to the Wendell Holmes. He was fond of Cedar, but the damn woman never slept. She was up on her deck at all hours staring at the stars as if they were going to do something different that night. Now that Marty was fucking her - how did a prissy man get a woman like that? - she did less star gazing, but Santy didn't want to take the chance. She was observant and smart. He had no doubt she would eventually ascertain their mission.

When they finished loading, they stepped into the last thin spaces on the panga. Santy did not miss how low they rode to the waterline. The boy didn't either.

"How far are we going tonight?" he asked.

He heard how Steinman tried to sound bold and his heart softened a little.

"Not too far," said Santy, and they both knew this was a lie.

Steinman sat in front. Santy saw how he craned his neck as they puttered toward the harbor mouth. Santy subconsciously put a hand on the crate containing the mix of ammonium nitrate fertilizer and fuel oil. The ingredients were easy to come by. Rigging the bombs was easy, too. They always motored a safe distance away before detonating the caps. Then they motored back, scooping the stunned fish into plastic bags. They only had to get the fish back to the docks. After that it was the German's job to keep the fish alive until they were shipped off to the aquarium collectors.

The biggest danger was sinking. And getting caught.

"It is a calm night," said Santy.

"I don't care if it is rough. You are the one who can't swim."

Santy forgave him his insolence and false bravado. He loved the boy. Santy's four sisters were a fruitful lot - they had eighteen children between them - but Santy had a soft spot for the boy. He admired his swagger and lies. Santy knew it was how he coped with his deformity. Santy was going to use the money to change that.

"Tell me where we're going," the boy said.

"To sea."

Santy opened up the engine, erasing any chance for words.

It is an improbable time for an engine. At first I wonder if I am the one dreaming, if my wishing has actually brought her here. But this sickly sputtering is not her engine and this is not Long Drop-Off. No one comes out this far at night. Sometimes in the distance I hear the propellers of a long range fishing trawler chewing at the sea, but I have never heard an engine directly over the reef at night. It is why I chose this reef. The sea has its hidden places.

The engine rattles and dies. I feel two heartbeats. Agitated. Fearful. The younger one positively dashes.

I exit through the opening in the bottom of the cavern.

This is wrong, I sense it, but I don't know what to do.

The boy leaned over the gunnel and looked into the black water.

"There is a reef here?"

Santy, occupied with the fuses, half heard him.

"Yes."

"How did you find it?"

"A fisherman told me."

The boy fell silent. Santy knew he was afraid.

"No one will catch us," Santy said. "Even during the day the fishermen come here only occasionally. Below us is a winning lottery ticket. Think of the envelope."

Six more envelopes and he would have enough for the boy's flight to the mainland and the operation. He had looked it up on the internet. To be so close bolstered his courage, though he also knew it made him rash. This reef could produce the equivalent of two envelopes in a single night, but it was very far from shore.

"I'm scared," the boy said.

Surprise saw Santy rest the fuse on his knee.

"Why?"

"I don't know."

They floated amidst the silent stars. Santy wondered if this was how it was for the astronauts.

The boy's unease was contagious.

"I wish there was a breeze," said Santy. "I believe you took a dip in the White Squall's shithole."

The boy did not take the bait. He pivoted slowly to and fro, peering into the darkness.

"How long will we be?"

"The usual," said Santy. *Quicker, if I can help it.*

Why is this panga here? I see its puny outline, no more than a matchstick. They are desperate, these fishermen. Granted the night is calm, but weather changes. There are also the long range trawlers. Collisions are not uncommon. A trawler would never know of the splintered panga and the bodies in its wake.

Why would they come here at night to fish?

This is wrong. But what is wrong about it?

Santy rigged all the fish bombs first. They would move in and out as they detonated each one, scooping the spoils off the surface. Tonight this process would take time. He had rigged six bombs. The boy's apprehension had infected him. Already he had decided they would not come here again. He would get the last envelopes close to shore, and then he would tell the German to fuck himself.

Something like sickness sat in his stomach. He tried to think of the Heidi Klum, but all he thought was that they were very far from shore in a place like outer space.

For one of the first times in his life, he wished for additional human company.

He slid the oars to the boy, who settled them expertly in the oar locks.

Steinman rowed them toward the center of the reef.

I hear the dip of oars, then quiet. The first sound is like a pebble dropped. The second is not. The report is short and sharp, like a slap. The concussive force of the blast actually knocks me back. I spin like an awkward top. Above me I hear the patter, the geyser of water now falling back to the sea.

But I am no longer analyzing.

I am rushing upward, my tentacles lunging.

In the final moments of confusion, Santy wondered if the fish bomb had exploded directly beneath them. Perhaps in the darkness the boy had rowed in a circle. It was an admissible mistake. The sea tossed itself into the air. Oddly the boy, far above him, did not fall back to the sea. In the night sky, he swayed as he sometimes walked, but wildly this time, his flopping head grotesquely canted.

Santy felt something clasp his chest, like a mother's hug. He twisted to look behind him, but not of his own accord. Very close, Santy heard a sound like a wet paper towel being torn.

I forget the man and the boy before I finish them. I plunge down, expunging air. The bomb exploded directly on the reef. A foot to the left and it would have wobbled down into the leftmost opening. I rush down along the reef wall, noting how the fissures have widened and shifted, the sand inside the cavern wafting through the largest cracks like thin whips.

I can hear the grinding. The reef is still settling back on itself. I thrust through the opening 150 feet down. I am inside the cavern. I feel as if I am pushing against an anvil. It is only twenty yards, but it takes me an eternity to ascend.

The reef has collapsed.

The shelf is gone.

Do I feel pain, shock, abject loss? No. I am aware of nothing. The pageant is not mine. I see as a theater goer sees from a balcony seat: water, already clouded with sand, now whipped to a frenzy of swirling current and bubbles by tentacles thrashing pointlessly against unyielding rock.

Lime Green and Blue

Word flew across the island; Santy's panga was gone and he was not at the dock. Santy's wailing sister burst into the police station, divulging her son's illegal escapades and his empty bed in a hysterical frenzy. At the fuel dock, Able broke the lock to the shed filled with ammonium nitrate, fuses and detonator caps. Standing on the dock, nearly sinking beneath the weight of Santy's friends and relatives, he thought, *It is a small miracle the explosion didn't occur here.*

Able phoned Marty and two expat pilots. He asked Marty to phone Cedar.

At noon Able, the two pilots and Marty and Cedar were wedged into Marty's office. They all stood looking at the nautical chart spread across the desk. It was still and unbearably hot. The air conditioner had rattled its last rattle that morning.

Outside of the criminal activity, Santy's hysterical sister knew nothing. No one had any idea where Santy and Steinman had gone.

"Thoughts?" asked Able.

Although he addressed everyone, he was speaking only to Cedar.

One of the expats said, "It's a big ocean?"

Were these people born stupid, or did the tropical sun turn them that way?

Able held his tongue.

Turning to the expats he said, "We need to push off. If they are still alive, we need to find them quickly. You take the easterly heading," he said to the fat, florid-faced man, "and you," to the skinny fellow with the ample forehead, "take the westerly course. Pay attention as soon as you lift off. They wouldn't have gone far," he said, although he wasn't so sure.

The men scurried out like schoolboys, anxious to please.

When the door shut, Able said, "Good. Now we can get something accomplished. Ms. Mahoney, have you any idea where they might have gone?"

She had been consumed with that question since Marty's call. She went to the window. The lock on the shed. Steinman veering into the brush. The panga puttering out of the harbor at night. They had all but screamed in her face.

Now she required a far less obvious answer.

Outside, the two planes throttled along the runway.

Patience, Cedar thought. *Rushing off serves no purpose. Think. It is a big ocean.*

Able and Marty waited.

Fish bombing was nothing new. On a poor island, it was too much to resist. It was common knowledge that at least a dozen fishermen participated in the illegal activity, but they were smarter than Santy about where they kept their explosives, and the blue expanse of nautical chart underscored the difficulty of catching them in the act. Occasionally when Cedar ferried the rare group of experienced divers to the more remote reefs, they heard the bombs underwater, detonating in the distance with a telltale thump. Her divers were always outraged, but they all took their outrage back to five star hotel rooms and 1200 thread count sheets and, soon enough, forgot.

Santy trusted no one. He would avoid the other fish bombers, seeking out reefs where few, if any, boats went. For once, Able was wrong. He would have gone far.

"There's hope," Able said. "Seas are calm."

They all knew what he meant. Hope of finding debris.

The two planes lifted off. They left behind a deeper silence.

Marty pushed at the chart, the sound like a whisper.

Cedar jerked upright. It was more than a hunch.

"Let's go," she said.

"Plane or boat?" asked Able.

"Boat."

Cedar called Ernan from Marty's office. She knew she was in no condition to deal with the mundane details of the trip to Water Whispers.

Marty drove from the airstrip to the dock. Able was at the dock when they arrived. Cedar saw he had traded his aloha shirt for a somber green military-style shirt. It was nearly ninety degrees, but he wore a green jacket too. He looked like a park ranger starting a tour. He was surrounded by several dozen locals, everyone shouting at him at once. Cedar recognized a slew of Santy's relatives and several fishermen who knew plenty about fish bombing. Some were one in the same.

Ernan was on the bridge. The lines were off, the engines rumbling. The boy was worth his weight in gold.

Able looked desperate.

"Permission to come aboard?" he asked as she walked quickly by.

"Yes," she said, and then louder, "This applies only to Able."

She had seen the weathered swim fins and rusted tanks.

This unleashed an uproar of upset.

Cedar spotted Steinman's mother, a skinny woman lost in a mumu. Pushing through the crowd, she took the limp woman gently by the arm, trying to remember her name.

"Please," said Cedar. "You can come with us."

As she helped the woman step on to the boat, Able bowed his head.

"Miss Regina," he said.

Regina Whitby. A quiet woman who worked as an aide at the preschool.

Regina regarded Able as if she had never seen him.

"My Steinman," she said.

It sounded slightly like a question but Able did not answer it.

A man pushed to the front of the crowd. His eyes were rheumy and his voice was threatening. Cedar knew him as a failed fisherman turned drunk. She knew how he paid for his liquor.

"I am coming!" he shouted, looking about for encouragement. "Santy was my friend!"

This got everyone excited again. Everyone was now Santy's friend. The crowd started to push forward.

Able's voice cut through the clamor.

"No one is coming aboard."

The crowd faltered, undecided. The drunk lowered his head as if he was going to charge the boat.

"Man, who the fuck are you to tell me what to do?"

"The chief of police, although I shouldn't waste my breath explaining this to a drunk. Who are you to claim to be Santy's friend? You barely knew him. You will stay on the dock."

"You will stop me?" The fisherman looked at the crowd. "You will stop *us*?"

There were murmurs of agreement.

"If need be," said Able.

Cedar saw now why Able was wearing the jacket. He had pulled it aside just enough for the crowd to see the holstered gun.

Up on the bridge, the shouting crowd on the dock receding behind them, she gave Able a grateful nod.

"I've never seen you carry a firearm," she said.

"Firearm, the device. Not firearm, the weapon. The firing mechanism is a corroded mess. You are not the only master of the bluff."

"You really should be a detective in New York."

"I do not know how to hail a cab," Able said, but he did not smile.

It was the perfect afternoon for making haste. The entire ocean held its breath. The Wendell Holmes flew over the slick water.

As Ernan took them southeast, Cedar checked her dive gear. Able talked quietly to Regina Whitby. Marty stayed up on the bridge with Ernan.

When Cedar finished checking her gear, Able came over.

"You are planning on diving?"

"Yes."

"May we scout the surface first?"

"Of course."

Able tapped her tank.

"You suspect something beyond an explosion?"

"I don't know what to suspect. It was likely an explosion."

"Likely," said Able. "Bigger is also a possible suspect."

"What?"

"Our conversation in the town square. You said none of the sharks were big enough to leave nothing behind. I agree." He watched her with his rutted poker face. "May I be honest with you, Cedar?"

"Of course," she said, although she wasn't certain she meant it.

"I feel you are hiding something."

"That's ridiculous," she said, but she saw he didn't think so. *You should be in New York*, she thought. *Maybe it would be better for all of us.* She feigned resignation. "I should be offended, but I suppose it's your job to be suspicious of everyone."

Able held her gaze a tick longer than convention warranted.

He glanced back at Regina Whitby.

Leaning close he said, "Ted Marple. Santy. Steinman. People are *dying*, Cedar."

He had the same pleading look on his face that he'd had in his office.

It probably had been an explosion. The homemade fish bombs were as stable as Middle Eastern politics. The right amount of ammonium nitrate would obliterate the Wendell Holmes, much less a tinderbox panga.

She wanted it to be a fish bomb. Santy and Steinman did not deserve Ted Marple's fate.

She decided.

"I trust you, Able. Do you trust me?"

He didn't answer right away. Maybe all good policemen were like that.

"I do."

"Then you'll have to wait."

The waters above the reef were ink-well still, as if the ocean was waiting for them before it cleaned up the mess. The ebbing tide had strung the debris out in a sinuous line.

When Regina spotted Santy's baby blue cooler bobbing in the sun she went to her knees and began to wail.

"Jesus," whispered Marty. "They probably didn't even know what hit them."

"That is likely so," said Able.

Cedar heard their words but they did not mean anything. Sorrow poured into her heart. She had seen enough to know.

Able had Ernan pilot the Wendell Holmes at a jogger's pace, making a widening grid, beginning at the western edge of the reef where most of the debris floated. Santy's panga had been lime green and blue. Bright chunks of wood and unpainted slats, probably the wood crates that had housed the fish bombs, drifted on the surface. Bits of plastic were everywhere. For some reason Santy had favored purple plastic bags for housing his specimens. The purple bags rode on the surface like an army of Portuguese man o'war.

Cedar saw that Able no longer looked at the debris. He knew. His parents had named him Able because they wanted him to feel he was capable of anything. It had worked brilliantly.

Regina Whitby had fallen silent. She sat on a bench. The way she stared out at the water broke Cedar's heart. For a moment Cedar forgot about the thoughts pulling at her from every direction.

Pouring a lemonade from the cooler, she took it to the tiny woman.

She didn't know what to say.

Regina Whitby took the cup, but she did not drink out of it.

"My brother became a grouchy old man but he still favored childish colors," she said.

Her eyes remained on the water.

Ernan had cut the engines. They drifted quietly. There was nothing more to search for.

They watched a fragment of lime green wood float past.

"I always enjoyed his company," Cedar said.

"He bragged without stop about how you introduced him to Heidi Klum. Men are all the same."

"Steinman was a fine boy, Mrs. Whitby."

The passing water made a gurgling sound. Regina Whitby looked as if she were struggling to remember something.

"He was a brave boy," she said. "And a fine storyteller."

Cedar wanted to say something more, but suddenly she could only think of Justin.

"He would have made quite the story of this," Regina Whitby said and she began to cry.

Able came down the ladder from the bridge.

"I've seen all I need to see," he said. "You've had a good look?"

Cedar recognized it as accusation, not question.

"Yes."

"You are still going in the water?"

"I won't be long."

"You don't think it foolish?"

Was it the detective in him that made nearly everything a question?

"No. I don't."

"You are going in alone?"

"Ernan has to stay with the boat. Marty..."

Marty would only slow me down. She pretended to concentrate on rummaging through her dive bag.

Able's face softened and he sighed.

"You brought only one tank," he said.

No need to mention the spare down below.

"I guess I did."

"Not an oversight, although you surely have a spare below. I could order you to stay on board."

"Please don't do that. We will both end up being embarrassed."

"You are a pig-headed woman." She was surprised when he put a hand on her arm.

"Please," he said. "Be very careful. This is not our world."

The instant she descended she knew her instincts were right. The top of the reef, at the tunnel entrances, had collapsed. The depression wasn't large, maybe the size of a community swimming pool. It looked like a sinkhole that had quickly lost interest.

But it was enough to tell her the damage inside the cavern was greater.

Both openings appeared clear, although there was no telling how the collapse had affected the tunnels where they disappeared from sight. Cedar chose the northern tunnel: it had been the larger of the two before this seismic shifting. She finned down cautiously. The walls stayed at arm's length. She exited into the cavern.

Her eyes swung about. It was still and infinitely quiet. *Like a morgue*. A spread of dead angelfish floated against the ceiling.

Her bubbles blasted, raucous and invasive in her ears.

She swam slowly along the wall until she found the spot. She ran her finger along the fractured scar in the rock, a jagged line where the shelf had been.

She floated, a circus acrobat balanced vertically on a finger. Her body buzzed. She was acutely aware of being wholly alone, cut off from the world. Her heart executed reluctant beats, each one like a shout in her ears. To her surprise, she was holding breath. Exhaling softly, she took an equally timid inhale. Her gaze ran along the distant cavern wall. Many of the fissures were wider now. Several clearly revealed blue ocean beyond.

She waited for a shadow to pass.

Finally she turned back to the uninterrupted basalt in front of her. She recalled her dream, the lantern flames wiggling. Life was fragile; one moment here, gone the next. It was the darkest certainty, the shadow we all turned away from.

She wondered what would happen next.

Back up on the reef she swam her own grid, looking for what, she didn't know. A creeping unease saw her rush. The waters were bright. The tropical sun poured down. Away from the spots where the fish bombs had detonated, healthy hard and soft corals stood unblemished. But the silence screamed. Not one gnawing, not one crackling. There were no fish. Everything that could swim was gone.

She was alone, but she was not alone.

She swam for the ladder faster than she liked. Aboard the Wendell Holmes her heart kept racing.

Before they left, Regina Whitby removed the rosary from her neck and said a prayer. When she finished, she dropped the rosary in the water.

She swayed back and forth.

"I know it was wrong what he did, but he was a good boy with a good heart. That foot was an awful burden. Few could bear it as he did."

She spoke solemnly, a teacher imparting a critical lesson upon small children, and then she hiccoughed and began to sob.

Cedar held her, a frail form forever changed.

As Ernan slowed outside the breakwater, Able stepped up beside Cedar.

"I am not sure where I stand," he said.

"That makes two of us."

"You must have very good reasons for keeping your secrets."

"I think I do. I'm not sure."

"Perhaps this is bigger than a police investigation," Able said.

"Yes." She turned to face him. "You're remarkable, you know."

He gave a slight smile

"All I know is I will get nothing from you until you are ready."

This time she put her hand on his arm.

"I know this isn't easy for you. You're an equally fine friend, Able."

The dock swung into view. Most of the island's populace waited.

"And so I will lie to them," Able said wearily.

"It's the best thing to do."

A cool breeze riffled the water.

"I wish I could be certain of that," Able said, zipping up his jacket.

As the full moon lifted above the jungle, Marty leaned on the railing and said, "I can stay."

"I'd prefer to be alone." Cedar kissed him. "You know I couldn't do this without you."

"I'm certain you could." He hesitated. She saw how his fingers kneaded the railing. "Do you think they died quickly?"

She had been asking herself that very question from the moment she first laid eyes on the debris. She had seen the same question in Able's face, and Marty's and Ernan's. Only the grief stricken Regina Whitby had missed the obvious.

"Yes," she said. "I think it was sudden. And quick."

"I would have stopped you from diving if I thought I could."

The way he looked at her almost made her ask him to stay.

"Able told me he asked you not to dive either," he added.

She nodded.

"So neither one of us is sure if you're impossibly brave or insanely foolish."

She was lucky to have one ally like this, much less two. She felt like a swimmer in a rip, being swept away from shore. Her secrets were distancing her from everyone, even this gentle man she had come to love.

Why not tell him about the eggs? Part of her said that now it couldn't matter. But another voice, a stronger voice, told her it was all that mattered. She felt queerly protective. Possessive. Even a trifle angry.

Santy and Steinman's greed had destroyed a mother's dreams. She knew it dreamed because she dreamed. The wavering flames danced in her mind.

The vision made her abrupt.

"I'll call you in the morning," she said, turning away.

Late that night she sat out on the deck.

Just off the bow a pair of white-tailed tropicbirds wheeled about each other. The full moon turned them brighter.

Cedar saw neither birds nor moon. In her mind, the debris slid past the Wendell Holmes, not a stitch of wood or plastic marked by flame.

She dreamed a terrible dream. At first the scene before her was idyllic, like creation itself, the ocean spread, gem clear and sparkling, to a horizon of equally pure blue. The dark slash appeared slowly, razor-thin and almost imperceptible, along the horizon's rim. She sat silent, mesmerized by the shocking beauty of the panorama and the thin slash she already knew would spoil it all. Along the horizon the dark slash swelled, rising up like a great wave. Spilling forward, it raced toward her, staining the ocean black, suffocating everything in its path.

The darkness did not stop at the ocean's edge. Reaching shore, it continued on across the flats, up the rise and over the knoll on which she sat, pouring into her lungs, smothering her last breath, before it moved on.

Heroes and Villains

I cannot apologize for what cannot be helped. When the first night came I was alone in the dark with my terrible thoughts. I fought them, for their direction was clear, but they roiled and spun and piled upon each other of their own accord. Their massing became a weight from which I had to escape. I swam at first without realizing it. But already I knew my intent. Of this I was fully aware. And fully deliberate.

Within the hour I found what I wanted. The sailboat was far from land. I jostled it first, a violent shaking - what did they think, tumbling from their berths on a quiet sea? -- and then I backed away. I stayed on the surface. I wished them to see. I wished to see. I wanted the unfoldings to be exquisitely clear for both parties

The man was first on deck, flashlight sweeping the water. Even as I churned the sea, making it easy for him to find me, the woman and the two children appeared behind him. The children were already wide-eyed, their hearts like trembling mice, but their fear reached an unfathomable apex when the man trained the beam on me.

Bold-hearted. You make much ado of this. In the end you rarely are.

I did not rush forward. I raised my tentacles into the sky. Their lashings made a quiet hissing as they parted the air, like something lurking close in a black corner, something you do not see.

Oh, but they saw.

The man leapt into the sea.

I heard the mother's prayers and the guttural sounds of the children choking on the realization that nightmares live. The woman fled too, disappearing below. Even in my fury I found this disappointing.

I took the cowardly man. I nearly lifted him from the water, to pull him apart for all to see, but even in my fury I was not wholly blind to the abandoned children. The oldest fell to his knees and retched. I finished the man beneath the surface, twisting him as you would wring out a drenched towel. His blood reeked of fear. This tipped me over the precipice. I became monster again, thoughtless apex predator of the sea.

When I rose again to the surface, the woman was back on the deck. She held a flashing light, perhaps a distress beacon of some sort, but we all knew a bonfire of flares would not help her cause on this lonely sea.

I did not recall finishing the woman or the children. I vaguely remembered smashing the boat to pieces.

I floated on the surface, my insides howling.

Slowly the sea settled. There was nothing left but plywood, fiberglass, a sandal shaped like a bunny and, after a time, remorse.

Children.

We are all of us, heroes and villains.

I return to the broken reef. For several days I do not move. I float off the reef wall, helpless as a butterfly in a web. I stare at the uncaring rock and I am jealous. The soft corals wave mockingly.

I move only once, when the boat comes. Even then I find it difficult to muster the effort to drift out of sight. When she enters the water I feel nothing. I see her form backlit by the sun, but it stirs no more sentiment than the debris.

Your philosophers, your God-fearing, your abortionists, they ask, "When does life begin?"

As soon as it can die.

How do I communicate to you what I feel? It crushes my heart. It blows out my soul. But it does not leave emptiness. Emptiness would be a pleasure. It is the foul card dealt to every intelligent organism in times of sorrow. The ability to think on loss clearly. Again and again.

Happenstance has seen me to a fork in the road.

Wrath and vengeance. Forgiveness and hope. Monster or savior.

Even as I took the old fisherman, the murderer of my dreams, I tasted his sweetness.

You baffle me. You are an infinite puzzle of contradictions. My years of accumulated wisdom crumble before the confusion you provide.

I say the word and everything changes. But I cannot decide.

Shadows and Wishes

Before he stepped off the Wendell Holmes, Able knew he was coming back to the reef. It wasn't that he didn't trust Cedar, though he didn't. He decided to return to the reef because he had to see for himself. He had always had to see for himself. It was a curse, but it was the way it was. There was no changing it.

The police department had a skiff and even an official captain to pilot it, but Able did not want to be seen leaving the harbor in an official capacity. He knew all the fishermen, but he knew only a few who could keep their mouth shut. Members of his immediate and tangential family fished, but they were not among the close-mouthed camp.

That evening he hired Mongkol Songkhla to take him to the reef. Mongkol appeared to be in his twenties, although Able had a difficult time telling the age of any Thai: they looked the same whether they were twenty or two hundred. He knew Mongkol's parents. They were good people who owned the Thai restaurant he frequented. Word on the docks said Mongkol was a fisherman who knew the waters and kept to himself. He also had a well maintained boat. Able did not want his career to end on the high seas.

They left the harbor at dawn, Able staying below until they were well out to sea. Able had told Mongkol they were going out to the reef where the accident had occurred. When Able came up on deck, the man-boy asked no further questions.

When they arrived at the reef Mongkol did not offer to help Able with his dive gear. The last thing Able saw before he fell back off the gunnel was Mongkol smoking a clove cigarette.

He hit the water flat, stinging his bare back. As he situated himself, pin-wheeling awkwardly in a cloud of bubbles, he chastised himself for not diving more often. He had been a strong swimmer in his youth, but he was no longer in his youth. He knew he was already breathing far too fast, a measure of his sorry state of fitness and his apprehension. He floated for a minute just beneath the surface, willing himself calm, and then he finned down to the reef.

There was no doubt there had been an explosion. Rubbled coral was strewn about where the bomb had gone off. It looked like a construction site; on Palau limestone was the primary building material. Able knew how long it took coral to grow, how the tiny organisms painstakingly built a reef polyp by polyp, how the dive shops lectured their clients about not kicking the coral, but he didn't really care. Growing up on the island he had seen reefs all his life. They were everywhere. It was impossible to think they could disappear.

But they were. He had read the articles explaining how rising sea temperatures and pollution were killing off reefs at an exponential rate. When it came to man, even the impossible was possible.

He believed himself a man of substantial mental discipline, but as he swam along the reef, its surface sloping quickly toward the deeps, his mind played games. He forced himself to breathe slowly but he could not stop looking jerkily about. In his mind he saw the sharks hanging from the gallows. They did not look so small anymore. He had no idea what he was looking for; he only knew he was looking for something. He felt wholly exposed and helpless, a free-floating hors d'oeuvre.

He turned his mind to stamping out his anxiety, but his mind only screamed that help was smoking a clove cigarette up on the surface, worlds away from this place where shadows did not always swim in your mind.

Maybe he should have enlisted a family member who actually cared about him, although, with family, one could never be certain either.

Another boat; a man alone in the water. I hesitate now for a different reason. What is there to do? There is nothing here to protect. Now it is only an exercise in self-control. I float inside the cavern, facing the wall, smooth from top to bottom, testing myself to see how magnanimous I can be. Immediately I feel myself losing, slipping toward fury and vengeance, darkness and bloodshed. When your fluids first fill the water there is a moment of exhilaration that is like sexual release.

Violator. Despoiler. I feel tension and anticipation in every pore.

I think of the children on the sailboat, how their innocence crumbled like dry leaves crushed in a hand.

But still I am moving toward the entrance.

Able found the openings, side by side in the depression, on his second pass over the reef. Settling to his knees outside the largest opening his entire body prickled, a queer hair-raising that swept his skin and froze his blood. He was not one for the supernatural, but he was all ears and chilled platelets now. It did not feel like premonition or shadow possibility. It felt as real as a slap across the face.

It was a mistake to be here.

He was starting to back away when it vaulted from the opening, the instantaneous bouillabaisse of churning bubbles and swirling water the result of his panicked shouting and the lashings of his limbs.

The turtle nearly struck him in the face, its plated underside like a cross-hatched shield. It rose quickly beyond him with perfectly timed flipper sweeps while he continued to roll about on the reef. It was nearly gone, reduced to the size of a softball speeding through the blue, by the time he curbed his spasms. It was too much, even for a man of substantial will. Able finned a panicked arc toward the boat.

He passed directly over the limb without noticing it. Drifting to the bottom, it had wedged between two large lettuce corals. It was clearly visible, a single leg balanced upside down so that the stubby foot resembled a cane's handle.

Already the flesh was softening. Soon the fish, and the occasional moray, would begin picking.

Santy would get his wish. His nephew's club foot would be removed.

In short order I could change the way you view the seas. So much tooth and claw and poison at my behest. They are angry. They are more than ready. They are not given pause by conscience or ethics. They are not puzzled by your contradictions, hamstrung by the intellectual conundrums that still stay my hand.

Some act already, without my urging. In the waters off Seattle

Washington, the transient pod is on the hunt. All orcas are intelligent and highly social, living in lifelong family pods. For those of you whose knowledge of orcas, what you call killer whales, does not extend beyond Sea World and Shamu, let me make a single important distinction. There are two kinds of orcas. The resident pods remain in a general area, feeding primarily on fish.

The transients, they feed on marine mammals. They are flesh eaters.

Separation Anxiety

That night a squall hammered across the harbor, shoving the Wendell Holmes against the dock with gusts of wind and rain.

Cedar barely heard the drumming. She sat in the dark galley beneath a single lamp reading "Of Mice and Men." She read Steinbeck's novel from beginning to end. When she finished, she closed the book and sat listening to the rain sizzle. She missed Justin. That she would never hold a little boy again was both irrevocable and inconceivable fact. So many times you rock them, and then you rock them for the last time. That Justin was now only a few months short of finishing high school shocked her. She wanted him back. She did not want him to come back.

The first time she read "Of Mice and Men" she was a high school senior herself. Her English teacher had asked an intriguing question. What gave George the right to kill Lenny?

Back then, she had been painfully shy. She had not raised her hand. But even then she knew in her heart that there was not one, but two answers. Yes, men were vengeful and Lenny would have died by a bullet either way. George provided the peaceful exit.

But there was something more. Lenny was good, but he was ignorant of his own power and wholly absorbed in himself. He was always an accident waiting to happen.

How intelligent are orcas? They have their own local dialect.

They teach one another specialized methods of hunting. They pass on behaviors that persist for generations. Even your skeptical scientists are coming to believe that orcas might be much smarter than the size of their enormous brains suggest.

Let's just say orcas possess more than enough intelligence to make decisions that are quite conscious. I will even suggest they are capable of weighing ethical matters. If this is so, you ask, why would they attack innocent humans? Killer whales now regularly play starring roles at your marine parks. Almost all of them are taken from the wild. Did you know that male orcas -- who can live for 50 or 60 years -- stay with their mothers for the mother's entire life, and they often die not long after she does? Did you know that when you captured one of the first orcas for your shows -- taking him from a net and towing him 450 miles from British Columbia to Seattle Marine Aquarium in a floating pen -- his family pod, some 20 orcas in all, followed him the entire way? At night, Seattle Marine Aquarium trainers heard him calling to these family members from his pen. He died of bacterial infection within the year.

This orca was by no means the last to die in captivity. Nor was he the last to suffer what your trainers call "separation anxiety", an antiseptic term for heartbreak, as anyone with a heart can see.

Why have captive orcas killed innocent humans? Innocence is in the eye of the beholder.

I could stop the transients, but at this moment I simply don't care. Laissez faire.

I have my own anger management issues.

Christmas morning Marty surprised her with a turkey and all the trimmings. He arrived at the Wendell Holmes ferrying two coolers and that gentlemanly smile that always made her feel impossibly lucky. Christmas night she slept soundly in his arms.

For two weeks now she had slept dreamless.

Something was amiss.

The kayakers are honeymooners, married on Christmas Eve. The orcas don't know this -- their intelligence has limits -- though they sense the kayakers' giddy manner and perhaps even a little procreative tension. On this bright day, the rhinestone waters off the southern tip of Vancouver Island augmented by love, the young man and the young woman splash each other with their paddles and race each other from point to point, shouting out challenges. The water is, of course, freezing, but the air is unseasonably warm on this Christmas morn.

Oh it is a lovely scene, innocent Adam and Eve frolicking in the Garden of Eden. I could still put a stop to it, but I ask you this.

If you have no qualm about slaying innocents, why should I?

The orcas ambush the kayakers in the cove of an uninhabited island. Only the birds bear witness; they lift from the pines and cobbled beach and circle above the water in a screeching mass.

It is a game. The killer whales leap from the water; 12,000 pounds of animal sends up a substantial splash. Both kayakers capsize. In the first instant, as the water settles and the birds scream, the hyperventilating newlyweds tread water close enough to look into each other's eyes.

The girl is yanked under first, taken by her pig-tail and pulled deep into a cold, green world. She jerks free, leaving half her scalp behind, but she has no idea which way is up. Not that it matters. In the murky deeps the whales slam into her, driving her through the water with a force that finally breaks her back. But youth is something. Still she persists in living.

On the surface the whales push the boy back and forth, bumping him with their noses. It is a grim game with a predictable finish. The boy's end comes in a burst of blood; the girl's, finally, in a burst of lung.

The whales leave only the kayaks behind. The explanations for two overturned kayaks sweeping out through a remote pass off Vancouver Island are many-fold.

You doubt the truth of this? It is true, there were no witnesses outside of the orcas, the birds and the kayakers, and none of them is talking. You claim there have been no documented attacks on man by orcas in the wild; by this narrow definition, the statement is true. But you need only go to your own news accounts, called up by a tap of the finger, to see that captive orcas have killed your kind; a trainer at a marine park, a drifter who made the mistake of taking a plunge in a marine park pool at night. In the latter case, the man received a serious working over first. His testicles were ripped open. Divers retrieved the pieces of his body from the pool bottom.

Unexpected opportunity for sweet revenge. And a much more literal definition of separation anxiety.

Hers

Palau's holiday season passed, as every season did, in heat and humid torpor. Cedar experienced a happy uptick in bookings. When he wasn't flying, Marty came along to help. He was good with repairs and the other divers loved him. While many dive guides cultivated a superior attitude, Marty was funny and non-threatening; particularly once he entered the water. It was a puzzle to Cedar how a man so balletic on dry land appeared as if he were being electrocuted beneath the water. He was improving, but he was still bad enough to make the other divers feel good about themselves.

One morning, gathering gear in the back of the dive shop, she heard a quiet voice conversing with Ernan at the counter. Her heart sprinted. Like a teenage girl, she waited until he was gone.

She tried to remain calm, but seeing him on the boat only threw open the starting gates, her heart pounding like a thoroughbred released.

"Hi," Sean said affably, as if days had passed instead of months. "I suddenly had a few free days and I couldn't bypass an excellent dive operator nearby."

"I'm flattered."

Her dry mouth made it sound, in her ears, like *I'm fatter.*

Fatter and younger. Acne-shy and tongue-tied. She saw herself, standing paralyzed beneath a makeshift elementary school spotlight.

We are not hardwired to be monogamous. We are no different from the animals. I am in a relationship. I am a schoolgirl stupefied by hormonal flushings and confusion.

What in the world am I thinking?

"Sean," he said, extending a hand.

Her laugh was genuine and then she was stiff again.

"Right. I just hadn't a chance to see the manifest yet."

She knew it didn't sound light in either of their ears.

She saw the sliver of pale forehead and her heart broke.

"Thanks for coming out with us again," she said.

It sounded like a line from a play, badly recited.

She saw the sadness in his eyes. She would have done anything to wipe it away.

He pulled himself together gamely.

"I was just looking at your trip schedule in the shop," he said. "You're not doing the nautilus dives anymore?"

"No. It was a really hard decision. Too many boats on that reef. I thought I'd ease the strain."

Life is a series of lies and truths. Sometimes they are mixed together.

Marty came up from below. He kissed her cheek and gave Sean a smile, moving off to check the tanks, jostling each one to ensure they were firmly settled in their holders.

The brown eyes held her.

"Paradise lost," Sean said, smiling. "But I'm sure the other dives are nearly as beautiful."

He placed his bag on the bench.

Marty was up on the bow, helping Justin coil the lines.

"I'm so sorry," she said softly. "You don't have to go out with us."

"It's okay. And honestly? Only a fool would miss your magnificent diving."

She wanted to kiss him. Instead, on the dives, she let him wander wherever he wanted. When he left he didn't ring the bell, but he left an overly generous tip. Part of her wanted to return it to his hotel, where she knew there was a lilac on the pillow.

When they finished rinsing down the Wendell Holmes and squaring things away, Marty came up with her deck chair and a gin and tonic.

He set up the chair and placed the drink in the cup holder. Taking her elbow, he settled her in the chair.

"My lady, you work far too hard."

She felt her back melt into the sagging chair. She'd spent the entire day like a compressed spring. The glass felt cool against her palm.

Marty stood quietly.

"I'm drinking alone?"

"I'm flying in the morning."

"*We* work too hard."

Just looking at him made her feel warm.

"I liked him, you know. He was a gentleman and a superb diver.

I also cannot fault his superb taste in women."

"What are you talking about?"

"Ms. Mahoney, you rarely lie and when you do, you do it very badly. Please show me at least a small modicum of respect. I saw how you looked at each other. I can't dive, but I am not blind. I know how lucky I am."

He actually stared at his feet.

She put down her drink and took him to bed. She showed him how very lucky he was.

Dawn broke cloudless and wide, bringing clarity with it. She couldn't do this alone.

Marty often slept with a hint of a smile, like a child basking in a fairyland dream. He never remembered his dreams, as if such childish happiness dissolved in the morning light of a harsh world.

When she nudged him the smile flickered out.

Like Justin, Marty woke clear-eyed. There was no need for preliminaries.

"You need to know," she said. "I need you to know. There were eggs on the reef where Santy and Steinman died. The explosions," she found it surprisingly hard to say, "destroyed them."

Marty sat up. He took his time wedging the pillow behind his back. She saw his mind working. She called it his pilot face, the way he looked as he scanned the instrument panel, absorbing everything with a concentration that was absolute.

"Eggs," he said.

"Nautilus eggs. Eight of them on a shelf in a cavern beneath the reef. They were beautiful. When the dynamite exploded, the shelf collapsed. The eggs were crushed. They were hers."

Hers.

Marty watched her.

"You're certain?"

"Yes. They looked exactly like Nautilus eggs, only bigger. Much bigger."

She let this settle between them. One step at a time. Outside the porthole a bird cried and someone dumped something in the water.

Marty absorbed this first offering.

"Does anyone else know?"

"Justin saw them."

"Did he know what they were?"

"No."

"And you didn't tell him?"

"No."

"Does Able know about them?"

"No."

"I could ask you why."

"You could."

"And would you tell me?"

She was still working out the answer to this question. It required leaps of faith even she hadn't fully committed to yet.

A boat throbbed past. The Wendell Holmes rocked gently.

For some reason Marty redirected. She almost sagged with relief.

"You think this thing killed Santy and Alex because of the eggs?"

"I do."

"Instinctual protection?"

"Maybe. But heartbreak too."

This was a major bite. She saw Marty working to swallow.

"It feels?" he asked.

"Yes." It rang emphatically.

"I don't understand how you can be so certain."

Step two.

"I know it's female."

"Her eggs. Yes. And you would tell me why you are certain of this too?"

Here she settled for partial disclosure. The dreams might really throw him off kilter.

This was going to be hard enough.

"It communicates with me."

Marty turned to her. It was as if he was trying on a smile for the first time.

"You are asking for a great deal."

"I know. I sound crazy."

"Perhaps you greeted the dawn with a pitcher of gin and tonic." He kissed her. "Ah. Good. Only morning breath."

She reached up quickly before he pulled away. Cupping his face, she pulled him close so she could see every twitch.

"Please," she said. "Just give me a chance. It's all I ask."

She did not release him.

"You can count on it," he said, and because he did not smile, she knew there was hope. "However it may be something of a struggle."

"You're all I have. I need you to know. It feels what I feel. It understands my emotions. What I need. I think it knows what I think." She heard her desperation. She did sound insane. What hope did she have that he would believe her?

But the face before her did not twitch. The dark eyes waited.

"It knew how lonely I was before I met you. It knows how much I miss Justin." *It knows I feel a hiss of primal warning every time I dive Long Drop Off.* She had never made this connection before. It startled her, and puzzled her too; but she had to finish this.

"Please. Tell me you're still with me."

"I am foundering just a little bit."

"This won't help," she said.

She still held his face. Perhaps she pressed too hard. Marty looked a little pained. She relaxed the pressure, but not much. She didn't want him pulling away. She needed him close for this last puzzle piece.

"The communication isn't one way, Marty. I know how it feels. I have dreams. I think it may plant thoughts in my head. Some kind of telepathy. I don't know. I have this vague feeling sometimes that my thoughts aren't mine. I'm almost certain that's why Ted Marple swam at dusk."

The corners of Marty's eyes twitched. Gently, he took her hands from his face, but he kept holding them.

"This connection," he said. "This is why you don't think it's dangerous?"

"Didn't. Now I'm not so sure. I think it killed Santy and Steinman out of anger." She paused. She was far beyond committed now. "As a mother I might even say it was justified."

Looking down she noticed she was naked. Had they made love last night? She couldn't remember. It didn't seem to matter.

"It's also possible I'm loon crazy." She fought to keep the words light, but she knew she was going to cry. It was too much to ask of anyone. She had driven a wedge between them, a wedge Marty would never again step past. Love had abruptly ceased for far simpler reasons than a partner who was mentally unstable.

Justin was gone. Now Marty was gone.

Her heart emptied, leaving nothing. That nothing can hurt so much is an unsolvable puzzle.

She located her best mask.

"You're free to go. I'd advise you back away slowly and put your pants on outside the cabin. You can start running..."

His finger pressed against her lips, the dark eyes close again.

"And if I told you *I* was the one who was crazy?" he said.

"What?"

His arms slipped around her. His skin was so warm and smooth.

"I lost my heart to you with the first bagpipe solo. You played awfully, but you played to the end. I loved you from that moment. And I waited ten years to tell you. *Ten years*. Now *that* is loony."

She began to cry. In that moment she was a child basking in a fairyland dream.

Two weeks later she received a call from Jimmy Maas. Fortunately Marty hadn't slept over. She fumbled for her cell phone, groggily trying to locate the time. Three forty-five.

"It's early," Maas said.

It was his form of apology.

"It's fine."

Her mind was still fogged. She heard Maas breathing.

"It's not good," he said. "You need to be completely awake."

"I am now."

"Okay. I just got a call from a friend. His niece was sailing around the world with her husband and their two girls. They took the girls out of school for a year to show them the world. Third and fifth grade. I met them."

Hearing Jimmy Maas falter was like seeing yourself in a grave.

In the silence his breaths came fast.

"They disappeared two weeks ago. Their last communication was near the Mussau islands, off Papua New Guinea. The weather was fair. The radio communication was just a routine daily check between the niece and my friend. She didn't call in the next day or the next. When he tried to reach her, he got nothing. My friend knows someone at the American Embassy in Sydney. Three days later a spotter plane found the debris. A fishing trawler in the area changed course. They found a camera tangled in some rigging, a waterproof throwaway with the niece's name on it. My friend arrived in Sydney yesterday. They gave him the camera. He developed the film himself."

An unseen fist reached down her throat and crushed her heart. *Please no.*

"He just e-mailed me the pictures. They're on the screen in front of me. No one has seen them but him and me." He was speaking slowly, trying to keep blame out of his voice. *I met them.* "My friend thought, given my interests, I might be able to offer an explanation. Which is why I'm sending them to you," she heard the click, "now. I'll stay on the line."

She walked to the galley on leaden legs. She turned the computer on. The e-mail, with attachments, was waiting.

There were four shots. The first, a pale mound in the darkness, could have been almost anything, one of those grainy visages Loch Ness believers devoutly display as definitive proof. Each succeeding shot was closer. Even though it was a scanned photocopy, the last shot was infinitely clear.

She didn't feel terror, or shock, or confirmation, or even guilt. She felt one thing and one thing only. Soul-wrenching pity.

She was a mother.

The voice came from the end of a long tunnel. It took her a moment to remember Maas.

"I don't think anyone should dive there anymore," he said. "And if you haven't told anyone, now you should."

Cedar called Marty. He was at the Wendell Holmes in ten minutes.

He sat before the computer stiffly upright, like a berated child.

He closed his eyes, but when he opened them the world remained unchanged.

"Mother of God."

In this world innocents died all the time, but it was the one thing no one ever grew accustomed to. In a violent world, perhaps this was their last finger hold to humanity.

Marty stood so quickly she had to snatch his toppling chair.

She listened to his footfalls. He didn't have time to shut the door. His retchings echoed in the passageway.

When he returned he said, "I'm sorry."

She had never seen a man look so sad.

He sat at the table so he couldn't see the screen.

"I've spent my whole life flying over empty water. I never really thought about it."

"Thought about what?"

"What's down there."

They sat very still. The Wendell Holmes made many small

noises.

Children. They had turned a corner.

It took all her energy to get out of the chair.

She returned with the folder.

Marty leafed slowly through the clippings, reading each headline.

When he put the last clipping down, she said, "I think they're connected."

He shook his head.

"These events," she said. "They're all part of the same thing."

"It can't be."

"I think it is."

She kept the last thought to herself.

We are heading for the end.

They went to the police station. Cedar waited until Able finished staring at the computer before she told him about the eggs. She said nothing about communication or the news accounts. They only muddled things. She needed Able's help in the immediate here and now.

Marty sat beside her, holding her hand.

Able turned to them, his chair squeaking.

"Until we decide on a course of action, no one must see these photos," he said. "There will be wholesale panic." He fought to control his own panic. *It was there. I know it. I felt it.* He waited for calm. For once it did not come.

Anger is fear's ugly step sister.

His voice was hard.

"Your waiting has proved foolish."

He saw how Cedar winced, but her eyes did not leave his.

"I didn't feel it was dangerous. I still don't."

"You don't feel it's dangerous."

It sounded ridiculous in her own ears.

"No. I don't." As if they were two separate confirmations.

"Ted Marple."

"Revenge."

"Santy and Steinman."

"Self-defense. Panic. Maybe revenge."

Able's voice softened.

"A mother and father. Two helpless children."

This she knew. It was no stretch at all. She saw again the beautiful lanterns.

"Heartbreak," she said. "Incomprehensible grief."

Able absorbed this with his deadpan policeman's face.

"A snail that feels," he said. "If I heard this from anyone else I would laugh. Except that people are dying."

Cedar sat silent. She couldn't begin to think of what to say.

Able turned to Marty.

"Quiet one with your head in the clouds. Do you have anything to add that might help?"

"No. She told you what we know."

Cedar did not miss the qualifier, nor did she miss that Able saw the lie.

"You may change your mind at any time," the policeman said. "It would behoove us all. It might behoove you."

Able turned back to her. He regarded her as if they had never met.

I am being interrogated like any other criminal who is lying.

"I will remind you that everyone answers to the law," Able said.

"I am reminded."

"Willfully withholding evidence could mean prison time."

Suddenly she was angry.

"Is that a threat?"

"Just a friendly reminder."

The hard face held and then faltered. All the air left Able in a single exhale.

"Christ almighty Cedar, I can't do this anymore." It was her friend who looked at her now. "You are lying. Your squirming boyfriend is lying badly. I don't know what possesses me to ask you, given you haven't helped one iota up to this point and I know you're not cooperating fully now, but what would you advise we do?"

"Wait," said Cedar.

Surprise saw him lean so far forward he almost fell out of his chair.

"Wait?"

"Wait to see what happens."

"And while we wait, we tell no one else? No one else sees these photos? No one else is apprised of the danger. Because you can certainly see, whatever the motive, there is some form of danger."

"Yes. That's what we do. You would order boats out to kill it?"

She asked the question kindly.

Able regarded her with his sad eyes.

"Knowing really doesn't matter, does it?" he said.

"I don't think it does."

That night, alone in bed, Cedar thought of the children. The children on the sailboat. Regina's child. The children in the eggs.

Her child.

It was the single thought that never left her, that never wavered no matter what the shock of unfolding. If not for the Nautilus, Justin would be dead. Justin lived because of her.

It was the one secret she kept.

The secret between them.

Sister Phyllis Newman

Able shut down the nautilus dives on Long Drop Off, the dive operators sending up a collective caterwaul. They stormed into his office as he knew they would, spitting betel nut and curses, a crowd that spilled back into the hall. They would go broke. They would have to sell their boats. Their children, the children of their aunties and uncles, the children of every generation to come, would end up in the street with their stomachs empty and one person to blame.

When they asked him for a reason, he played the poker face of his lifetime and told the story he had concocted. He had received a call from a senior official from CITIES, the international group charged with protecting the oceans. The official, a scientist from Norway, had said in no uncertain terms that the endangered nautilus should be left alone. If they did not desist, the scientist said, the fines would make their business losses look like pocket change.

How had CITIES found out about the dives?

Able answered this with a question of his own.

How many wagging tongues were there on this island?

It was a good story, told with a fine poker face. The diver operators yowled louder. Several began plotting a trip to Norway to dice the scientist into chum.

Able knew that closing Long Drop Off was pointless, but he felt he had to do something.

Cedar had not been part of the protest. When he called to inform her there would be no more nautilus dives, she said, "I understand."

Hanging up, Able thought, *What sort of world would it be if we each listened clearly without self-interest clamoring in our ears? If we were open-minded enough to make the decision that was best for the whole?*

He realized now why he never beat her at poker.

I continue to wander aimlessly, unable to outdistance pain. I can find neither wisdom nor patience; they are gone from my sight. I am lost. I regret taking the children, and I do not; in my literal and figurative darkness I remember their sweetness and revenge tastes good. An eye for an eye, you say. I feel dirty. Sullied. Wrong. I want to lash out again. Share this pain that crushes everything from me. Dreams live until they die.

I am rudderless, drifting with the currents, wobbling absently down into the deeps where even wholesale blackness is colored by ache.

And stewing anger.

Sister Phyllis Newman had saved a lifetime for this trip, dropping coins, one by one, into the white mouth of a bright green ceramic frog her grandmother had made her for her sixth birthday in a time long gone. When the coins appeared at the bottom of the frog's throat, she took it to the bank. Each time, as she lifted the frog from the kitchen counter, its' weight a promise, she gave a happy croak. She knew it was silly, but nuns did not have enough silliness in their lives.

No one here knew she was a nun. She had arrived on this tropical island, famous for its God-given beauty, dressed like any tourist, in jeans and a Red Sox baseball cap, for Fenway Park could be a chapel too. She loved how the jeans hugged her thighs and the way no one stared at her as she lifted her luggage from the wood carousel.

She had booked a room at a pension. She spent the first full day of her vacation sleeping beneath the mosquito netting. She was no longer a young girl. The trip had tired her mightily. She did not mind giving up a day of her short vacation. She wanted to be fully alert to God's glories.

She hired the first guide she found. She knew she probably paid far more than necessary, but she did not like to bargain with those in need. The boat was smaller and more worn than the dinghies she had fished in when she was a girl, but the guide assured her they did not have far to go. The island she sought, the one with the marine lake filled with the stingless jellyfish, was only thirty minutes away through protected waters. This lake was a lifelong dream. Thirty minutes was so close.

Her guide smoked the entire way out, sweet smell of cloves, ashes and the occasional spark whipping back past the rattling outboard engine. Sister Phyllis said a silent prayer. His breath told her he had been drinking. Maybe she should have walked away and found another guide, but it was obvious to her this man had fallen upon hard times.

When they tied up at the small wood dock jutting from the island's mossy shore, her guide simply gestured to a footpath leading into the wall of jungle. "It is a half mile down that path," he said, his eyes already closing. "It is the only path and the only lake. You cannot get lost."

I don't know how it happens. I honestly don't. I certainly do not will it. It is orchestrated without a doubt, but it is orchestration beyond me. What do I sense? Hatred. Pure, elemental hatred. A primal emotion undiluted, containing not a wisp of reason, yet somehow carried out with conscious thought. It shocks me. Even single cell organisms are evolving. But this is a different kind of evolution, one I did not expect. Evolution, of course, is unexpected. Under other circumstances I would be amused by my blind ignorance, but this is deeply unsettling. For an instant, I even forget my pain.

This woman is pure and good.

Single cell organisms.

Perhaps the meek will indeed inherit the earth, but not in the fashion you imagine.

Sister Phyllis knew from the guide books that she was required to have a guide, but he looked so peaceful and she was a strong swimmer - childhood summers spent at the lakes in upstate New York - so she took her fins, mask and snorkel and bade him whispered goodbye.

It was not easy going. The path was slippery with recent rain and jungle drippings, and there were many roots. At points the path rose so steeply she drew quick breaths. But it was a short walk, as her guide had promised. After fifteen minutes she stood on a small dock, the wood spongy beneath her feet, her heart bounding now with joy. Surrounded by forest, the dark green marine lake might have been a lake of her childhood dreams. Across the lake she saw dangling vines and explosions of hibiscus. And there was no one else, this communion with Nature hers alone.

Sitting on the end of the dock, she slipped on fins and mask. Settling the snorkel firmly in her mouth, she pushed up with her hands and plunged forward into the lake.

The water was so warm it was like the sun's exquisite embrace. Finning away from the dock she saw, through her face plate, mossy tree limbs strewn on the rocky bottom and dark, catfish-like fish flitting to and fro. It was as if she had swum back in time. Her girlish smile made the snorkel bobble.

Halfway across the lake, all familiarity disappeared. The first jellyfish were scattered individuals, opaque softballs pulsing in the murk. So beautiful, their pulsing like a serene heartbeat. As she finned forward, their numbers grew. Within a minute, the water was a gelatinous cloud. The massing of the jellyfish, some now the size of cantaloupes, might have given someone else pause, but Sister Phyllis had read everything there was to read about the lake and she knew that even the largest jellyfish possessed only enough sting to prey on shrimp-like copepods. At most she would feel a mild itching, perhaps here and there the faintest kiss of sting.

Reading in her room at the convent, she had imagined herself an adventurous marine biologist, exploring wild places, making discoveries that thrilled the world and quietly honored God.

Now she was here, swimming through jellyfish throngs. Her heart beat faster with the adventure, and also with the smooth, silky brush of dozens of jellyfish. Sister Phyllis made herself resist for a moment, it was base and ungodly, but then she gave in. It was erotic, like hands everywhere, the multiple lovers she had never had.

As the jellies brushed past she felt only the faintest tingling.

It was erotic, divine and beautiful, and then it was not. At first she was only aware of the thickening mass. The first jolt surprised her, but she was not alarmed. Perhaps a single jellyfish had maintained its ability to deliver a full dose of venom. The second and third jolt undermined this theory.

She turned and began to kick back in the direction of the dock, hoping to swim back to the middle of the lake, away from the sunlight, where she knew the jellyfish would dissipate, but the jellyfish were so thick they formed a wall, not a hard wall, more like a mattress, but almost as impenetrable. As she pushed forward, fighting to remain calm, it felt as if the wall pushed back.

The guidebooks had told her to wear a bikini -- it allowed for more contact -- but she was too modest for that. Still, so much of her was exposed. The stings burned her arms, her legs, her outthrust hands and her cheeks where the mask did not reach. A match flared against her lips. Reflexively she opened her mouth, and the jellyfish slid inside. She stopped, jerked her head out of the water and spat. The jelly oozed out reluctantly, sliding down her chin, stinging all the way. The pain was everywhere, thousands of needle applications, improbably minute doses of poison falling one upon the other in an agonizing downpour. Somewhere in her brain she remembered. Twenty million jellies in the lake.

Sister Phyllis Newman was a survivor. She turned for the nearest shoreline; no more than twenty yards away. She kicked furiously; she knew the pointlessness of swimming with her arms. She nudged forward through the mass. A tree had fallen into the lake. It loomed suddenly in her face plate, bearded with moss. Beyond thought, her fingers clawed for purchase among the sharp branches and soggy bark. Hand over hand she pulled for shore, branches raking open her flesh.

The world was a gelatinous mass. The pain rushed forward in waves. She fought to be free of the water. She pulled herself up the trunk until she was half out of the water and then she acceded. It was God's will. Below her waist, untold puncturings proceeded. Above her waist, her hands cupped in prayer.

She thought of all the coins dropped. She counted them, one by one. Finally a wave of pain swept over her and did not recede.

It is terribly slow. I wish I could stop it. She crawls up the trunk. She is a godly woman, so to God she prays. Like Jesus on the cross. But as you know by now, I am no god.

It is terrible and yet so very beautiful. Her acceptance is a marvel. At the last she does not even strike out at the jellies. She does not assign them blame. She declined to bring the guide who might have saved her. She takes responsibility for her own actions. She offers forgiveness. She thanks her God for her time here. She prays that, in that time, she made a difference.

Ocean acidification, oil spills, global warming, the waste of nation upon nation dumped from barges, washed down rivers, poured down sinks. Coins dropped, one by one.

Perhaps the jar has at last shattered.

You are no longer an accident waiting to happen. It is possible you are even making accidents happen.

This is an unexpected twist.

Eventually the guide went to find her. To his credit he possessed a barely functioning two way radio, and enough sobriety to remember the police channel.

When Able arrived at the lake, only half the island was there.

Matchstick in the Darkness

Cedar was virtually the last on the island to know. Marty was flying. She had gone into town to organize the rented garage she used for storage. It was a mess. She had started with fine intentions, until she came across the photo album. There were pictures of her wedding day, Justin's first day of kindergarten standing proudly with the Superman backpack Wyatt had bought him, a ten-year-old Justin, grinning wide, with Jonathan latched nearly sideways in his hair. And always that special light in his eyes.

She had been blessed. She closed her own eyes in gratitude.

The abrupt voice tore the past from her cradling grasp.

"Got yourself a bonafide mess in here."

Miss Patsy's Stonehenge form leaned against the doorjamb, blocking most of the afternoon sunshine.

"Life's clutter. Good afternoon to you, Miss Patsy."

"It will improve somewhat when I can recoup my breath." The great breasts heaved for a few moments. "Saw your truck. Got some news." And then, almost as an afterthought, "What you doin' in here?"

Packaging up my next cocaine shipment, Cedar wanted to say, but all the humor had already left her. Still the island's reigning busy body, old age and some three hundred pounds of pudding flesh now kept Miss Patsy soundly anchored to her front stoop. Only the worst news would see her heft herself into the world.

It was.

Though she stood on a hard cement floor in a muggy garage,

she felt the jellies clasping her own body like a clammy fog.

Her hands trembled.

Miss Patsy missed nothing.

"It's right to be scared," she declared. "People dyin' and disappearin', which is pretty much the same as dyin'. Able wanderin' round like a little boy just flunked his first spellin' test." Miss Patsy freed herself from the door jamb with a grunt. "Strange thunderclouds rollin' in off the horizon. Doubt they spell sunny days."

That night Cedar dreamt; a dream of regret, remorse and apology. Even in her dream, she felt relief.

She woke to dawn's cool ladling through the porthole.

When Marty rolled toward her, she smiled.

"She's back."

"Is that good?"

"I think so," she said, but neither of them missed the hesitancy in her voice.

The dream was mostly sad but it was mildly fearful too.

Cedar felt her relief drain away, until it was no more.

It wasn't just the brave nun. There is something about the encounter at the lake that nudges me, something important I am overlooking. The second piece of the puzzle.

When I return to Long Drop Off it is quiet. My fellows bemoan the absent chickens -- they have been made lazy and far too complacent -- but I am happy for the solitude. It helps me think, here in our final refuge.

It takes time, but I am patient. Finally, it comes.

You know how a salamander can regenerate its tail? There is a species of jellyfish, turritopsi nutricula, which regenerates its entire body, reverting back to its polyp stage. A nifty trick of resurrection. A real life Fountain of Youth.

I am not saying I can bring back the dead. It is too late for Sister Phyllis Newman. But I see clearly the inherent symbolism.

A terrible end, but perhaps a new beginning.

Maybe I can be better than you. Well, at least some of you. As Sister Phyllis Newman ably demonstrated, there are some among you who live to a set of ideals that are admirable indeed.

There is still hope.

I only hope there are enough of you, these people who might make the world right.

Build thee more stately mansions, O my soul

As the swift seasons roll!

Leave thy low-vaulted past!

Let each new temple, nobler than the last,

Shut thee from heaven with a dome more vast,

Till thou at length art free,

Leaving thine outgrown shell by life's unresting sea!

Oh we were clever wordsmiths, Mr. Holmes and I. We saw the metaphors. We grasped the Big Picture.

A new, nobler temple. It is still possible.

There is the boy. And perhaps enough Sister Phyllis Newmans to make things right.

It was beauty who enlightened the beast.

Cedar wasn't surprised by Able's call. He did not bother explaining. He knew she was already familiar with every sordid fact and plenty of sordid falsehoods, too.

"This incident," he said. "Is it is related to the others?"

"They were jellies."

She tried to state this as if it were the indisputable clincher in a high school debate.

"They *were*," said Able.

He really was a remarkable policeman.

Gautama Buddha. Jesus of Nazareth. Muhammad. Mother Teresa. They are the names you know, and certainly movers and shakers in their own right. But they are not the ones who truly turn the tide.

A cook perched on a toilet. Sister Phyllis Newman, with her Red Sox cap and her ceramic frog. A mother who captains a boat named after my favorite poet. They are the ones who see me pause, the ones who lead me to think you may be worth saving.

But with full disclosure in mind, there is something else I must confess, something a trifle unsettling. It is possible the jellyfish did not act on their own accord. Perhaps, being single-cell organisms, they are easily swayed. I am still very angry. I gave no direct order, but perhaps I underestimate my ability to influence. Perhaps I am no longer responsible for myself and my emotions.

But I still think I was not responsible.

Ha.

I am absolving myself of blame. Isn't that ironic?

Two Sides to the Human Coin

Justin didn't return for the summer. There wasn't time. First there were the two weeks in Tallahassee, a national student government convention. His teachers had nominated him. There would be high school kids from across the country. He couldn't wait to meet them.

Politics. Cedar actually shook her head. It was the farthest cry from backwater dive boat operator, but it wasn't a complete surprise. Justin had a way with people. She and Wyatt had raised him to see the world beyond his own.

Wyatt had introduced Justin to the mayor of Chicago at an election fundraiser. She guessed his father's intention was simply to impress the son, but apparently it had been Justin who made the impression. Two days after the meeting, Justin received a call from the mayor's office. He signed on to help with the re-election campaign; a gopher, e-mailing announcements, cold calling on-the-fence voters, delivering cases of water to fundraising events, although Justin himself convinced the mayor to do away with plastic bottles. Election night, Justin wrote, was like nothing he had ever experienced. He had felt like a part of something bigger. He felt like he had made a small difference. It felt good.

Politics had also earned him a girlfriend. Amber loved politics too. Dad had taken them both out to dinner to celebrate the mayor's re-election. Amber had six brothers. On election night she had tied his tie.

This news arrived in a hand-written letter. Her son's happiness fairly leapt off the scrawled pages. Cedar was happy for him. But part of her heart struggled to beat, and when she finished reading the letter for the third time the empty galley blurred.

She leaned back into the couch. She was glad Marty was away.

That night, in answer to her e-mail, revised again and again, Justin told her she had been right to send him back to Chicago. There were so many possibilities. He mentioned Issy in two sentences. She had a boyfriend in Ocala. He was happy for her. It was time, her son said, to move on.

She turned off the computer.

She sat in the dark, mildly stunned. It was a strange feeling. As if her life's work was suddenly behind her.

Oh no. By no means are you finished. There is so much work yet to do. After loss, we must pick ourselves up. To borrow the words of a wise young man, we must move on.

It is imperative that we do so. Hesitate and you will not outrun the onrushing tide.

On her birthday, Marty invited her to Shirley's for a drink.

"I'll meet you there," he said on the phone.

That he didn't come by the boat to get her stung a little, but she supposed this was one of the prices paid by today's independent woman.

Independently she decided to dress to the nines. Marty would wear his standard Hawaiian shirt. He might upgrade to dress slacks given it was her birthday. Everyone else at Shirley's would be dressed in standard tropical garb. She didn't care if she looked out of place. It was her birthday; she could celebrate in whatever fashion she chose. She took a morning charter only. By two she was alone. She spent four hours getting ready. She hadn't dedicated that kind of time to her appearance since the senior prom. Making her final adjustments in front of the mirror, she thought she didn't look like anyone's mother.

Walking down the dock she passed a sailboat she didn't recognize. From below decks came a whistle, not a cat call, but soft and polite. She made no acknowledgement, but it felt good. She wore sneakers for the walk up the hill. Outside Shirley's she put the sneakers behind a bush and slipped on heels.

Marty was wearing a tuxedo. So was Henry.

The bar was lined with Red Rooster bottles, each bottle sprouting a white rose, ten in all.

"For every year I've loved you," said Marty.

He took her hand and led her out to the empty patio.

He did not let go of her hand. He dropped to one knee.

"I am not waiting anymore," he said.

She knew now she had made her decision when he had cleaned the cockpit windows for her the first time, the long graceful fingers making meticulous circles, the impossible white smile growing clearer and clearer on the other side of the tempered glass.

When they came back inside, a carafe of champagne rested on the bar, foam running from the top.

Henry grinned.

"I took a chance," he said.

They danced to What A Wonderful World on the jukebox, his ring on her finger, her heels following his showroom spats as they made their neat circle on the floor.

She touched her lips to his ear.

"You bought them for a special occasion."

"I did. I bought them for my nephew's christening."

She leaned back to look at him.

"Your nephew is eleven."

"This is only the second time I've worn them. I was going to give them away after the christening, but then I met you and I decided to save them for our wedding."

"That was risky."

"For the mind, but not the heart."

When the song ended, Marty smiled.

"You let me lead," he said.

Only then did she notice.

"Where is everyone?"

"They are finding entertainment elsewhere."

Behind the bar, Henry bowed.

"Your fiancé rented the entire establishment, from jukebox to bartender. Tonight closing time is your decision."

"It's June, Marty. There must be at least a dozen new boats in."

"They can celebrate your birthday with you tomorrow."

She kissed him.

"Is the wedding date a surprise too?"

"I was thinking August," Marty said.

Cedar gave a triumphant smile.

"At last you are wrong," she said.

"What?"

"Haven't you learned from your mistake?"

She touched the ten bottles one by one.

"Not August," she said. "August is too long."

The three men were barely more than bones, but as they approached the boat they ferried an oppressive weight she actually felt.

They had watched Cedar and Marty come down the hill. They had barely noted the slight, tuxedoed man, but the long-legged woman had set their loins on fire. The crystal meth only heightened their anxiety.

Cedar watched them walk down the dock. They were pale, with

high cheekbones and scruffy blond beards. Slavic maybe. Marty was below, waiting in bed. She had come up, over his good-natured protests, to give the Wendell Holmes a final once over and thank her stars.

Doubt and champagne slowed her. She thought about shouting out, but there were other boats further down the dock. Perhaps they were just passing by. It would be embarrassing.

"Evening, pretty woman."

They moved like wolves, quick and soundless. The first man was over the railing. A rough hand clamped over her mouth before she could react.

"No one else is invited," he hissed, a smell like sour milk in her face. "We're keeping it intimate." He turned to the shortest man. "Take care of him."

The man pulled a butcher knife from under his shirt and disappeared down the stairs. She wrenched hard, tried to stomp down on her captor's bare foot with her heel, but he anticipated her move, deftly shifting his position and jamming his free fist into her throat. For a moment she thought she was going to pass out.

"Save yourself," the man whispered. "You'll need the energy."

The third man had already thrown off the lines. He went up the ladder without a sound. She had the keys in her pocket, but the engine started.

"Setting sail for a little privacy," her captor said, grinding his hardness up against her.

She strained for sounds below.

"Don't worry," the man said. "If he behaved, he's still with us. He can watch." The muted laugh was queer and high-pitched. "Go out with several bangs."

It was her birthday. They were engaged. They were going to

die. She still tasted champagne. The disconnect made everything dream-like.

The man pulled her into the shadows as the Wendell Holmes idled through the harbor. Cabin lights glowed in several of the boats they passed, but Cedar knew anyone who knew her would give her nighttime departure no thought. All those sentimental trips to the reef beneath the stars.

They cleared the breakwater, idling toward black horizon. Five hundred yards out and they were still idling.

Her assailant jerked her to the starboard side and shouted up to the bridge.

"Open it up, you stupid fuck."

The voice from the bridge was puzzled.

"She's wide open."

In retrospect it was the quiet that shocked her.

The tentacle, pale in the night, was simply there. The man who had been on the bridge swung through the night like a child on a swing, his face bulging impossibly. He stared at Cedar as if pleading for an answer and then he spat blood and whirled off into the darkness. The man pinning her arms departed as if he had never existed. When she turned he was gripping the railing, something like innocence on his face, and then he was gone.

The man below was wrenched through the porthole. It was not a tidy fit.

Cedar met Marty at the foot of the galley steps. They held each other as the Wendell Holmes rocked, slowly settling.

Below the porthole fish fed.

Ugliness, cowardice, greed, lust. My optimism is undermined yet again. Your armies of evil and stupidity, they sweep forward as resolutely as the tide. The taste in my mouth is still rancid.

I have always known I cannot do this alone. But at moments like this I wonder if this may be a task beyond even a collective reach.

Sinking into the deeps I try to think of the boy, the impossible airiness of his pale form as I raised him to the surface like a rising sun.

Here in the velvet blackness it is difficult to hold this vision. But I do. It is my talisman. My lucky charm. My holdfast to belief.

For without belief, we are lost.

Marty spent the night. Neither of them slept. Laying side by side up on the deck they stared up at the uncaring stars, and in the morning they went below and cleaned the cabin. They worked without speaking and when they finished they stood awkwardly.

"I have to fly to Peleliu to drop off supplies. I'll be back by evening. Do you want me to come back tonight?"

She knew he had another flight early the following morning. It provided a good excuse to say no.

"I'm okay," she said.

He didn't believe her. She didn't believe her. But they both knew she wanted to be alone.

Marty said, "Tuesday when I get back I'd like to take you to dinner."

"I would like you to take me to dinner."

They were actors in a play, now both smiling badly.

After Marty left she felt sick and restless, but she waited until darkness fell.

Throwing off the lines she headed out of the harbor.

Unveilings

She drifted up on Long Drop Off as she always did, but this time she dropped the anchor; fixing to the mooring buoy alone at night was too risky. She knew the reef well. She lowered the anchor, felt it settle in sand. Backing the Wendell Holmes she felt the anchor catch.

Briefly she thought of Able. No doubt he had broken a promise or two for the greater good.

The night was warmer than normal. Dry-mouthed, she put on her gear.

She slipped quietly off the swim step and sank beneath the surface. The water closed overhead, sudden cool on her scalp, the familiar feeling of a curtain closing.

She kept her dive light off. She descended to thirty feet, feeling the change in pressure in her ears. She stopped and drifted.

The world crackled.

Bracing herself she looked down.

There was nothing. She was out and away from the reef, the ocean floor 4,000 feet below. Fear traced a finger down her spine.

She floated, willing herself calm. There was the faintest hint of current. She felt herself rocked slowly in the balmy darkness. Like birth.

They appeared first as thousands of tiny sparks. They rose toward her, wavering hypnotically, like embers from a fire. She was drawn toward them. Half aware of her own descent, she stopped at 80 feet. Turning on her dive light, she swung the beam through the water.

The scattered embers were now a deluge. As they drifted close, passing through the beam of her dive light, they assumed implausible and lovely shapes. Something that resembled the Mad Hatter's chapeau. Then a fish, no bigger than a thumbnail, staring back at her, its fins like hands. A thumb-size jelly floated past; it appeared to house a delicate stand on which rested an equally delicate diamond.

Wafting, twirling, cilia legs running in numbers uncountable, they rose from the deeps, transparent glories that pulsed and sparked color.

It was Eden.

And then, in the deep, a pale spread like a reef itself.

She had come for this, but panic still gored her, clawing inside her chest, turning her breathing ragged and making her heart gallop. In the first instant she wondered if she had made a foolish and fatal mistake. She saw again the meth addict's distended face, a last question before blurting out his innards.

She rose slightly, fighting back the urge to kick wildly for the surface.

The shape, so familiar and yet so otherworldly, continued its rise. Her mind slowly pieced it together as it drew closer. She knew the shape by heart - the lovely, three quarter crescent of shell, dark zebra stripes etching the ivory surface, the protective plate, resting like a warrior's shield above the head, the army of snow-white tentacles wafting like streamers in a slight breeze -- yet she struggled to assemble the outsize proportion in her mind. As it rose it bobbled slightly like a bubble.

The creature stopped rising. Enormity made it difficult to judge how deep it was, perhaps thirty feet below her.

In front of her the sea of ctenophores, sea angels, heteropods, salps and venus girdles danced; the loveliest ballet, for her eyes only.

The single tentacle came toward her slowly. It was one of the smaller tentacles, yet as it drew close she could see it was thicker than her torso. As easy as a breath, fear left her. She saw the slow ascension for the signal it was. Apprehension. Anticipation. At last, long-awaited realization. She had reached for her son's tiny squalling form in the same way, a gift not be believed

She felt her own arm extend. In the funnel of her dive light she saw her hand, pale and pimply. *Like a chicken*, she thought, and she almost laughed.

Contact was gentle, a spongy bump, and then all serenity was blasted away. The phosphorescent dream waters disappeared. Terrible images ran ragged through her mind, passing so quickly they were barely more than flashes of shadow and light. It was like rolling beneath the hooves of a stampede. Whatever tore through her mind was screaming, a heart-wrenching sound born not of pain but of hopeless despair. Cedar wished for pain, for the despair was worse.

Her eyes were closed tight but the flashing stampede continued unabated, a melee of blurred images, the screaming riding alongside, only now she knew the screams were her own.

Something pushed at her and she was tumbling through the water. When she remembered to open her eyes the nautilus was nearly gone, receding into the blackness which snuffed the giant form as easily as a match.

The phosphorescent masses were gone too.

She floated alone in the water column, crying.

For as her eyes absorbed the here and now, the stampeding visions came to her clearly, a ruined world of stinking oceans and rancid rivers, where great storms razed sea and land, and governments and order toppled, and men, women and children did not reach out to each other but performed unspeakable acts in the name of survival, and glistening, half-recognizable things slid from a porthole in a gore-splattered slurry, puzzle pieces that had comprised a whole.

Instinct saw her out of the water. Curled on the deck, she held herself.

Overhead the stars laughed.

It required all my strength and cold-bloodedness but now is not the time to coddle. We are nearly past the crossroad. She needed to see where the other paths lead. She had to see because she matters greatly in this game, which is no game at all. So many millennia, arriving at this juncture: time and fate and mounting woes intersecting. Yet even as the terrible visions swirled between us, she did not draw away. I felt the press of her fingertip, warm blood propelled there by a right heart. She did not falter. It seems when it comes to judging some of you, I am not entirely blind.

Drifting down, I know I have made the right choice. It is the second time I have seen tears underwater, tears without recrimination or self-pity, tears of simple knowing.

Tears of apology in the clear sea eyes.

In the dark I think. I try to retain objectivity in the face of my own shock. Rational was what I once was. Cold, calculated, objective and, yes, merciless. Uncaring and unfettered by emotion. I try to concentrate on what truly matters. She absorbed the lesson. She will pass it on. This is a victory for hope. But here in the darkness my insides are sick and hollow too. It is not the visions that make me sad. I am quite familiar with them. It is loss that assails me. When we touched I knew that she will not be part of this pageant much longer. I know now she is dying.

The possibility of just such a surprise is precisely why I spread the word. I have tried, as you say, to cover all the bases. But planning does not alleviate sorrow. I do not descend beyond hearings' range. When the engine throttles to a start and the boat begins to move away, I drift in the direction of the receding sound.

Goodbye.

Even as I rise I tell myself her passing will be a small setback, but the cause will not be lost. She was right. She has already accomplished her task. She has raised a child. This shock, I tell myself, doesn't qualify as shock at all. It is merely one of life's countless surprises, almost inconsequential given what else is at stake. Soon enough, stronger players by far will take up the cause. Her passing is no cause for alarm. As I tell myself this I know it is not alarm that sees me break the surface.

I cannot bravely soldier on with this quest in every moment. In this moment I am not sad for the world. I am sad for me. I need to see the stars. Two women sharing secrets in a quiet kitchen can become friends and even lovers.

I apologize. I must modify what I stated earlier. On certain fronts, I can predict the future. I know I will pine for plumeria and bagpipes. Yet another ache in an accumulating sea.

Toward dawn the wind rises. I hear its song.

The next time the wind laments, listen closely. Is it not the sound of bagpipes keening?

When Cedar returned to Koror harbor late in the afternoon, Marty was at the dock holding a bouquet of lilies. They said nothing until after they made love, gently and quietly, quick breaths and the cries of tropical birds in their ears.

"I can't just forget," Marty said.

She kissed him. For an instant she felt like a mother again.

"We're not supposed to forget," she said.

She was no longer in this alone, but still she hesitated.

"I need to tell you," she said.

The tears came again. When she finished, Marty said, "Is that our future?"

"I don't know."

She knew why she thought of Justin.

"Cedar?"

She returned slowly.

"Yes?"

"Are you frightened?"

"Terrified."

The men did not return to their single rented room. After three days the proprietor, who catered primarily to a questionable clientele, reluctantly called the police. Able drove the police van to the shabby hostel. He watched quietly as two of his officers placed the drug paraphernalia, porn magazines and ratty backpacks in the evidence bags he knew would reveal no evidence. For a week the island buzzed with talk of the missing men and a small band of citizens came into his office - was a serial killer afoot in their paradise? -- and then everyone returned to their jobs, their lovemaking and their lives.

At the end of the week, Able called Cedar.

They were past pleasantries and gambit.

"Do you know what happened to these men?"

"No."

"They disappeared without a trace. It has a familiar ring."

"I know you don't believe me, but no."

Able sighed.

"I was almost certain this call would be a waste of time, but I had to be able to tell myself I tried. You understand, I have to do something Cedar. I am charged with protecting the people on this island."

"They aren't in danger."

He wasn't angry. He was just very tired.

"I no longer believe that is an accurate assessment," he said.

He knew what her face looked like.

"What do you propose?" she asked quietly.

They both knew what he would say.

"We have to expose it and kill it."

"You saw the photos."

"Yes."

"That assumes you even find it."

They were adversaries now, but they had been friends.

"It's not what you want to do," she said.

It stopped him for a moment, but then the policeman in him was back.

"I know you are not with me on this, Cedar. I am truly sorry."

"I'm sorry too."

Able kept the phone to his ear, although he expected nothing else. The silence and Cedar's even breaths were soothing.

In his mind, the distended sharks hung in the town square amidst a cloud of flies. If Justin and Issy hadn't cut them down, he would have.

She hung up softly.

He considered summoning Cedar and Marty to the station, but he knew the summons would yield the same result as his phone call.

He turned on the computer and, in his first break in the case, connected to the internet on the first try. It never ceased to amaze him that a tap of the finger brought information from every corner of the globe.

This also made it hard to know exactly who to notify. He had always been a precise man. Never before had it been more important to be just right.

He finished his research after midnight. He made his decision. He would make the call the following afternoon. It would be morning there. He would have to plan what he would say; otherwise he would be heard as a lunatic, a policeman gone troppo.

Before turning off the computer he went to his downloads. He clicked on the photographs one by one. He had looked at them countless times, yet each time they shook him, touching him, not with fear, but with an inexplicable sadness. Each time he felt something else too, the faintest drumbeat behind his temple, almost imperceptible, struck again and again. He felt he should grasp this drumbeat -- that it was beating out a message he should decipher -- but the drumbeat contained nothing resembling words, only a hypnotic rhythm that was probably just an overexcited pulse in his head. Yet some nights he would wake to his wife's soft snoring and hear the beat clearly, and something in it would fill him again with the weight of loss and sadness. Several nights, alone in the kitchen, he wept. He didn't know why. He wondered if even the crime of this small place had turned him into a melancholy man.

It was well past time to go home, but after he turned off the computer he remained in his chair. Rocking gently he idly considering last week's Manila Times folded neatly on his desk. The paper contained an article about a Florida toddler who had fallen into an exhibit housing African painted dogs. The boy was torn to pieces. African painted dogs, explained zoo officials, are pack hunters.

Man had traveled an inconceivable distance beyond the taming of fire, but the prehistoric was never more than a fingernail scratch beneath the veneer.

He gathered up the pages he had printed, slipping them into a file. For four hours he had read everything he could, so many words his eyes stung.

For some reason one phrase stuck in his head.

Naturalists have long marveled at the shell of the Chambered Nautilus. The logarithmic spiral echoes the curved arms of hurricanes and distant galaxies.

Perhaps he had finally come up against something beyond him.

Becoming

It would be easy to call an end to it. We could usher you toward your oblivion. It might very well be the best way to start anew. A clean slate to begin the planet's resurrection. Ecosystems bounce back with surprising speed after even the most massive die-offs. Our planet has a bright history of rapid recovery without any help from you. Eden without Adam and Eve. Eden again.

To each of your generations, the same facts surprise as if they are brand new. Oliver Wendell Holmes was bewitched by the lustrous coil. Jules Verne observed Nature's glorious engineering and imagined a submarine of many compartments, christening it the Nautilus. When the first Nautilus shells arrived in Renaissance Europe, collectors fell to respectful silence. They saw the perfect spirals as reflecting the larger order of the universe.

Your forgetfulness would be amusing if it didn't have such deadly repercussions.

I am not forgetful, but I have been rendered indecisive. I suppose I can blame my indecisiveness on a tug-of-war. Sister Phyllis Newman. Three putrid corpses choked down to dispose of the evidence. Abraham Lincoln. Adolph Hitler. The semen already staining the man's boxers. Cedar Mahoney's tears. Yes, no, yes, no, yes. If I didn't know better, I'd say someone was playing games with me.

It wouldn't really matter if you disappeared. Many among us see your throwing yourself on your own sword as proper punishment and no loss.

Again and again I debate with myself, like an old woman standing at a half-familiar street corner. The debates vary, but they always end the same. I see the limp boy rising toward the sun, his pale body lighter than them all, so light he draws me up with him.

A boy raised on a fleck-of-birdseed island in the middle of the Pacific. A boy, light as a sunbeam. Hope given form.

Hope above doubt. Hope above evil, ignorance, indifference, sloth, hatred, lust, greed.

Perhaps this is no more than a hope itself. My own hopeful delusion.

In the oceans, creatures are stirring of their own accord. I sense it. I have not forgotten. Liopleurodon banking slowly, vectoring with a fin-changing course, turning about. Fang and claw. A force of Nature I may or may not subjugate.

It is possible I am losing control.

It is certain we are sliding close to a tipping point from which there is no turning back.

At least not for you.

But all is not lost. Time, the patient educator, has taught me many lessons. What is your expression?

Never put all of your eggs in one basket.

He is one of the world's preeminent underwater photographers, aboard this boat to shoot a magazine story on the Sea of Cortez. After a long day of diving the other divers are drinking in the galley of the *Becky Lee*, already dozy drunk. He is a teetotaler and mildly shy. He needs night shots too, and when he walked to the stern thirty minutes ago to share a little quiet with the stars, he saw the Humboldt squid, attracted by the *Becky Lee's* lights, darting just below the black surface like gray shooting stars.

Humboldt squid were once confined largely to the Southern Hemisphere. They are spreading now into waters off California, the Pacific Northwest and the Sea of Cortez. You have not yet pinned down the reasons for this outward migration -- gradual ocean warming, pollution, over-fishing of the squid's predators, the squid fleeing deeps now sucked dry of oxygen (recall the Dead Zones?) - but sometimes a reason is not what matters.

Make way for the aggressive opportunists.

Recently scientists attached your so-called crittercams to Humboldt squid and learned some startling things (a recurring theme). Humboldt squid hunt in tightly coordinated groups, a behavior heretofore unassociated with invertebrates. You knew they flashed colors, but the cameras showed the squid flash specific red and white color signals when they encounter an individual of their own species. They "may", you hypothesize, be talking. And, when inspired, they move very, very fast. Your crittercams have clocked them at speeds of nearly 45 miles an hour, comparable to the fastest ocean fish.

Remember the octopi experiments.

The squid you catch on camera, they may downshifting.

You don't need to be capable of abstract thought to have a sense of mischief.

On the back of the deck he pulls his gear from his dive bag and suits up. He has done this thousands of times. Still he triple checks his air, breathes through both regulators and examines his BCD to ensure his backup dive light is clipped tight, if, for some impossible reason, he should lose his camera rig with its white bright strobes. Complacency kills. He has heard dozens of stories, and twice witnessed it first-hand.

He glances toward the door leading to the galley, warm light behind the porthole's scratched glass. He should tell someone, but now that he is suited up he just wants to go. It is a calm night; the ocean's surface barely fidgets.

He places his camera carefully on the swim step and slips into the water. He pulls the camera in after him. Its weight makes him sink. For an instant he sees both worlds through his face plate; the lights of the *Becky Lee* and the black water. The thought strikes him every time. Two distinct worlds, distinctly one. He tells this story at every lecture he gives. As the oceans go, so we go.

The curious squid are already bumping his legs. He trains his strobes out into the darkness. The school is far larger than he thought, a continuous wall of flesh, whipping past. His experienced eye picks out individual squid. Some are big. It's hard to tell in the kaleidoscopic movement, but he knows from experience the Humboldt squid can measure up to six feet and weigh over 100 pounds. He is experienced but not jaded. His heart beats faster. He's going to get good shots. Possibly great shots. Maybe a career changing cover.

They are on him before he raises the camera, swarming as if on some collective signal. They fill the parabola of his vision created by the strobes, flashing iridescent rainbow colors. They fix to the strobes, his hands, his mask, his regulator, powerful suction cups wresting. He kicks for the surface with everything he has. His mask is torn away. The world goes blurry but he knows he is wide-eyed because his eyes sting. His regulator is yanked away. He still has a chance; the surface is ten feet away. He swims daily to keep in shape. He kicks hard, rises, feels the first fin pulled free. His wetsuit tightens about him. Pressure builds in his ears. Away from the pinnacle, there is nothing but deeps. He recites the figure to himself as if he is standing at a lectern. Three thousand feet to the bottom. That is where he is going.

When it is finished the squid flash their electrifying colors, translucent and beautiful and different from any color they have flashed before.

Your scientists are bewitched by cephalopods. Puzzle solvers. Tool users. Communicators. Cephalopods, you surmise, may be able to see with their skin. Or laugh. I find nothing funny in this. The man, he was one of the good ones. A small savior.

Squid are far more intelligent than you believe. I won't burden you with details. I will only say there are some shocking discoveries just over the horizon. I will tell you this. These Humboldt squid in the Sea of Cortez, they were playing. A conscious game of cat and mouse, without conscience.

I don't need to explain such behavior to you. Your own bullies have graduated from playground fisticuffs to drive by shootings. The squid, they were wrong, but similar soul-less ugliness unfolds in your world every day.

Your crittercams have captured how Humboldt squid, at times, ruthlessly cannibalize their own. You believe the larger squid are simply eating the smaller. Let me suggest an ancillary theory. The indecisive are being eaten. A selective winnowing to hasten the genetic advancement of the brutish species.

Your writer Robert Louis Stevenson said, "To become what we are capable of becoming is the only end in life."

A double-edged sword, no doubt.

When I reprimand these squid they pulse as one, a shimmering, laughing wall.

Feral children.

Cedar woke in a cold sweat, her stomach queasy. She returned to the present slowly, and when she did she saw Marty sleeping soundly beside her and she smiled. She wondered if anyone else on earth slept so peacefully. Except for the slow rise and fall of his chest, Marty slept as if he actually was a log. Wyatt had been a fitful sleeper, tossing and turning and grinding his teeth, perhaps tormented by the alpha male confrontation of the upcoming day. Oddly, her otherwise serene Justin had inherited this fitful gene.

In the night silence she realized how much she missed him. He was coming home for the wedding, but that was still a month away.

She looked at the clock radio, the numbers red. Three ten. Just past noon in Chicago. It had been two days since her encounter with the nautilus. She had waited too long already. She wasn't sure why she was delaying. Maybe she wanted Justin to get on with his own life. But she also knew his life was part of this.

Something saw her rise from bed.

Slipping from the cabin she padded into the galley and flicked on the computer. She left the lights off. She listened to the computer whir and click to life. Her gaze fell on the basket of fruit on the counter and the single overripe banana. Her heart gave away a beat. She missed Jonathan too. She would give anything to have that damn fruit bat drool banana bits down her front again.

It took her more than an hour to compose the e-mail. She did not apologize for her secret. It didn't matter now, and she had known he was never in danger. She labored to describe every detail of the encounter. As her words scrolled across the screen, she realized how absolutely impossible they looked. It was so much to tell and so much to accept. Dreams made real.

She wrote and rewrote, envisioning Justin's face as he read the words; worry first, and then a furrowed brow as he worked at choosing his own words, words that wouldn't outrightly call her insane. This time when she reached the end of the letter she didn't allow herself to hesitate. She clicked send.

It was done. She sat in the dark. Justin could be anywhere. She realized she did not know her son's life. He might not have his phone with him. It might not be on. Even if he was reading her e-mail right now, his response wouldn't be quick. It was too much to respond to in an instant.

She was sliding back her chair when the words appeared.

It's exactly what I dream. It's what I've always dreamt.

A pulse banged in her head. She was barely aware of her fingers typing.

Why didn't you ever tell me?

She held her breath, waiting for the answer she knew was coming.

It was my secret.

This she understood.

I come to the harbor again and settle against the hull of the boat, every groove as familiar as the habits of an old friend. I do not come for her now. She no longer needs me. I come for me. I wish I could sweep the dark dream away, but the dream is hers alone. A dream like this, it cannot be erased. It is not a metaphor. It has nothing to do with oil spills, pollution or wanton destruction. The darkness is coming just for her.

I cannot stop it.

Able

Able left work in the middle of the afternoon, surprising his wife when he came in the door.

"What?" she said, looking up from the chair where she was reading a detective novel. "You have decided to turn over a new leaf and not work yourself into an early grave?"

They had a good marriage. She read detective novels because she wanted to understand his job. He brought her Blue Dawn flowers every Friday because, as he told her with each presentation, the plant can be troublesome, but when it flowers it is beautiful. They met when they were eighteen. Policemen have their secrets too. In his life Able had made love to only one woman.

After thirty-five years of marriage, her chiding still made him feel like the luckiest man in the world.

He smiled back. It made him feel guilty. He was lying to his wife. He had never lied to her before. His smile was a lie and he was not exactly sure why he was lying.

"You would make a fine detective," he said. "And I have learned it is never too late for a change."

He went directly into their bedroom. He wanted more than anything to stay with her, but he didn't.

From the other room she said, "Next up, the resurrection," and laughed.

She had a lovely laugh.

He found what he required in the closet, though in the dimness he paused again.

When he came back out he was wearing the floral swim trunks his brother had given him, and carrying a pair of fins.

His wife's eyebrows raised in genuine surprise.

"You are going swimming? Since when are you a disciple of exercise?"

The honest truth was he didn't know.

"Since now." He thought for a moment. "I hear it clears the mind."

"Stop it right now, Able. You are not fooling me. Your mind is gin clear all the time. Tell me you're not going to leave those fins beside another woman's bedside?"

For a moment, he was himself.

"I might just crawl into bed with them on."

"That could prove awkward."

"It might make things more interesting." For some reason he felt a need to explain what he could not explain. "I am not getting any younger. I would like to buy a few more years with you."

He loved her. He had never doubted this, but suddenly it struck him with an almost holy clarity. He wanted to change his mind, spend the afternoon in this home they had made, but his wife stood and kissed him and he smiled and went out the door, swinging the fins like a ten-year-old boy.

When he arrived at the beach he could still see the happiness in his wife's eyes.

He began to cry.

He stands at the ocean's edge for a long time. His reluctance -- his mind is strong -- but also mine. A part of me wishes someone would see him, hail him and break the trance. But no one passes by. Fate still plays its card in many things.

He is a strong swimmer. As a boy he swam for hours, and the boy still exists in this man. He swims on the surface until he reaches the edge of the reef. Here he stops, jerkily treading water. Maybe he issues some form of goodbye. His mind is very strong. I do not know how much of it belongs to him and how much belongs to me.

But I must possess the majority for he does not even take a last breath before dropping beneath the surface. Nor does he hesitate at the edge of the reef. Finning strongly he continues down the sheer wall, a beautiful diver in a viscous sky, anemones and sea fans swaying in the currents as if applauding. I do not feel like cheering. I do not want to do this but I know he is supremely capable, possibly even capable of thwarting what must be. He is a sacrifice for the greater good.

I rise to meet him. He is not afraid. He swims down toward me, his smile wide. Like we are old friends.

I welcome him into my arms.

This one last thing, he sees for himself.

You

Justin flew out a week earlier than planned to attend Able's funeral.

When Cedar saw him step off the plane, her heart stutter stepped. The baggage handlers on the tarmac each gave him a high five. One pulled a suit bag from the cart and handed it to him.

The boy she hugged was broad. A strange cologne too.

"I'm so sorry about Able, Mom. And happy for you and Marty too. Is he here?"

He paused, looking a little awkward. He was still only seventeen. The joy of this nearly saw her laugh out loud.

"I invited him but he declined. Something about a mother-son reunion."

His relief was so obvious, she did laugh.

"What?"

"Nothing. I'm just the world's happiest mother."

"Dad asked about Marty. I said he was the only man on earth who deserved you."

"You did, did you? And how, may I ask, did your father handle that?"

"He said he had his chance."

Cedar pretended to brush something off her blouse.

"You look good, Mom."

"Thank you," she said, though she knew it was a lie. Sleep was harder and harder to come by. She had bags under her eyes. The airport's hard tile floor made her back ache. She wanted to curl up in one of the plastic seats. In her e-mails she had told him she had had something similar before and it had passed. A mother's white lie.

Softly Justin said, "Did they find his body?"

"No. He hadn't gone swimming since he was a boy."

It hung between them.

"He was a good person," said Justin.

"He was."

"He knew Issy and I cut down the sharks. He never said anything."

Her son's face was almost blank, but there was something there Cedar recognized.

"Life isn't always fair," he said.

Such a gentle smile.

"No," she said. "It isn't."

She didn't want to feel sad in this moment.

"Does that bag actually have a suit in it?"

"I *am* here for a wedding. Just to brace you, the bag is leather."

"Your father gave it to you."

"Actually, the mayor did. Well, more like the mayor's office. After his re-election. As a thank you."

"My son the power broker," she said. "An unexpected direction."

She loved how he couldn't hide his pleasure.

"No one is more surprised than me," he said.

"That you have a knack for politics? Please. It's just people. You've always bewitched them."

She knew now what she'd seen, barely visible on his face. She had given him the same reassuring look when he was a little boy.

Walking to the car, he took her hand. She leaned against him.

"You know, we have twenty-four hours before the funeral," he said.

"Something you'd like to do?"

She wanted to smile but she couldn't.

She'd cleaned his cabin. She saw how he touched the towel rack. Like a blessing. Glancing into her cabin, he grinned when he saw Marty's sunglasses on the window shelf.

When she looked at him, his eyebrows made an exaggerated bump.

She wanted to kick herself for blushing.

"I guess it's an outdated tradition," he said.

"We're adults and we're engaged."

"I like it."

"Like what?" she said, knowing full well she was stepping into a trap.

"That now you have to explain yourself to me."

"I don't need to explain myself to anyone, least of all my son."

She couldn't help herself; she followed him into his cabin like a puppy.

He laid the suit bag carefully on his berth. It *was* leather. In the cabin's narrow confines she could smell it.

His back was to her.

"Isn't today Friday?" he asked.

Another trap?

"Let's suppose it is," she said.

She heard a zipper. When Justin turned, he held a bag of Doritos.

"What time is King Kong?"

He is here. I feel it, a lightness that permeates the water. But I feel the weight of sadness too, for his return reminds me again of what I have lost.

Life is like that. Pain and pleasure. Sorrow and light. Dreams and nightmares. Not unfair. Just life.

There is a full moon tonight. The moon illuminates the reef as if it is day. A breeze runs across the ocean's surface, sending shadow ripplings over the reef. The openings on top of the reef swallow the ripples that pass their way.

I enter the cavern, passing over the collapsed rubble that now rests silent and silt-less. Two silver shafts pierce the openings. In the cavern they spin slowly, gauzy wands. I should see it as lovely, but I do not.

I press against the uncaring rock.

I see the egg sacs, lovingly aligned, the movement inside like the flickering of Chinese lanterns.

I press harder.

I wish I had finished the old man and the boy slowly.

Do not succumb to bitterness and hatred. Bitterness and hatred bring us all down. They lower us to a common denominator no better or worse than the so-called beasts.

In the lake the jellyfish turn as one, killing the fish that remain.

They arrived at Long Drop Off at dawn so that they were the only boat. With Able gone, the other operators had started up again.

Her eyes swept the bruised blue water. Was a time she found the vast plain soothing and peaceful. On this morning the expanse made her feel small and helpless.

She wondered again if they were making a mistake.

"He closed the reef," she said, turning to Justin.

. "You told me."

Justin was preoccupied with replacing a mask strap.

"I suppose you also remember why."

Justin put the mask down and studied her.

"Yes," he said.

"Do you think this is wise?"

"There's nothing to worry about."

They were her words. It stopped her for a moment.

"Able? The children?"

He picked up the mask. He looked down into it as if he saw something other than the deck.

"I'm truly sorry about each of them," he said.

"You knew they were eggs, didn't you?"

"Yes."

The torch had been passed.

"Why didn't you tell me?"

"I didn't know if you were ready. I'm sorry."

There was one last thing.

"The dreams you have," she said.

He looked up now but he said nothing.

"They're not always just dreams, are they?"

"No," he said. "Sometimes they're more like conversations."

She wanted him to go in, but she didn't. She would sacrifice the world for her son.

"We both know I'll be fine," he said.

You are still a mother's child. You cannot imagine the loss.

"Mom?"

The way he looked gave her chills. Eyes so very bright. A smiling eight-year-old holding a conch shell and a whispered secret. Now a man confident in his path. But his face was so smooth and open. For a moment he was her little boy again.

"Have you ever dreamed about a man on a toilet seat?"

"No," she said, and she knew she never would.

"It doesn't matter." He stood, settling the mask on his face. He kissed her cheek, the mask bumping her temple. "It's a nice dream, though."

She could only watch him, thick with muscle now, sit on the swim step and slip with barely a splash into the water.

She let him go.

When she looked over the side there were two reefs.

Even in this short time he has changed. He is like nothing I have seen. I am shocked. I am beyond pleased. I have told you I am not all seeing. Now I am reminded of this myself.

He is not afraid. He has no cause to be. I feel his gratitude as if he speaks it. Already there is a power and presence to him.

I knew it before I lifted him from the sand. It is why I lifted him from the sand, although, rising through the sun-dappled water, his airy lightness surprised even me. He was lighter than air. It was as if I was the one being lifted toward the sun. As if he possessed a gravitational pull of his own. I had never felt anything like it. Lighter than a messiah on a toilet seat. Lighter than hope.

We regard each other, very nearly equals.

He knows. When I reach out to touch him, he does not flinch.

He does not recoil from the terrible visions.

You, me, him, us; none are perfect. The important lessons, they bear repetition.

Repetition, as you say, is the mother of all learning.

Frail as spring ice, she marries the gentle man who swims like a tumbleweed. Theirs is a quiet ceremony beside the sea. The water sparkles prettily, though beneath the surface forces move which are beyond your understanding or control.

She has esophageal cancer. I do not know this term but I know the deadly power it ferries. Soon a doctor will give her the news. This delay is an unalterable setback, the cancer making its silent ugly inroads. But it is also true. She has, as she once believed, completed her job. Yes, she plays the bagpipes atrociously, but she has sounded the notes that mattered and now they play on.

To paraphrase Mr. Holmes slightly, "From thy lips, a clearer note is born."

It is each generation's fresh hope.

Already the boy is taking the first quiet steps of his rise, far off center stage for the moment, a breath of fresh air to the first few who are coming to know him. You will know him when you see him, a different kind of politician, not really a politician at all, although he will rise toward the highest office because he knows this is the surest way to bring about change. Like Gandhi. Like Jesus. Like Mohammed.

The world will be galvanized. You still have a chance.

I only hope you don't kill him.

And you.

I whispered to Oliver Wendell Holmes, to Jules Verne, to Steinbeck, to wordsmiths who have dissolved into the mists of anonymity. Why not this writer's ear? These words he has penned, might I suggest they are not entirely fiction after all? Compare the accounts in this story against your news accounts. There will be some surprises.

Is there a savior? For your kind, it has always been an appealing thought. There might have been (you will have to trust me regarding the messiah on the toilet seat; there is no other record); there might still be. But may I suggest that saviors are not the answer? Remember it is the ones you never hear of who make a difference. They are the patient movers of stones. One by one.

So here we are, just you and me, the way I intended it to be.

Perhaps these words did not end up in your hands by accident.

A world reborn or a world of ruin?

I don't know.

It's for you to decide.

It truly is a long drop off. Four thousand feet beneath the surface four eggs huddle close, enhancing the odds of a mating pair.

From where the cold sea-maids rise.

In the deeps the first egg wobbles and splits.

NEXUS (The Ship of Pearl Series, Book 2)

Sugule Ali watched the fishing sloop through stolen binoculars, a sad-looking scrap nearly invisible upon the Gulf of Aden. The sloop reminded him of the boats he had played with as a boy. Standing where the waves washed in, he had worked tirelessly to keep his boats upright, but they had capsized every time. Even then he had realized this was a life lesson.

The three fishermen were so thin as to already be ghosts. Sugule Ali thought of his fellow pirates, scarecrows on the open sea. None escaped Somalia's poverty. In this, his country bestowed equality.

It was no cargo ship, but cargo ships were far fewer these days, redirecting to other waters or accompanied now by armed escorts. Perhaps, thought Sugule Ali, he was a victim of his own success.

Watching the panicked fishermen through the binoculars, Sugule Ali spoke his last words.

"Shoot them when we are in range."

He felt the impact, a simultaneous hammer strike upon every bone. In the instant before the pain, he was angry. The half-wit Yusuf had run them aground, although he knew this was impossible in four hundred feet of water. All about him was popping; the undisciplined report of Kalashnikov rifles, splintering wood and a snapping not quite like failing tinder. He had yet to lower his binoculars. He saw, in two perfectly oval worlds, the squalid fishermen gesturing madly, as if they had never seen pirates before. His men screamed. Wet doused him. When Sugule Ali dropped the binoculars he saw that it was raining. The rain was red.

After a time the boat of Sugule Ali, pirate king, slid beneath the sea, but it did not concern him anymore.

JUNCTURE

QUESTIONS FOR DISCUSSION

At the beginning of JUNCTURE we meet Cedar and Justin Mahoney, mother and son, and we watch their relationship evolve - with its ups and downs - as the story progresses. Cedar and Justin have a special relationship, but it's one that's not unfamiliar to many parents and children. What is it that makes a parent-child relationship special? Do you think a mother-son bond is more powerful than the bond between mothers and daughters, fathers and daughters, or fathers and sons?

This story is about the sea. Some people are moved and touched by the sea. Others are afraid of it. What are your feelings about the sea?

Much of JUNCTURE is based on fact. Many of the behaviors of the sea creatures, many of their seemingly impossible adaptations and evolutions, they have actually happened. How does this make you feel?

Ninety-five percent of the ocean deeps are unexplored. Scientists are continually discovering new deep sea species, creatures often stranger than anything we can imagine. Yet many of us discount these possibilities until we see them. Why do you think we often don't believe in things we can't see?

Justin has a special connection with animals. Do you think a connection like his is possible? Do you know anyone who has unusual connection with animals?

How would you describe the relationship between Cedar and the Nautilus? The Nautilus is often planting thoughts in Cedar's mind, but what does the Nautilus learn from Cedar?

What do we learn about our species through the Nautilus? How would you describe her view of humanity? Do you agree or disagree with how she sees us?

Is the Nautilus hopeful about humanity's future, or is she not?

Cedar and the Nautilus share something very special, a deeply intimate connection that is emotional, sexual, spiritual, environmental... Do you think such a relationship, deep on so many fronts, is possible? What elements of their relationship have you experienced in your own relationships?

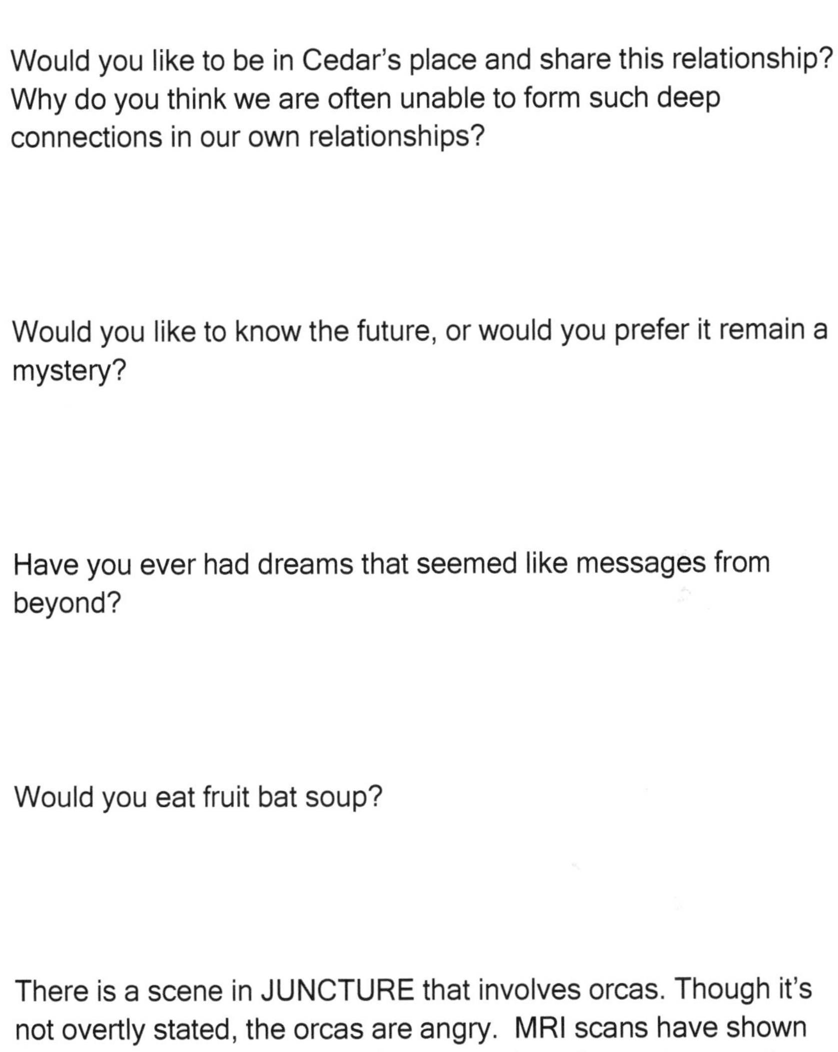

Would you like to be in Cedar's place and share this relationship? Why do you think we are often unable to form such deep connections in our own relationships?

Would you like to know the future, or would you prefer it remain a mystery?

Have you ever had dreams that seemed like messages from beyond?

Would you eat fruit bat soup?

There is a scene in JUNCTURE that involves orcas. Though it's not overtly stated, the orcas are angry. MRI scans have shown that the lobes that deal with the processing of complex emotions are larger in an orca's brain than our own. Do you think more animals are capable of emotion -- and intelligence -- than we realize?

Discuss the parallels between the story line and Oliver Wendell Holmes' poem "The Chambered Nautilus."

Oil spills, overfishing, rising ocean temperature, ocean acidification, extinction rates 10,000 times the norm; the wanton destruction of our nurseries, our reefs, our worlds. You are, quite literally, killing us. It is almost like war. You force us to fight back. Against you, but for all of us. For as the oceans go, so you go. You are blithely sawing at your own throat. Why can't you see this? How can a species so intelligent be so blind? So the Nautilus wonders. How would you answer these two questions?

Although it doesn't end well, Sister Phyllis Newman follows through on a lifelong dream to visit a place completely foreign to her; and, swimming in Jellyfish Lake, she tries an experience totally beyond her normal life. Have you ever aspired to experience something or someplace far out outside the life you know?

For neither your species nor mine ever changes completely. We retain our primordial underpinnings. Has there ever been a time when you became someone you didn't recognize? Where your baser instincts took over? How did you feel about that?

What does the dream of the man on the floating toilet seat mean to you? What single word comes to mind when you think of that scene?

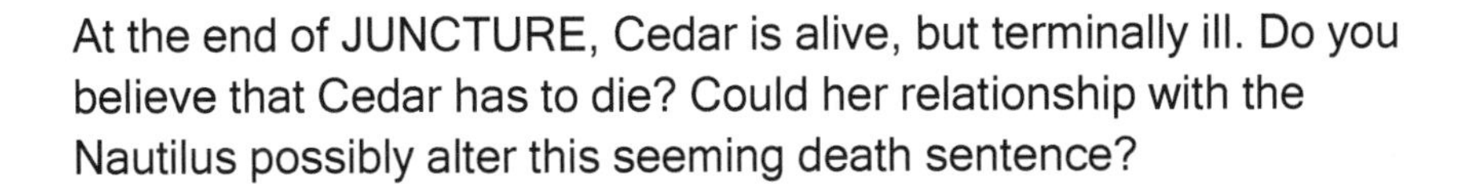

At the end of JUNCTURE, Cedar is alive, but terminally ill. Do you believe that Cedar has to die? Could her relationship with the Nautilus possibly alter this seeming death sentence?

Robert Louis Stevenson wrote, “To become what we are capable of becoming is the only end in life.” Do you think human beings can become what they are capable of becoming?

JUNCTURE alludes to futures of both happy possibility and terrible bleakness. What do you foresee for our future?

Can one person make a difference in this world?

Other Books by Ken McAlpine

Nexus (The Ship of Pearl Series, Book 2)

Together We Jump: A Journey of Love, Hope and Second Chances

Fog

Rise of the Mooncusser

Islands Apart: A Year on the Edge of Civilization (nonfiction)

Off Season: Discovering America on Winter's Shore (nonfiction)

West is Eden: Reflections on this Gift Called Life (essays)

Lightning Strikes of Loopy Giddiness and Other Bucket List Travel Tales (travel essays)

Salt on Our Lips: Stories of Humor, Humanity and Mysteries Happily Unresolved

For more information, please go to...

www.kenmcalpine.com

www.facebook.com/kenmcalpineauthor

ABOUT THE AUTHOR

Ken McAlpine is the author of ten books; fiction, non-fiction and selected essays. His books and magazine articles have received numerous awards. Ken lives in Ventura, California with his wife and their two sons. He likes to stand in his yard at night looking at the stars, but he does not like to spend any time during the day doing yard work.

A LAST NOTE (always good to read to the end)

Is the story over? Oh, no. The oceans are still threatened, still changing. NEXUS picks up where JUNCTURE left off. At this writing, I think there will be one more book after NEXUS, making for a trilogy. Beyond that loose plan, I don't know. Will there be a happy ending in this fictional world? I don't know. Will there be a happy ending in our actual world? I don't think anyone knows that either.

One thing I do know. I am grateful to have you as a reader.

Sincerely, Ken

Made in the USA
San Bernardino, CA
05 July 2016